"Doesn't this kitten look familiar?"

Dr. Augustin held Randy up under the lamp. He looked momentarily perplexed, as he studied the kitten's markings. Then he smiled. "Arnie Silor's cat, Pearl."

"There must be a zillion cats in this town that look like Pearl," I said.

"I doubt it. Not white with blue eyes and an odd dark band across their noses . . . Give Mr. Silor a call. See how Pearl is doing. Try to find out if she's had a litter of kittens recently. Without mentioning the money or sounding like you're accusing Arnie of anything, of course."

"Of course," I said.

I went to the lab and dialed Arnold Silor's number. A man answered on the second ring.

"Mr. Silor?" The guy didn't sound like Arnie.

"Mr. Silor is unavailable at the moment," the man said. "May I take a message?"

"Do you know when he'll be back?"

There was a muffled sound, like the guy had his hand over the receiver. Then a different voice came on.

"This is the Brightwater Beach Police. May I ask who is calling?"

I hung up. Then I rushed into Dr. Augustin's office . . .

Don't miss the first Samantha Holt Mystery,
Eight Dogs Flying—
as Samantha and Dr. Augustin enter the high-stakes, low-life world of dog racing
to chase a cle

"Delightful Florida se
ful animals, and a dr
could you ask for?"

KAREN ANN WILSON

COPY CAT CRIMES

A Berkley Prime Crime Book / published by arrangement with the author

PRINTING HISTORY
Berkley Prime Crime edition/September 1995

ISBN: 0-425-14932-3

Berkley Prime Crime Books are published by
The Berkley Publishing Group,
200 Madison Avenue, New York, NY 10016.
The name BERKLEY PRIME CRIME and the BERKLEY PRIME CRIME
design are trademarks belonging to Berkley Publishing
Corporation.

PRINTED IN THE UNITED STATES OF AMERICA

10 9 8 7 6 5 4 3 2 1

For Doris and Russ, who have adopted more than their share of strays

ACKNOWLEDGMENTS

•

I wish to acknowledge the technical assistance of the following people: Richard L. McClelland, Special Agent in Charge, and Rob Buster, Special Agent, Department of the Treasury, U.S. Secret Service, Tampa; Detective Richard Howard, Clearwater Police Department; Deborah A. Edwards, DVM, All Cats Hospital, Largo; Roy Finley, MD. As usual, any errors are entirely my own.

I want to thank my readers, Bonnie Goldman and my father, Donald F. Wilson, for their helpful suggestions. Special thanks go to Catherine Koogle, Wm. Paul Mitchell, and Rod Perry. I also would like to express my appreciation to my agent, Robin Rue, and my editor, Ginjer Buchanan, and, most of all, to my husband, Robert A. Knight, for their continued support.

PROLOGUE

•

People steal for a lot of different reasons. When I was ten, I lifted a carton of cigarettes from the convenience store down the street. I can't remember the brand. It wasn't like I really wanted them. My father, a surgeon, had explained to me on numerous occasions and in graphic detail what happens to a person who smokes. No, I stole them because the kid next door double-dared me. I would have gotten away with it, too, except it is tough to conceal a carton of cigarettes under your shirt when you are ten and flat-chested.

Until I came to Florida, I never actually met anyone who stole because they had to. Everyone I knew back home in Connecticut had money to burn. The fact that people invariably got burned in the process is what finally drove me away. At the age of thirty, I found I needed to rethink my life. I'd grown soft, evidently, and overly sensitive. Less daring. Not a good thing to be where I come from.

I ended up in Paradise Cay, on Florida's west coast, a suburb of Brightwater Beach, because, according to Jimmy Buffet, everything moves more slowly in paradise. I always thought it was due to the heat, but if you believe the rumors, it is because half of Florida's human inhabitants have one foot in the grave and the other in the poorhouse. It is true we have a lot of AARP members trying to thaw out after decades of shoveling snow. And we have more than a few lonely widows attempting to survive on Social Security. Most of them keep a pet for company, if the traffic in and out of Paradise Cay Animal Hospital is any indication. So, it isn't surprising one or two might pocket a can of cat food or a rawhide chew toy now and then.

My boss, Dr. Louis Augustin, usually looks the other way. He says if they care enough about their pets to bring them to his clinic, then they deserve a break. The truth is (and he knows it), our elderly female clients would almost rather pass the afternoon hours at our clinic than at the local bingo hall. In fact, women of all ages are drawn to Dr. Augustin like moths to a bug light.

Little do they know he spends his free time snooping into people's private affairs. He isn't above a little breaking and entering, either. He does this in the name of justice. Personally, I would like to see him give the local police a chance, but Dr. Augustin does not have a high regard for government officials. He is convinced Brightwater Beach would fall into the sea without his help.

Where he gets his boundless energy is a mystery to those of us who know him. It certainly isn't his diet. If anything, all the fast food he eats should slow him down. In an adult, sugar is supposed to induce sleep, or so I thought. Anyway, he seems to enjoy playing Robin Hood immensely and thinks nothing of sending his not so merry little band out in search of the evil sheriff.

When one of our clients is found faceup in a nearby canal the same day someone leaves a basket of kittens and $300 in stolen funny money on our doorstep, naturally Dr. Augustin cannot stick to doctoring. This time, though, it nearly puts an end to his extracurricular activities once and for all. And for me, it reinforces that old adage, "Never take anything at face value." Because people kill for a lot of different reasons, too. Even in paradise.

CHAPTER 1

•

Monday, July 6

The patrolman, his yellow poncho half blown away by the wind, appeared out of absolutely nowhere. In the rain, he looked like Big Bird, feathered arms swinging pendulum fashion to indicate a detour down Fourth Street. I slammed on the brakes. My car slid sideways a few feet before I managed to regain control and turn right. The cop gave me a dirty look. Behind him, an array of red and blue lights flashed disharmoniously through the downpour.

Somebody must have taken a nosedive into the canal, I thought, relieved it wasn't me.

In July, it rains nearly every day, usually in the late afternoon but sometimes in the morning, if the wind is out of the west. It is a great sobbing torrent that temporarily overwhelms the drainage system and makes crossing intersections a little like riding a jet ski. An hour or two later, except for the humidity, it is difficult to tell it has rained at all.

When I finally got to the clinic, the deluge had subsided. The sky was still leaking a bit, so I grabbed my purse and dashed across the parking lot, hopping over puddles as I went. Frank Jennings, our kennel manager cum rock musician, opened the door for me.

"Hi, Samantha," he said, smiling. Actually, it was more like a leer. "How goes it?" He looked particularly seedy that morning in his black *Death Watch* T-shirt, its bearded demon laughing at me in red and gold Technicolor.

I shuddered. Frank gives me the willies. He is reliable and

conscientious and loves animals. I know the long hair and jeans with the knees torn out are simply part of his act. Dr. Augustin puts up with his attire and the fact that he occasionally comes in late after a "gig," as he calls it. But I keep my distance whenever possible. I think it has to do with Frank's attraction to me, something I have never been able to understand since, at thirty-two, I am fours years older than he is and cannot name a single Pink Floyd number.

"So far, so good," I said. I avoided looking at him and walked resolutely down the hall to the lab.

Frank followed me like a puppy. "You're not going to believe what I found out back."

"What's that?" I poured water into the coffeemaker and took a packet of coffee out of the cabinet over the sink.

"I'll get it," he said. "You wait right here." He scampered off.

After I dumped the coffee into the filter basket, and the coffeemaker was hissing and gurgling, I went into the darkroom to check the automatic processor. When I came out, Frank was standing in the doorway to X ray holding a small wicker picnic basket.

"You're not going to believe it," he said again. "Go on, take a look." He was like a little kid who'd discovered that boys were different from girls.

I peered in the basket. Three tiny, wet balls of fur shook and tottered unsteadily around, mewing feebly.

"Poor little guys," Frank said gently. "Out in the rain and all. Whoever left these kittens meant for us to find them, though. They were on the ground next to the door."

One of the kittens was noticeably larger than the others, and I picked it up. The mewing intensified.

"They're probably freezing," Frank said. "No telling how long they've been out there. I almost tripped over them when I went to the dumpster." He placed the basket on the X-ray table and lifted up the two smallest kittens, holding them snugly against his chest. The demon on his T-shirt licked at them with its tongue.

There was something unsettling about that image. Suddenly, I wanted to get the kittens away from Frank. "Let's put them in a cage in Isolation until Dr. Augustin gets here," I said quickly.

I walked across the hall and opened one of the intensive care cages. I placed my still complaining kitten on a clean cage pad and turned the heating element to low. Then I stood back to let Frank add his two.

"They look really weak," he said. " Especially these." He touched the two smallest on the head. "Like they haven't been getting enough to eat."

I nodded. "It's almost like they're from two different litters." I closed the cage door and headed for the treatment room. I had things to do. "Why don't you mix up some formula and have it ready? We can feed them after Dr. Augustin checks them out."

"Will do," Frank said. Suddenly, he was right behind me. "Samantha?"

I turned around.

"My band is playing at the Chilly Bin tomorrow. Ladies drink free from nine to midnight." He was staring, his eyes doing a slow, head-to-toe appraisal of my uniform.

I tried not to sound too repulsed. "Can't tomorrow, Frank. I already have plans. Maybe another time." I opened the refrigerator and took out a vial of insulin.

"Sure, Sam," I heard him mumble. "Another time."

Cynthia Caswell, our receptionist, was shaking out her umbrella. Through the plate glass window that makes up most of the clinic's front wall, I could see it had started to rain heavily again.

"Great hair day, isn't it?" I said, fingering my blond Little Orphan Annie look.

Cynthia grimaced from under a transparent plastic rain bonnet.

"Did you happen to notice if the cops were still blocking Nautilus Avenue?" I asked. "Somebody apparently slid into the canal."

Cynthia shook her head. "I took the bus today. That's why I'm late. My car is in the shop. That's twice in one month for the same problem. Now they say I need a new carburetor."

She frowned. "When I was your age, a woman trusted men to take care of things like automobiles. We didn't need to know what a carburetor was. And we never read the fine print. I'm not even sure there *was* fine print in those days." She put her hands on her ample hips and looked at me. "Now you can't trust any of them. Men, that is."

Cynthia is my mother's age and, like my mother, still reeling from the consequences of a divorce late in life.

"Yes. Well," I said, "you know how I feel about men." I pointed toward Dr. Augustin's office. "Incidentally, is *he* here yet?"

"No. The only surgery scheduled for today is a tooth extraction, so he'll probably be a little late. After all, his plane wasn't supposed to get in until sometime last night." She went around behind her desk. "I certainly hope he had a good time. For our sake as well as his." She looked down at the appointment book. "And I hope no one comes in today with anything complicated. He'll need a chance to get back into the swing of things, I imagine, and we've got a full schedule."

I gasped. " I almost forgot."

Cynthia looked at me.

"Frank found a basket out back with three kittens in it. Abandoned on our doorstep, apparently. They can't be more than a couple of weeks old. And they were drenched. I hope they're okay."

Cynthia followed me into Isolation. We stared at the infants through the glass door. They were nearly dry and had fallen asleep in a tiny mound in the middle of the cage. They looked a lot better.

"Oh, they're adorable," Cynthia exclaimed. "Somebody probably found them. You know, a lot of stray cats live over on Sunset Beach. They have their kittens under the houses there. Did Frank find a note in the basket?"

"I don't think so."

We went into X ray. I got the basket and pulled out a soggy, blue towel. An envelope lay under it.

"Well, what do you know," I said. I tore open the envelope and extracted a sheet of notepaper. Clipped to the note was a small stack of crisp twenty-dollar bills. I counted them. "Fifteen twenties," I told Cynthia. "Three hundred bucks. That's a lot of money for someone to leave out in the open like that." I read the note out loud. " 'Dr. Augustin, please help these poor kittens, if you can. I hope three hundred dollars is sufficient.' It's signed 'A Concerned Pet Owner.'"

Cynthia and I studied the note. The handwriting was small and neat, almost cramped. It was written on a piece of paper torn from one of those notepads pharmaceutical companies give away as a form of advertising. The product name was Theo-Dur.

"Well, that's a switch, isn't it?" I said. "Leaving us money, I mean." I handed the bills to Cynthia. "I guess you can put this in the cash drawer until Dr. Augustin decides what he wants to do with it."

The telephone rang. Cynthia took the money and trotted down the hall. I went into the lab, poured myself a cup of coffee, and tried to gear myself up for Dr. Augustin's first day back from vacation.

The demon had returned. Now it stood in the doorway, life-sized and three-dimensional, black eyes shining, hairy jaws working on a piece of gum. I stumbled into the exam table, knocking over a plastic spray bottle filled with disinfectant. It rolled noisily across the stainless steel and hit the floor with a thud.

"You don't look happy to see me, Samantha," said Dr. Augustin. Straight, white teeth flashed through the beard. Then he blew a nice round bubble and caught it before it popped.

"No, I am, really. You look . . . different, is all." I gripped the edge of the table. He is enjoying this, I thought. He gets some perverse pleasure out of watching people come unglued.

He laughed. "So, what do you think? Should I keep it?" He touched the wiry growth with his fingertips. It was almost a caress.

Dr. Augustin has long, slender fingers, and he keeps his nails short and immaculate. His hands seem inappropriate for someone so muscular. It's as if they were intended for somebody else, and a mix-up occurred at the factory.

"Give me a little time to get used to it," I said.

"Sure. I'm going to let it grow another couple of weeks at least."

He leaned over and picked up the spray bottle, then handed it to me. His hair, normally on the long side anyway, was even longer. It fell an inch short of his shoulders in loose curls, accentuating his beard. He was wearing a purple and black pullover, jeans, and his leather hiking boots. He seemed taller than I remembered.

"So, how did Larry do while I was away?" he asked. "Our balance isn't all that great. You people did come to work every day, didn't you?"

"No, we went to the Keys for two weeks," I snapped, regretting it instantly.

He stood by silently, while I finished cleaning the exam table and put the bottle back on the shelf. Then I turned around to face him.

"You know perfectly well that your regular clients won't bring their animals to anyone but you, unless they absolutely have to. No matter how good Larry Wilson or any other relief vet might be."

He wanted to hear me say it, of course, wanted to know that he was missed, that his female clients just couldn't live without him. All he had to do was look at the appointment book to see it was filled to capacity for the next several days.

"Besides, June is always a slow month," I added, just for spite.

But he only heard what he wanted to hear. "Cynthia said something about kittens in a basket by the dumpster." He glanced at his watch. "Let's take a look at them, before our ten o'clock arrives."

We went into Isolation. I opened the cage door and scooped up all three kittens and put them on the exam table. Their tiny cries echoed off the metal cages.

"They're hungry," I said.

Dr. Augustin picked up one of the kittens. It was jet black, except for a few white hairs on its chest. He looked under its tail.

"A female," he said. He pulled down on her lower jaw with

his index finger and peered inside her mouth. "Wonderful," he muttered, and furrows appeared in his forehead.

He put the kitten down and picked up another—a cream and tan male. He looked in its mouth. He repeated this with the largest kitten, a white male with faint points on its ears and feet and a grey smudge on its nose. In the light from the overhead lamp, I could see pale grey tabby stripes halfway up its legs and tail.

This time, Dr. Augustin took his stethoscope off the wall and listened to the animal's chest. Then he hung the stethoscope back on its hook. He put the kitten down and leaned against the sink.

"Let me see the note," he said.

I took it out of my pocket and handed it to him. "What's wrong with them?" I asked. It was obvious something wasn't right.

He read the note, turned it over to check the back, then reread it. When he was finished, he put it on the counter and picked up the black kitten. He pried open her mouth again and held her under the light.

"What do you see?" he asked me.

I squinted at the tiny opening, but the canyon in the roof of the animal's mouth was hard to miss. "Are they all like this one? Even him?" I touched the largest kitten.

"Yes, although his cleft isn't severe, which probably accounts for his size. A cleft palate makes nursing difficult, if not impossible."

Dr. Augustin put the kitten down. It moved over to sit crouched next to its siblings, tail curled tightly around its little body, a look of confusion and fear on its face. I could see that the kitten's mouth didn't close properly, and its nose was off-center. It was something I should have noticed right away.

"If they don't die from lung problems associated with inhaling small quantities of milk," Dr. Augustin continued, "they starve to death. Someone has to have been feeding these kittens with a stomach tube. Someone experienced at that sort of thing." He picked the kittens up, one by one, and put them back in their cage.

"It's pretty unusual for an entire litter to be affected," he said. "I'd say the mother was probably exposed to some teratogenic agent during pregnancy. Some toxic chemical or a drug like griseofulvin."

He turned to go. "Have Frank mix up some formula. You can feed them if you want. For now." He wouldn't look at me, but I knew what he was implying.

"If this one isn't as bad as the others," I said, picking up the kitten with the smudge on its nose, "couldn't you repair his palate? I'd be willing to feed him, until he's strong enough." I paused. If I couldn't convince him, maybe money could. "I mean, they left us three hundred bucks."

Dr. Augustin stopped briefly in the doorway but did not turn around. "Have Cynthia deposit that money, but tell her not to record it. Not yet. Just put a note on my desk." He continued across the lab into his office and shut the door.

If there is such a thing as a base revenue in the practice of veterinary medicine, then Glynnis Winter would be a contributor. A major contributor.

Mrs. Winter, the wife of the late Circuit Court Judge Jameson Winter is, at the age of forty-six, filthy rich and apparently bored to distraction. She is also extremely attractive, although, with her money, it is safe to assume Mother Nature had more than a little help.

Her dog, a Maltese by the name of Frosty, has never seen a fire hydrant or, heaven forbid, grass. According to Mrs. Winter, he does his business on newspapers in the guest bathroom of their new (and, no doubt, spacious) fifteenth floor condo. I imagine he spends his afternoons gazing out at (but not smelling) the surf from the glassed-in lanai or watching Lassie reruns on his very own television in his very own bedroom. I do know he eats the kind of dog food that looks and smells like beef bourguignon and comes in those tiny little cans with no meaningful nutritional information on the label.

Frosty suffers from a variety of digestive and skin disorders. It is a toss-up as to whether the dog's diet or Mrs. Winter is more to blame. In any case, Mrs. Winter feels that these problems require Dr. Augustin's attention at regular intervals, usually every two weeks. If Mrs. Winter were a guinea pig, I would say that this was the length of her heat cycle.

It didn't surprise me to find her name at the top of Monday's appointment sheet. Cynthia posts one on the hall bulletin board every morning. She had written "Diarrhea/Vomiting" after Frosty's name.

They arrived at 9:40. Mrs. Winter looked smashing, as usual. She had on a royal blue crepe de chine skirt that reached nearly to her ankles. Her blouse, of the same material, was pale lemon, very baggy, very airy, and potentially very revealing, since the first button was halfway to her navel. She wore shoulder pads that made her neck appear longer and narrower than it really was, like a peacock's neck thrusting up out of an explosion of gaudy feathers. She finished the outfit off with a wide silver belt that made her waist look about as big around as a broom handle, and earrings the size of silver dollars, engraved with a sign of the zodiac. Scorpio.

Her pheromone du jour was Safari. I knew that, because I sometimes help myself to the "tester" bottles on the cosmetic counter at Dillards. Just for fun. Dr. Augustin frowns on his employees wearing perfume or cologne. He says it irritates the animals. Cats, in particular. I think it irritates him, but I would never tell Mrs. Winter that, of course.

"Good morning, Mrs. Winter," I said, smiling. Frosty panted from the crook of her left arm. His hair ribbon matched her skirt.

Mrs. Winter thrust a small yogurt cup at me. "Frosty's 'poo-poos,'" she said with obvious distaste. She held it like it was a hand grenade whose pin had just fallen out.

I took the container and led them into Room 1. "Dr. Augustin will be right in," I said. "You have a seat."

"Thank you, Miss Holt," she said, rather primly.

As I was pulling the door closed, I saw her lean over and touch the chair to make certain it was clean.

Dr. Augustin rearranged his face into a wide smile before opening the door. "Good morning, Glynnis," he said heartily upon entering the exam room. "How is that sweet baby of yours today? Not feeling too spunky?"

It was all I could do to keep from gagging.

He scratched Frosty's head while Mrs. Winter did a quick assessment of Dr. Augustin's overall appearance. She lingered over his beard.

"I approve of the beard," she said. "It makes you look a bit like a new wave film director." She smiled, so he could appreciate her dental work. "Very avant-garde." Like she knew a whole passel of new wave film directors here in Florida, the film capital of the world.

"Why, thank you, Glynnis. I haven't decided yet if I'll keep it. Florida is almost too hot for a beard."

He reached for her dog, and she handed him over, willingly. Something she never does with me.

"Frosty and I will be back in a flash," he told her. "Before you know it, in fact." He winked at her. Then he and I went into the hall, and he pulled the door closed.

"Pouring it on a little thick, aren't we?" I asked him, once we were in the treatment room.

I held Frosty while Dr. Augustin drew a blood sample. Whether we do this sort of thing in the exam room or in the treatment room depends on the client. Mrs. Winter is one of those people who puts body fluids in the same category as hazardous waste. Well, most body fluids, anyway.

"It doesn't hurt to be congenial, Samantha," he said. "It's good for business, don't forget."

I didn't say anything.

He did a quick examination of Frosty. The animal winced when Dr. Augustin prodded his upper abdomen.

"What do you want to bet Frosty has a touch of pancreatitis?" he asked. "Too much liver pâté or whatever she feeds him." He shook his head. "Let's do a CBC and a fecal for starters. Depending on what those tell us, we may want to do a chemical profile." He labeled two collection tubes, then handed them to me. "I'll have her wait."

I nodded. "By the way," I said, "how was your vacation? You took lots of pictures, I hope."

"A couple of rolls," he said. He thought for a minute. "They should be ready by now. I dropped them off at Eckerd's on my way in." His eyes locked onto mine. "Would you mind getting them for me over lunch? I have a tooth extraction to do. Just ask Cynthia to give you a twenty. That should cover it." He didn't wait for me to answer. He picked up Mrs. Winter's dog and headed down the hall toward the exam rooms.

"Sure," I told the doorway. "I'll be happy to."

Our laboratory technician quit shortly before Dr. Augustin left for vacation. She finally got tired of him criticizing her all the time. He never actually came out and told her she did a lousy job. He doesn't work that way. He laughs, pokes fun, makes snide remarks. When she broke down and cried once, he backpedaled and said he never meant anything by it, that he was just teasing. But he started in again the following Monday.

"He's only doing it because you let him, P.J.," I told her.

We were eating lunch in one of the exam rooms. Dr. Augustin had been in a bad mood all morning and had taken it out on P.J. Cynthia hadn't been able to cheer her up, so now it was my turn.

"Try ignoring him. Just do your job and pretend you don't hear him. After a while, he'll learn to leave you alone. If he can't get a rise out of you, it won't be fun, and he'll quit." It sounded like we were talking about how to stop a cat from pestering the family dog. "If that doesn't work, just let what he says slide right off your back. After all, if he didn't like the job you were doing, he'd fire you."

"You should talk," she said. "You're always afraid you'll screw something up, and he'll find out and get on your case. How can you put up with that? I'm a nervous wreck." She threw her half-eaten sandwich in the trash can under the sink.

"I don't know," I said. "Maybe it's because he pays better than most." I grinned. "How many bosses do you think spring for pizza whenever it's someone's birthday?"

She didn't seem amused. "I don't even like pizza," she said.

So she quit.

We'd posted a notice on the Employment Opportunities board at the junior college. Unfortunately, Dr. Augustin's reputation was scaring off potential applicants. If it got too bad, I figured I could go out and recruit someone personally. Lie about Dr. Augustin, if necessary.

Anyway, for the time being, I was doing the job of two people, trying to be in two places at once, and not succeeding very well. Fortunately, Dr. Augustin was still mentally hiking some alpine trail and didn't notice or didn't feel compelled to comment.

At lunch, I dutifully walked up the street to the drugstore and retrieved Dr. Augustin's pictures. I stood next to the counter for a minute or so after getting my change, trying to decide if I should look at them. The clerk had suggested I check to see if there were any shots the lab had messed up that I wanted redone. I didn't tell him they weren't my pictures. Finally, I peeled open the envelope and slid out the packet of prints.

They were beautiful, all green trees and snow-covered mountains and crystal-clear streams. A number of shots were of moose, most of them in the process of leaving the field of view. One was a picture of a brown bear. The image was tiny, but unmistakable. I wondered what size lens Dr. Augustin had used.

I was about to put the prints back in their envelope when I noticed a person standing at the base of what I presumed was a glacier. The glacier itself was turquoise and white, really spectacular, and I almost missed the woman. It was the last print of the first roll. Quickly, I opened the second envelope and pulled out the pictures. There she was again, this time sticking her head out of a tent. She had a toothbrush in her mouth, and she looked surprised.

I hurried through the rest of the pictures, but only one additional shot included the woman. That time, Dr. Augustin was sitting next to her on a ledge overlooking some river valley. He had his arm around her, and they were both laughing. She was very pretty, about his age, and appeared incredibly fit. Like she spent a lot of time wrestling lions and tigers. His kind of woman.

I put the photos in with their negatives, made certain both envelopes were sealed the way I had picked them up, and left. On my way back to the clinic, I stopped at Wendy's for a salad. I had brought my lunch, leftover barbecued chicken from a Fourth of July party at my apartment building, but decided I could stand to lose some weight. I put fat-free dressing on the salad. It was awful.

When I got to the clinic, Dr. Augustin was nowhere to be seen. I put the envelope on his desk, along with his change, and went into Isolation to check on the kittens. I wanted to feed them again, before I got involved with the afternoon's appointments. But when I looked in their cage, I saw only the kitten with the smudge on its nose. A cage card read: "Stray—Male; no food or water in cage." It was Dr. Augustin's handwriting.

CHAPTER 2

•

Tuesday, July 7

Cynthia had gotten her car back. It was parked in its usual spot out front.

"I see they fixed it," I said, as I walked in.

She took a sip of coffee and nodded. "It cost me a small fortune," she said glumly. "At least it runs now. I should be thankful, I suppose." She smiled.

She had done something to her hair. I wasn't sure what. It was still grey, but it looked different somehow. I could tell she was waiting for my reaction. When I didn't say anything, she went back to reading the paper, and I hurried into Isolation to check on Randy.

It is unwise to name an animal you can't keep or one that isn't expected to make it. You are more likely to become attached to it if you do. That's Dr. Augustin's theory, anyway.

I had decided the night before to call the kitten Randy. I liked the name, and continually referring to him as the "Stray" seemed a bit cold-hearted, not to mention confusing, since we often took in abandoned animals. Now I was worried he might be dead. By naming him, I had doomed him to join his brother and sister in kitty heaven. But there he was, still very much alive and obviously very hungry. He stood up when he saw me and came over to the cage door, mewing frantically.

I opened the door and picked him up. Instantly, he began to purr, a resonant, nasal rumbling that seemed entirely too loud for such a tiny body.

"All right, all right." I laughed. "Give me a chance to warm it up first." I took a container of formula out of the refrigerator, while Randy began to claw his way onto my shoulder.

"Samantha!" Cynthia sounded upset.

I put Randy back in his cage and went up front.

"Remember that police business on Nautilus Avenue yesterday?" she asked me. She had the local section of the *Times* in front of her.

I went around the desk and looked over her shoulder. She pointed to the lead article. The headline read "MUTILATED BODY FOUND IN CANAL."

"The poor man drowned," Cynthia said. "And someone cut off his hands." She shuddered. "There certainly are a lot of sick people out there." She looked up at me. "Nautilus Avenue is less than a mile from here."

I continued to read. "It says here he'd been dead for two or three days."

The police had failed to identify the man at press time, according to the article, but said he was white, about six feet, 180 pounds, with grey hair and brown eyes. That sure narrows it down, I thought.

A car pulled into the parking lot. Both Cynthia and I looked up. It was Dr. Augustin.

"Either he's early or I'm late," I said. "In any case, I'm in trouble, since I haven't done treatments yet." I sighed and raced down the hall. Poor Randy would have to wait.

The heartworm test on the Peters dog was positive, the first positive we'd had in four months, thanks to Mosquito Control and Dr. Augustin's rather unorthodox methods.

Despite protests from Cynthia, Dr. Augustin keeps a jar containing a preserved dog heart on the reception desk. The dog, an ex-patient, died of heartworm disease. Long, white spaghetti strands explode out of the animal's heart like straw out of an overstuffed scarecrow. People either put their dogs on heartworm preventative or get the jar stuck in their faces every time they come in. A few clients have elected to go elsewhere, but that hasn't stopped Dr. Augustin.

I knew Mick Peters had Jonesy on heartworm medication,

because he came in regularly to purchase it, complaining each time about the price.

"It's too bad I don't have stock in this company," he said on one occasion, holding up the paper package containing six foil-lined tablets. "What they charge for these things is highway robbery. I spend more money on that mutt than I do on myself."

Although I hear this from time to time from clients who really don't mean it, Mick probably wasn't exaggerating. According to Cynthia, his little computer business was struggling to make ends meet, which was unfortunate for a couple of reasons. Mick was trying to raise a four-year-old daughter alone, after his twenty-one-year-old wife died of cancer. His teaching job at the junior college barely covered the cost of daycare, let alone groceries and rent. But more to the point, Mick really knew his stuff when it came to computers. Following months of dickering and shopping around, Dr. Augustin finally agreed to purchase a new computer system for the clinic from Mick. I felt certain if Mick had it to do again, he would have sent us to his competitors. After the system was installed, he spent weeks babying us—Cynthia, in particular—through the learning process. I told him he might as well move his office to our clinic, since he was there so much of the time.

"Jonesy has heartworms, I'm afraid," said Dr. Augustin.

Mick stared at him. "Heartworms? But, how is that possible? I swear I haven't missed a single pill. Never."

He was a cute guy, with hair as long as Dr. Augustin's and a baby face that made him look a lot younger than his thirty or so years. He was always clean but usually dressed in worn, ill-fitting clothes that seldom matched. As if appearance was low on his list of priorities. Certainly not the best attitude for a computer salesman. I noticed his daughter, Cindy, always looked picture perfect, however. She usually came to the clinic with him. That day he was alone, and I wondered where Cindy was.

"Jonesy may have spit a pill or two out, when you weren't looking," I offered. "Dogs and cats can be very sneaky. Hide the pill under their tongue, until you leave, then jettison it across the yard."

I scratched Jonesy's head. After a few seconds, he got this "died and gone to heaven" look on his face—eyes closed, jowls slack, ears at half mast. Jonesy was part shepherd, part beagle, part terrier. He had a terrific personality and rotten skin, the kind of dog you can smell before you can see him.

"Or he may have gotten heartworms despite the pills," added Dr. Augustin. "They're not one hundred percent effective in all cases. That's why we do an annual heartworm test even when the dog is taking medication to prevent the worms. And we follow up a positive test result with an X ray."

Mick looked at Jonesy. "Can you treat him?"

"Yes," said Dr. Augustin. "But treatment puts a lot of stress on a dog, particularly its circulatory system. You need to know that. After the initial treatment, Jonesy will need several weeks of rest—no exercise, no excitement. And some dogs can get pretty sick from the chemical we use. We may need to stop treatment, then start it up again, if that happens."

He looked at Mick. I knew he was waiting for some indication that Mick was willing to cooperate. If not, the dog would have to stay with us for a month or so, and that could get expensive.

"Whatever you think is best, Doc," Mick said. He gave Jonesy a hug, and the dog bathed his face in saliva.

Dr. Augustin lifted Jonesy off the table and handed his leash to me. "Don't worry about paying for this right away, Mick," he said. "We'll work something out. Maybe do a little trade. I'm sure Cynthia would love to see your face around here again." He smiled.

"Hey, I'll be happy to help you guys out with the computer," Mick said, a little too enthusiastically, "but I can pay. The business is doing pretty good right now." He avoided eye contact with Dr. Augustin or me. Instead, he fumbled with Jonesy's collar, making sure the rabies tag was facing the right way.

I glanced over at Dr. Augustin and shrugged, then opened the door. It was obvious Mick didn't want charity, and I felt embarrassed for him. I hurried down the hall, with Jonesy tap-dancing along behind me.

• • •

I stuck a Melba Round in my mouth, just as a car pulled into the parking lot. It was one o'clock, and Cynthia was at lunch, leaving me to man the reception desk.

I chewed slowly and watched as two very tall, very official-looking men got out of the vehicle. They were dressed in nearly identical charcoal-grey suits with white, button-down shirts and dark ties. They both had short, neatly styled haircuts and nice tans. One was in his forties, the other I guessed was about my age. Their faces lacked expression, as far as I could tell. They were on a mission. They look like government men, I said to myself. All they need are matching sunglasses to fit the stereotypical Hollywood image.

I was glad Cynthia had gone to lunch. Despite her own problems and my resolve never to get romantically involved with a man again, she was determined to marry me off and checked out every male who came into the clinic as though taking job applications. These two looked like her kind of groom material.

I sat up and brushed crumbs from my uniform and the desk, then glanced around the room. I wanted to make sure no one had secretly piddled on the floor or the furniture, not that I could do anything about it at that point. I spotted a wad of hair lurking under one of the tables. It reminded me of something out of *Star Wars*. I prayed it would stay put.

The older of the two men pulled open the door, then followed the younger one in.

"Good afternoon," I said pleasantly. "May I help you?"

"Hello," said the older man. "Is Dr. Augustin around?" He smiled. He seemed friendly enough.

His companion was doing a careful survey of the reception room. His eyes wandered slowly over the notes on the bulletin board, the magazines on the end tables, and the food display. Suddenly, he spotted the dog heart. He stepped back two paces and paled noticeably. This caused the older man to look at the heart.

I reached over, picked up the jar, and placed it on the floor behind my chair. "Sorry," I said.

Both men looked relieved.

"Dr. Augustin . . . ?" said the older man.

"He's at lunch," I said. "Perhaps I can help you."

The man appeared torn between telling a lowly assistant (and a female one at that) his identity and mission and going home empty-handed. He was spared from having to decide. Dr. Augustin opened his door and stepped out into the reception room.

"I'm Dr. Augustin," he said. "What can I do for you?"

The older man took a business card from out of his pocket and handed it to Dr. Augustin. Then he flashed open a two-by-five dark blue folder. The photo inside was not very flattering. "I'm Special Agent Daniel Nelson, U.S. Secret Service. This is Agent Jackson Held." He indicated his partner.

I felt my eyes bug out. I had to fight to keep my mouth from dropping open. Was the President in town and in need of a veterinarian. Or had Dr. Augustin finally flipped and sent a letter bomb to Washington?

"What brings the Secret Service to Brightwater Beach?" Dr. Augustin asked calmly. He hadn't offered the man his hand, so I knew he was on the defensive. Of course, Dr. Augustin is suspicious of anyone even faintly associated with the government, and these guys were about as close as you could get.

Agent Nelson hesitated a fraction of a second. He glanced over at me.

Dr. Augustin picked it right up. "This is Samantha Holt, my technician," he said, putting his hand on my shoulder. The hand indicated I was to stay right where I was.

Nelson smiled. It might have been an involuntary twitch for all I knew. He and Dr. Augustin were like two tomcats forced by circumstance to reside in the same territory. Fighting was pointless, but that didn't mean they had to be friends.

"We received a call from your bank this morning," Nelson said. "It seems you included some counterfeit twenties in your deposit last night." He waited for Dr. Augustin's reaction.

Mine was quicker in coming. "Counterfeit!" I exclaimed.

Dr. Augustin shot me a warning glance.

"Yes," said Nelson. "Fifteen twenty-dollar bills. Good quality, too. Some of the best we've seen lately." He looked at me, then back at Dr. Augustin. "Do you have any idea who might be the source of those bills?"

Dr. Augustin, who never cooperates with the authorities unless he has to, looked about as innocent as Sylvester the cat. "No, I'm afraid not. Someone—I don't know who—left three stray cats on our doorstep yesterday, along with three hundred dollars. I never saw the money. I expect my receptionist included it in our deposit." He smiled faintly.

"Was there a note? Was the money in an envelope or a container of some kind?"

Dr. Augustin shook his head. "Afraid not."

I stood up. "There was a wicker basket. And a blanket. I'll get them."

Dr. Augustin glared at me.

"No, that's all right," said Agent Nelson. "If we need them, we can contact you." He looked at Agent Held, then back at Dr. Augustin. "We have to leave for Tampa. If you think of anything, or if the person who left the stray cats turns up, please give me a call." He stuck out his hand.

Reluctantly, Dr. Augustin shook it. "If anyone claims them, we'll let you know."

We watched the two men get into their car.

"Agent Held must be a deaf mute," I said, as they drove off.

Dr. Augustin obviously didn't think this was funny. "No," he said, "Agent Held is Agent Nelson's subordinate. And a good subordinate knows when to keep his *or her* mouth shut."

"I was trying to help," I said. It came out like a whine. "I thought maybe you'd forgotten about the basket. Why didn't you give them the note?"

"Because I wasn't ready to give it to them," he said. He went into his office and closed the door.

Cynthia turned into the parking lot. I decided to be a good subordinate and keep my mouth shut. Cynthia would have to find out about this on her own.

Our three o'clock appointment was a beautiful black and tan Doberman pinscher by the name of Dresden. I went out to the reception room to get him and found his owner, Vivian Porter, in a heated discussion with another woman—actually, Miss Porter was doing most of the talking—concerning the pros and cons of ear cropping. Dresden's ears were long and free-flowing, according to the style in England.

The other woman apparently was a new client, because I had never seen her before. She had an adorable boxer puppy with her. The puppy was about eight weeks old and appeared to be quite healthy. It squirmed and struggled in the woman's lap, trying to get down. I was glad the woman had a firm grasp on her pet. It would have made a tasty snack for Dresden.

Miss Porter, Vivian, was dressed in a denim wraparound skirt, white cotton blouse, and sandals. She is a large, broad-shouldered woman, about sixty, robust, with rosy cheeks and a Julia Childs type of voice. I can picture her in the woods somewhere, armed with binoculars and a copy of *Field Guide to the Birds of North America*. Cynthia and I agree, instead of a Doberman, Vivian should have an Irish setter or a King Charles spaniel.

On the other hand, maybe Vivian Porter is a retired army medic. A sergeant. The kind who sticks a thermometer in your mouth immediately after your teeth and the steering wheel of your car have become intimate. *That* Vivian would most definitely own a Doberman.

Whichever one she is, Vivian has strong opinions about things and doesn't mind sharing them with others. That day, she evidently was trying to convince the boxer's owner to leave the puppy's ears "au naturel." In vivid and somewhat exaggerated detail, she was describing the ear crop procedure to the woman.

Cynthia pecked away at the computer terminal. I could tell she was trying to block out the discussion. She looked relieved when I walked in. She quickly picked up Dresden's file and handed it to me.

"Okay, Dresden," I said, "you're next." I smiled apologetically at the new client, who was watching Vivian with obvious resentment.

Vivian and her dog followed me into the exam room. "I am so glad that Dr. Augustin does not do ear crops," she said. "What a barbaric practice." She handed me a small brown paper sack, carefully folded over and labeled "Dresden" in neat penciled letters. Like Dresden was a child, and this was his lunch.

I took the offering. "He does them, Miss Porter, he just

doesn't like to do them. He tries to talk the owner out of it first."

She seemed shocked. She didn't say anything, as I drew a sample of Dresden's blood for a heartworm test. I was halfway out the door, when she cleared her throat.

"Well, I suppose he has to make a living, doesn't he," she said.

I turned around. "Dr. Augustin will be right in, Miss Porter. I'll start these labs tests and be back to help with the exam." I left her sitting in the corner, a curious mixture of anticipation and disappointment on her face. I was glad she hadn't asked me if Dr. Augustin declawed cats.

"Doesn't this kitten look familiar?" asked Dr. Augustin. He refused to call the cat Randy. That meant he didn't plan to keep him around very long.

We were in Isolation. It was six o'clock, and the last client had just walked out the door.

"What do you mean?" I asked.

Dr. Augustin held Randy up under the lamp. The kitten complained and wiggled violently. "Come on, Samantha, doesn't he remind you of another cat we see from time to time?" He looked momentarily perplexed, as he studied Randy's markings. Then he smiled. "Arnie Silor's cat, Pearl. If I'm not mistaken, Pearl is supposed to be part Siamese. Lilac point maybe."

"I thought you spayed Pearl last year," I said. Come to think of it, Randy *did* look a lot like Mr. Silor's cat.

"He never brought her in, and I forgot about it."

"There must be a zillion cats in this town that look like Pearl," I said.

"I doubt it. Not white with blue eyes and an odd dark band across their noses." He put Randy back in his cage. "Give Mr. Silor a call. See how Pearl is doing. Try to find out if she's had a litter of kittens recently. Without mentioning the money or sounding like you're accusing Arnie of anything, of course."

"Of course," I said.

I went to the computer terminal in the lab and called up

Arnold Silor's number, then dialed it. A man answered on the second ring.

"Hello?" he said.

"Mr. Silor?" The guy didn't sound like Arnie, but it was difficult to tell, since Arnie hadn't been to the clinic in a while.

"Mr. Silor is unavailable at the moment," the man said. "May I take a message?"

"Do you know when he'll be back?" I asked.

There was a muffled sound, like the guy had his hand over the receiver. Then a different voice, one I vaguely recognized, came on.

"This is Detective Sergeant Robinson of the Brightwater Beach Police. May I ask who is calling?"

I hung up. I stared at the phone like it had just burned my hand. Then I rushed into Dr. Augustin's office.

He was sitting at his desk, looking at his vacation pictures. He had taped the photo of him and the woman to the wall next to his chair.

I tried not to stare at the picture. "I called Mr. Silor's house," I said. "A cop answered the phone."

"Yes? What did the cop say?"

"Nothing. I hung up."

Dr. Augustin stared at me. "You what?" If he had been a cobra, he couldn't have struck me with such force.

"Well, he caught me off guard," I stammered. "I didn't know what to say, what you'd want me to say, so I didn't say anything. Besides, it was that Detective Sergeant Robinson from Homicide. You remember, the one who investigated Harvey Snead's murder in February."

Dr. Augustin's ex-wife, Rachel, had been accused of Harvey's murder, and Dr. Augustin had turned the entire clinic upside down for several weeks, while he found out who really killed Harvey.

"Well, never mind," he said cheerfully. He tossed the pictures on his desk and stood up. "Let's finish doing treatments and go home."

I followed him into the kennel. That was too easy, I thought suspiciously. Entirely too easy.

CHAPTER 3

•

Wednesday, July 8

Normally, Wednesday is my day off. The clinic is closed, and Dr. Augustin does treatments. Cynthia's nephew, Terry, cleans and feeds. That Wednesday, however, Dr. Augustin needed help with Jonesy Peters.

We'd gotten the results of Jonesy's blood work back the night before. His liver and kidney functions appeared normal, so Dr. Augustin had scheduled his first heartworm treatment for 9:00 A.M. Three additional treatments, at twelve-hour intervals, would be required, assuming Jonesy tolerated the drug. Dr. Augustin planned to spend Wednesday at the clinic doing paperwork, so he could keep an eye on the dog. He said I could go home after the morning treatment, but I'd have to come back at nine that night. I didn't really mind. The overtime was nice, but it meant I had to get up early.

I try to jog three miles every other day, usually in the morning. I'm not a "runner" by any means, but on a good day I can finish three miles in under twenty-seven minutes.

That morning, I struggled to make two miles. It was already seventy-eight degrees out and so muggy I felt like I was breathing through a wet washcloth. I had to walk three times and finally gave it up. My next-door neighbor, Jeffrey Gamble, dressed in grey sweatpants and a navy singlet, was on his way out but stopped at the foot of the stairs when he saw me approaching. I didn't have to look in the mirror to know my face was beet-red. Sweat trickled down my neck and arms, and I was still breathing pretty hard.

"You okay, Samantha?" he asked. He looked half asleep. His hair was flat against his head on one side, and there were creases in his face, the kind a bunched-up pillowcase leaves.

Jeffrey is not a morning person. He works the dinner shift, waiting tables at a local restaurant and generally doesn't get home until midnight. He sleeps until ten, usually, then runs five or six miles before heading to the beach. He is twenty-four, energetic and fit, but even he had begun to feel the effects of the heat. As a result, he was having to run after he got home, when it was still oppressive, or sacrifice sleep for the slightly cooler temperatures of early morning.

I shook my head. "I had to walk home. I felt like I was suffocating. It's too damn hot to run." I collapsed on the steps.

Jeffrey smiled. He is extremely attractive, in a feminine sort of way, with brilliant blue eyes and curly auburn hair. "At least you tried," he said. "That's what counts." He leaned against the banister and began his stretches. "You should run in one of the beach races. They're not too bad, really. The sunsets are spectacular, and a terrific breeze comes in from the Gulf." He stuck his right leg out behind him. "There's a 5K this Friday, and I'm off. How 'bout it?"

I got up. "No way. It's all I can do to shuffle along in private. I don't want to be run over by a bunch of zealots. And don't try to tell me it's a fun run, either. No one but a masochist would run at that time of the day. And on wet sand, no less."

Jeffrey sat down on the grass, extending his long legs out in front of him, and wrapped his hands around his feet. His agility was depressing. I started up the steps toward my apartment.

"Want me to bring leftovers home tonight for the cats?" he asked, changing the subject. "It's supposed to be pork spare-ribs with some kind of glaze."

My cats, Tina and Miss Priss, look forward to Jeffrey's little midnight visits. A veterinary technician should know better, I realize. Pork spareribs, Szechuan chicken with peanuts, and beef enchiladas are not particularly good for humans, let alone cats and dogs. How could I find fault with Glynnis Winter, when I was just as guilty?

"No, Jeffrey, not tonight. Thanks, anyway, but Miss Priss

absolutely has to lose two pounds. I could stand to shed a few myself."

"Okay," he said. "I'll bring you the leftover veggies and salad stuff." He hopped to his feet. "Well, I'd better get going. I'm doing ten today." He looked toward the sun, still low in the sky but climbing rapidly. "I hope," he added.

"You're crazy," I said, and we both laughed.

After showering, I fixed a bowl of cereal and sat down at the kitchen table to read the paper. I usually don't have time in the morning for such luxuries, but I decided to pamper myself. It *was* my day off.

I was about to put a spoonful of raisin bran in my mouth, when I saw a picture of Arnold Silor. The accompanying headline read, "BODY IN CANAL IDENTIFIED." The article was written by Michael Halsey, a reporter friend of mine. According to Michael, the police had determined that Arnie was murdered, but they had no motive for the killing or the mutilation. The investigation was continuing.

It was pretty obvious they hadn't found any funny money at Arnie's house, or if they had, they weren't talking about it. It was also possible that Dr. Augustin was way off base about the kittens being Pearl's.

I got to the clinic at 8:30. The front door was unlocked, and I could hear Dr. Augustin back in the kennel yelling at the dogs to shut up.

"Great," I mumbled. "Terry must be late." I took a deep breath and started down the hall. When I got to the kennel, Dr. Augustin swung open the door, nearly striking me in the face.

"Samantha," he yelled, "Terry is sick, and I couldn't reach Frank. Get in here and help me clean up this mess." He pushed the door all the way open, until it caught. "I swear I'm going to fire that kid."

I wasn't sure if he meant Frank or Terry. It really didn't matter. I knew he wasn't serious.

I unlatched Charlie's cage, and the clinic's mascot—a large black cat with emerald eyes and the soul of a pirate—hopped to the floor and disappeared into the surgery. Then, while Dr.

Augustin led the dogs outside, I gathered up soiled newspapers and food dishes.

The racket in the kennel was awful. We were full of boarders because of summer vacations, and Frank had resorted to wearing a Walkman headset to help drown out the noise. Of course, considering what Frank listened to in the way of music, the barking dogs might have been easier on the ears.

It took Dr. Augustin and me nearly an hour to finish cleaning and feeding. I saved Randy for last. His purring had a soothing effect on my nerves. Even Dr. Augustin seemed to enjoy handling Randy, and I hoped that meant he would spare the kitten.

"What are you doing later this afternoon?" Dr. Augustin asked me, after he had put Jonesy back in his cage.

Amazingly, the dog had cooperated and remained still while Dr. Augustin gave him his first IV injection. I prayed he would continue to be a good boy. Jonesy weighed forty-five pounds and tended to be a little rambunctious.

"I'm going to the mall," I said. "Byron's is having a sale today only, and I need a few things." Luckily I had seen the ad on TV. I hadn't planned to go, but the last time I told him I wasn't doing anything, it nearly got me arrested for breaking and entering.

"Can you be back around three?" He was using his eyes on me.

I could feel my resolve slipping. "I guess," I said.

"Good. Meet me here, and we'll drive over to Arnie's and see if we can find Pearl. I guess you know it was Arnie's body they found in that canal. Anyway, with Arnie dead, Pearl is probably roaming around scared and hungry."

I followed him into his office. "But, what about Jonesy? Shouldn't somebody stay here in case he gets sick?"

"Jonesy will be fine," he said. "I'll check his urine before we go. Don't worry, Samantha. That dog isn't going to perish in the space of a couple of hours. Trust me." He picked up his AVMA journal and propped his feet up on the desk.

"Well," I said, " I guess I'll be going."

He didn't look up. "See you at three. Don't spend too much money."

On the way home, I thought about Arnie Silor's missing

hands. I knew Pearl was just an excuse for Dr. Augustin to snoop around. His curiosity had been aroused, and he had an annoying habit of sticking his nose where it didn't belong.

"What Dr. Augustin needs," I said out loud, "is a hobby."

CHAPTER 4

•

We took Dr. Augustin's Jeep. Never in a million years would I want him as a passenger in my car. It would be like sharing a cell with the Marquis de Sade. Worse.

"So, what did you buy?" Dr. Augustin asked me, as I settled myself in the passenger seat.

"Buy?" Suddenly I remembered the sale at Byron's.

"The mall. Weren't you going there today?"

"Yes," I stammered. He was grinning at me. "The sale prices weren't all that great. I decided to leave my money in the bank."

"Ummm," he said, as he pulled out into traffic. He was still grinning.

"Why do you think they cut off Arnie's hands?" I asked hastily. The best defense is a good offense.

Dr. Augustin shrugged. "If this were a Mafia killing, I'd say Arnie took something that didn't belong to him."

"You mean like money? Freshly minted twenties, perhaps?"

"Seems reasonable to me."

"But what if it wasn't the Mafia?" I asked.

"Maybe the murderer watches a lot of television."

Arnold Silor lived in a typical beach bungalow a block from the Gulf. It was small, white, and had a screened-in back porch. There was a large hole in the screen near the door. A toolshed, the kind you can get ready-made at those do-it-yourself home improvement places, stood at one corner of the house. A sea grape tree cast a shadow over most of the tool-shed and the porch, providing some relief from the afternoon sun, which was intense. Three clusters of sea oats and a spindly cabbage palm were the only other vegetation.

Arnie's front yard was gravel, like most of the lots on the beach. His backyard was loose sand. Large concrete circles, like scales on the back of some prehistoric reptile, snaked their way from the street to the front door and from the back door to a narrow asphalt driveway, where an old Dodge Dart was parked.

We left the Jeep at the curb in front of the house. Even from the street, I could see the yellow police tape across the door.

"The cops must not be finished in there," I said, hopeful Dr. Augustin would take the hint. The words "Police Line—Do Not Cross" hadn't stopped him in February. Of course, this time his ex-wife wasn't in jail accused of murder.

Dr. Augustin muttered something I didn't catch and went around to the back of the house. I followed him.

"Pearl," I called. "Here, kitty, kitty."

Dr. Augustin peered in the Dodge. Then he went up to the screened porch and tried the door. It was unlocked, so he stepped inside.

"Here, Pearl," I called again. I figured I could always say we came for Arnie's cat. Even if I knew better.

"She's hidin' out under my house," said a gravelly voice behind me.

I jumped and whirled around. I think my heart must have come to a complete halt for several seconds before starting up again.

An elderly woman wearing faded red clam diggers and a man's red and white striped pajama top grinned at me. She was about five foot six, extremely thin, with equally thin yellow-white hair obviously cut with no regard for fashion. Tiny wisps of varying lengths fluttered about her face like moths. She wore thongs. Her toenails were the color of amber and needed trimming.

"I said Pearl is under my house. You deaf or what?" She was missing a couple of premolars.

"No, I heard you," I said. "You just startled me. Are you a neighbor of Arnie's?"

She ignored the question. "You can prob'ly get her to come out with some tuna."

I heard Arnie's screen door open and close, and then Dr. Augustin was standing next to me.

"I'm Arnie's veterinarian, Dr. Augustin. We're looking for Pearl. Have you seen her?" He smiled congenially, but the beard made him look a little lecherous.

"I just told your wife, here, she's under my house." The woman stared up at Dr. Augustin. "A vet, you say? Where's your bag?" She seemed suspicious.

Dr. Augustin pointed toward his Jeep. "It's in the car. You want to see it? I'll get it, if you want."

I was amazed we were having this conversation. The old woman obviously belonged in the local loony bin, and Dr. Augustin was acting like she was one of his best clients.

"Sure," the woman said. "Bring it on over to the house."

She pointed across the street at what would have been a carbon copy of Arnie's place, except it was several years overdue for painting. And the yard, if you could call it that, was totally overgrown with sandspurs.

She started to go, then turned back. "And your wife can come along, too," she said, looking at me like I had just slithered in out of the swamp.

"This is Samantha Holt," said Dr. Augustin. "My technician." He paused. "Nurse."

The woman shrugged, but I could tell she hadn't changed her opinion of me. "Come along, then."

We followed her, pausing long enough for Dr. Augustin to get his bag out of the Jeep.

"Why are we doing this?" I whispered.

"Because that old woman might know something about Arnie's death," he said. "It's pretty obvious nothing around here gets by her. Let's just play along and see what transpires."

"I thought we came here for Pearl." It sounded like an accusation.

"That, too," he said.

The woman was waiting for us by the front door. "Hurry," she said. "Can't leave the door open. Somebody might take off."

An image of Hansel and Gretel flashed briefly in my head. I stopped abruptly, but Dr. Augustin grabbed my arm and pushed me inside. The old woman brought up the rear and quickly closed the door.

It wasn't what I expected. The living room reminded me of the library stacks at college. Bookshelves, crammed to capacity with books dusty and yellow enough to be first editions, lined three of the walls. Additional books and magazines were piled on the floor and on nearly every table and chair visible. And on top of every pile was a cat. Green, copper, and blue eyes blinked at me from an assortment of body sizes and colors. Some of the cats had long hair, some the slinky lean torsos of more exotic breeds. A few were missing parts of their tails. A few had tattered ears. They all looked clean and well fed.

An argument began suddenly in one corner of the room. An enormous orange cat, its tail thrashing, its ears pointed backwards, was attempting to take possession of a worn brown recliner positioned in front of an old console television. His target, a small but plump white cat with one green eye and one blue eye who, apparently, had been curled up in the chair, was preparing for flight.

"Garfield, you leave her alone, do you hear me?" The woman clapped her hands together, and the orange cat reluctantly hopped off the arm of the recliner and walked away. The white cat relaxed.

The woman lifted magazines and a brown tabby off two of the chairs. The tabby took a couple of steps, then settled down on the floor between the chairs.

"Have a seat," said the woman. She had to raise her voice because of the rattle her window air conditioner was making. "I'll brew us some tea." She picked up the white cat and thrust the animal at Dr. Augustin. "Look at Angel's paw," she commanded. "Bite wound. Abscessed, most likely." She attempted a smile, then hurried out of the room.

Half of the cats jumped to the floor and hurried after her,

crying and meowing, their tails held high in a swaying field of question marks. I sat down.

"Bet you're sorry we came now," I said.

Dr. Augustin handed me the cat, then went over to the air conditioner. He pushed up on the unit's frame, and the rattle stopped. He came back over to his chair, sat down, and opened his bag.

"No, not really," he said, taking out his stethoscope. He grinned at me. "You mean you're not having a good time?"

He listened to Angel's heart and lungs, looked in her mouth, then examined her paw. He took a thermometer out of his bag, along with a tube of K-Y jelly.

"Help me out here, Samantha," he said, handing me the lubricated thermometer.

He held Angel, while I took her temperature. She really was an angel, and I figured she must be pretty sick to let complete strangers get so personal. But her temperature was only slightly elevated.

"One-oh-three," I said, squinting at the thermometer. How can anybody read in this dim light? I wondered.

Dr. Augustin let go of the cat, and she dashed over to the recliner. "A little antibiotic, and she'll be fine," he said, putting his stethoscope and the thermometer back in his bag.

The woman appeared, carrying a tray. She put the tray on the floor in front of us. Three delicate pink and white china teacups with matching saucers sat on the tray, along with a small bowl of sugar, three spoons, and a white enameled teapot. The woman squatted down by the tray.

"The tea is ready," she said. "Shall I pour?" She lifted the pot.

"Please do," said Dr. Augustin. He winked at her.

I must be imagining this, I said to myself. I closed my eyes, then opened them. I half-expected to see a white rabbit with a pocket watch sitting by the recliner, instead of Angel.

The woman poured. "Sugar?" she asked.

"No, thank you," I said, taking a cup from her.

After a moment, Dr. Augustin cleared his throat. "You have us at a disadvantage," he said to the woman. "We don't know your name." He sipped his tea.

The woman put two spoonfuls of sugar in her cup and stirred. Then she stood up and went over to the recliner.

"Sarah," she said with her back to us, like the name embarrassed her. "Sarah Milton."

She sat down, and Angel jumped up into her lap. The rest of her feline entourage began to filter out of the kitchen. There was much lip smacking and face washing taking place.

"Did you look at Angel's paw?" Sarah asked.

"Yes," said Dr. Augustin. "You were absolutely correct. It is an abscess, but it appears to be draining, which is good. I'd like you to stop by the clinic and pick up some medication for Angel. Tablets or liquid, whichever is easiest."

Sarah took a long drink of tea, made a face, and stirred some more. "Can't," she said. "No car."

"Then I'll bring it by later," he told her.

"How much?" she asked. "I can't pay much, you know." She stared off across the room.

"It's on the house, Sarah."

Her head turned and she smiled broadly, exposing the gaps in her dentition. "That's fine," she said. "Real fine. You see, I take them in off the street. They're hungry and sick, and I help them. But I don't get much from those bastards in Washington." She frowned. "Social *Security*. That's a laugh. It's hardly enough to keep a body together. And there's sixteen of us." She waved a hand airily around the room to indicate her feline family.

"They need to be vaccinated," said Dr. Augustin. "Every time you bring in a new one, you're risking the health of the others. And they need to be neutered." He looked at a few of the cats. "I don't see anyone obviously pregnant. What do you do with the kittens?" It was so casual, the way he asked it.

Sarah ran her fingers down Angel's back. "The County helps with the neutering," she said. "Oh, I get a few pregnant ones. When the kittens are weaned, the Humane Society comes for them. People want kittens, you know. They don't want the already grown ones."

"What'll happen to Arnie's cat, Pearl?" I asked. "Will you take her in?"

Sarah shook her head. "Tried. All those strangers in and out of Arnie's house spooked her. She ran off for a spell, then came back pregnant. But she wouldn't go inside Arnie's house again. Took to hiding in the toolshed or under my house. Now I put a dish of food and a bowl of water out for her."

"Are the kittens under your house?" asked Dr. Augustin.

"Nope. Not in the toolshed, either. Raccoon must have got 'em. Or a dog."

"That's too bad," said Dr. Augustin. He put his cup and saucer on the tray. "Strangers, you say? You mean the police?"

"Way before the police came snooping around. Way before that."

"How did they act, these strangers?"

Sarah looked hard at him. He was prying, and I could tell she didn't like people who pried. Getting information out of her was tough. Dr. Augustin is not a patient man, usually, but he was doing his best not to scare her off.

"I'm just curious," he told her. "I don't mean to be nosy, but Arnie was a friend, as well as a client. I'd like to know who would want him dead."

Sarah closed her eyes and leaned her head back against the recliner's headrest. She continued to stroke Angel, as if the action helped her think.

"Nobody decent would," she said finally. "Everyone liked Arnie. Felt real bad when Ralph got sick."

"Ralph?" I asked.

"His son. Twenty-six. Has some kind of hereditary liver disease. Doctors told Arnie the boy has three or four months. Maybe a little longer. Maybe a little less. He needs a new liver."

"A liver transplant is expensive," said Dr. Augustin. "Does Ralph have insurance?"

"Couldn't say," said Sarah.

"Did you ever know who these people Arnie got involved with were?" asked Dr. Augustin.

Sarah put her cat on the floor and stood up. "I said they were strangers, now didn't I?" Her voice had an edge to it.

"You did say that, yes." Dr. Augustin paused. "Did Arnie have any friends that you know of? Other than you, of course."

"Can't say. He and Ralph spent time at the Paper Moon before Ralph got sick. Ask there." She picked up the tray and headed for the kitchen. Several cats followed her.

Dr. Augustin stood up. "Thanks for the tea, Sarah. I'll bring that medicine by tonight. Do you want tablets or liquid?"

"Makes no difference to me," she said. "I can do either."

"Great. We'll just show ourselves out, then."

"Make sure you close the door good," she shouted.

We looked under the house for Pearl, but the crawl space was too dark. Dr. Augustin didn't feel like going to the Jeep for a flashlight.

"I'll see if I can get her out later tonight, when I bring Angel's medication."

"She's an interesting woman," I said, after we were under way. "Odd but interesting. I wonder why Animal Control hasn't been after her. Although, everyone looked pretty healthy."

And there hadn't been any evidence of animal waste on the floor, either, to attract roaches or the health department. Not even any litter box odor. With fifteen cats, there should have been *some* odor. Something other than the unmistakable aroma of old age—that dark, slightly musty, yet comforting smell that conjures up images of crocheted doilies and wing-backed chairs upholstered in velvet and brocade. And a grandmother's touch.

"Do you think she left Pearl's kittens at the clinic?" I asked suddenly.

"It's difficult to say. She doesn't have a car, and she seems pretty hard up for money. Would you give away three hundred dollars, if you were financially strapped, to save three newborns instead of fifteen healthy adult cats?"

"Probably not."

"Then again, she obviously knows her way around a medicine dropper. Could be she knows how to use a stomach tube." He drummed his fingers on the steering wheel. "Maybe she knew the money was fake and didn't want to draw attention to herself or Arnie by spending it at the grocery store." He rolled the window down and rested his arm on the door. "I'll see if I can get her to tell me anything more tonight."

But I wasn't really listening. I was thinking about Sarah's red and white striped pajama top. I wondered who had owned it first and where the bottom half was.

CHAPTER 5

•

Thursday, July 9

Randy had quadrupled in size overnight. Actually, it was Pearl staring out at me from the cage next to Randy's. The kitten, a near replica of his mother, was investigating this new arrival with typical kitten daring. He had his paw stuck through the narrow opening near the door hinge and was attempting to reach into Pearl's cage. Pearl, for the most part, was ignoring him.

"There were four kittens, originally," Dr. Augustin said from the doorway. "Born June eighth in Arnie's toolshed. Sarah said one of them looked like Pearl."

"So, where's the fourth one?"

"Beats me," he answered.

We went into the lab, and I poured myself a cup of coffee.

"According to Sarah," he continued, "they disappeared a couple of days after they were born. She thinks Arnie knew where they went but wouldn't tell her."

He pulled a tissue out of the little box by the microscope and began polishing the eyepieces. Most people smoke or bite their fingernails or go for a walk when they are trying to work a problem out in their head. Dr. Augustin cleans. I can always tell when something is bothering him. He wanders around the clinic looking for dirt. If there isn't any, he invents some. Needless to say, the clinic is spotless most of the time.

He wadded up the tissue and threw it into the trash can under the sink. Then he went into the treatment room. I followed him. He took Jonesy's file out of the basket on the counter.

"She last saw Arnie on Friday. Told me he was pretty excited about something. Happy. She seemed to think it was about Ralph."

"Could she describe the people who visited Arnie?"

"She said, and I'll quote her, 'I don't have the eyes of a cat, you know. I can't see in the dark.'" He chuckled. "She does have a cat's curiosity, however, because apparently she went over to Arnie's house one night and, through a window, overheard a strange man talking. Or trying to. She said he sounded like an old steam engine."

"What does that mean?"

"You'll have to ask Sarah," he said. "I couldn't get anything more out of her. I guess she figured she had paid for Angel's medication with what she told me, so at ten, she threw me out. Said she was an old woman and needed her rest."

Dr. Augustin opened Jonesy's cage and lifted the dog up onto the table. "Heard from your buddy Michael Halsey lately?" he asked, seemingly out of the blue.

I stared at him. "No, not in a couple of weeks. Why?"

"Oh, nothing," he said. He was examining Jonesy's leg, checking for any signs of inflammation around the catheter. "I just thought he might know something about Arnie Silor's death that wasn't in the paper. Something about the counterfeit money, maybe."

"I thought you hated reporters and didn't approve of me dating Michael."

"I haven't changed my opinion, Samantha. I just thought if you talked to him, you might find out what he knows."

"Well, I haven't talked to him," I said caustically. "But when I do, I'll be sure to file a report." I was furious and didn't mind advertising it.

Dr. Augustin looked at me, but his eyes were vague and unreadable. He turned back to Jonesy. "You're a good pup, Jones, my man," he said. "Ready for another dose?"

Jonesy wagged his tail briefly. He didn't look like he trusted Dr. Augustin all that much.

I don't blame you, Jonesy, I almost said to the dog.

• • •

As if obliging Dr. Augustin, Michael Halsey dropped by the clinic at 11:30. He looked very tan and handsome in his aqua polo shirt and grey slacks. But the creases at the corners of his eyes were like tiny white fingers grasping at his receding hairline. They made him look old, even if they were from squinting into the sun.

He gave Cynthia a hug, and for a second I thought she was going to faint dead away.

"Isn't it wonderful, Samantha," she said, somewhat out of breath, "our Mr. Halsey is back safe and sound." She always sounds like a schoolgirl around him.

Michael had taken his forty-foot boat, the *Serendipity*, down to St. Thomas for two weeks. He'd asked me to go with him, but I couldn't because Dr. Augustin was planning to be gone. Michael was clearly disappointed. So was Cynthia, since she was hoping for a December wedding. Michael Halsey was at the top of her "groom list," even though I had all but hit her over the head with the fact that Michael and I were just friends. Of course, I was also having trouble convincing him of that.

"You've cut your hair, Cynthia," said Michael. "It suits you." He was leaning on Cynthia's desk, trying not to look at the dog heart.

Cynthia smiled and fluttered her eyelashes. If Michael was a few years older, I think Cynthia would claim him for herself.

"Thank you so much for noticing," she said, glancing over at me with one of her best hurt expressions. "No one around here has."

"Well, I think it looks wonderful."

Our last appointment of the morning, an elderly couple with an equally elderly poodle named Booboo, drove up and parked. I had to give the old guy and his wife credit for taking care of themselves and their dog without any help, but the way they moved, it was like watching a film in slow-mo.

I knew it would take them a while to get it together, so I steered Michael into an exam room. I left the door open.

"Welcome back," I said, giving him a hug.

He kissed me, but it was tentative, like he wasn't sure where he stood with me. I hadn't wanted him to kiss me at all, which was why the door was open. Now I was disappointed he hadn't shown a little more determination.

My feelings for Michael were in a constant state of flux. He is a perfect gentleman, kind, compassionate, with his feet firmly planted and his mind focused. He is handsome, still fit at fifty, and financially secure. My mother, like Cynthia, would find him the ideal catch for someone with my "breeding." My female friends back in Connecticut would be envious. Still, somewhere deep down, I wished he had stayed in the Caribbean.

"I've missed you, Samantha," he said. "You would have loved St. Thomas. The weather was sensational." He grinned. "I ate lobster every day."

"You sure know how to rub it in, don't you?" I said. "But I just couldn't get away."

"Maybe next time."

The wistfulness in his voice reminded me suddenly of Frank Jennings, and I cringed.

"Maybe," I said.

Cynthia knocked lightly on the open door, as if reluctantly disturbing some passionate love scene. She actually looked disappointed when she saw we were standing on opposite sides of the exam table.

"The Petchivics are ready," she said. She smiled at Michael, then went back to her desk.

Michael started to go. "If you're free tomorrow, how about dinner?" he asked. "That steak place up the road. Freddy's." He paused, eyes pleading with me.

I remembered the beach race. It would have been a perfect excuse.

"Okay," I said reluctantly. "Is eight o'clock too late? You know how this place is on Fridays."

"Eight is fine," he said, obviously relieved. "I'll pick you up at your apartment."

We walked out to the reception area. The Petchivics and Booboo were at Cynthia's desk. Mrs. Petchivic looked even more stoop-shouldered than she had on their last visit, and I resolved to drink more milk.

Cynthia handed me the poodle's file. I looked at it. The dog had lost weight. She was down to four pounds. The complaint was "Not Eating."

I waited patiently by the door to Room 1, while Mr. and Mrs. Petchivic, Mr. Petchivic holding Booboo under one arm, shuffled down the hall. After the man helped his wife into the room's only chair, he put the dog on the exam table.

Booboo sat down and sniffed the air. She was blind, both eyes the color of skim milk. But it never seemed to bother her.

"Dr. Augustin will be right in," I told them, smiling. I put the file on the counter and pulled the door closed.

I went back to Cynthia's desk. Not surprisingly, Michael was still there.

"I almost forgot," I said to him. "Arnie Silor, the man they found in that canal, was a client."

Michael grimaced. "Nasty business. I'm glad I didn't get to the scene until after the body was bagged." Like Arnie Silor was a pile of grass clippings.

He sounds more and more like a cop every day, I thought.

"Dr. Augustin wanted me to ask you if there was anything about Arnie's death you didn't put in your article," I said. I looked over at Dr. Augustin's door. It was closed, but I lowered my voice anyway. "You know how he is."

Michael nodded sagely. "Indeed I do." He shrugged. "I pretty much wrote everything I was able to find out from the police. Except the fact that whoever removed Mr. Silor's hands knew what he or she was doing. It was a very neat job. Oh, and Silor was knocked unconscious first, before he drowned. Someone hit him with a heavy metal object, like a hammer or a crowbar."

Cynthia paled. "Can't you two talk about something else?"

Suddenly, the door to Dr. Augustin's office opened, and I bolted for the hallway.

"See you tomorrow," I said over my shoulder. I didn't wait for Michael to answer.

CHAPTER 6

•

Friday, July 10

Pest control is big business in Florida. Not to belittle the hurricane trackers, but insects are the *real* price we pay for living in paradise. Everything is bigger and healthier here. And oh so fruitful.

Grooming kennels and veterinary clinics make a lot of money attempting to rid people and their pets of fleas. Frank spends a good two or three hours every morning trying not to get mauled while bathing and dipping a variety of less than enthusiastic cats and dogs. Fridays and Saturdays are his busiest days.

A few of our regular baths are dogs who have grown used to their weekly visits and don't seem to mind being lathered up, rinsed, then stuffed into a dryer cage. Rosco Friedman, an eight-year-old basset hound, fell into that category. Basset hounds generally are slow, placid animals who periodically surprise you by chasing after a toy or paying attention when you talk to them. Rosco was pretty energetic for a basset, but he and Frank appeared to get along okay.

Every Friday, Edna Carlyle, the Friedman family's live-in maid, would drop Rosco off at the clinic around 8:30, then return for him at five.

Rosco's owner, Dr. Norman Friedman, an internist at St. Luke's, never appeared particularly interested in the dog and hadn't graced us with his presence, at least not during the two years I had worked for Dr. Augustin. It wouldn't have bothered me if he never did, either. According to Cynthia who had seen him once or twice when Rosco was a puppy, he was pompous and overbearing and a know-it-all. I imagined he was a lot like my father in that respect. A friend of Cynthia's told her he was working on wife number five, having discarded or driven off the first four.

Edna, by comparison, was a kind, patient woman with a heart of gold. Why she continued to put up with Dr. Friedman was beyond me. Cynthia said it was because she had been in his employ for over twenty years, had never married, and, at the age of sixty-four, was too old to start looking for someplace else to live.

Edna usually brought some tasty treat for us when she came with Rosco—coffee cake or cookies. Homemade stuff filled with lots of saturated fat and calories. That morning, Edna's Tupperware contained two dozen sweet rolls.

"You're determined to make us all fat, Edna," I said, opening the box and releasing a delectable odor of yeast and cinnamon.

"You're talking to an expert on fat, Miss Holt," Edna said, chuckling.

The side seams of her starched grey and white uniform showed signs of a recent retrofit.

"Fat is a form of potential energy," I said.

Edna started to laugh, then got so carried away, she had to grab onto Cynthia's desk. "Then I got me a whole lot of potential," she said finally. She took a deep breath, then looked down at Rosco. "You be a good dog, Rosco, and do like Miss Holt tells you. I'll be back for you later."

Rosco lifted his head and stared at her with his sad eyes. He wagged his tail.

"Thanks for the goodies, Edna," I said, taking Rosco's leash.

"Goodness, you don't have to thank me. You just keep on taking care of my Rosco."

She waved at us from the door, then waddled across the pavement. I watched her climb slowly and heavily into an old Mercedes sedan, one of Dr. Friedman's castoffs, undoubtedly.

"Why doesn't Dr. Friedman just give Edna that dog?" I

asked Cynthia. "From what you say, he doesn't seem like the type to keep a dog. Especially a basset hound."

"It was his son's dog. Mark. He died several years ago of complications from cystic fibrosis. According to Edna, Dr. Friedman and wife number two—the mother—had a terrible falling-out over Mark's illness. She left him right after the boy died. Dr. Friedman would probably rather not have the dog around to remind him of Mark." Cynthia shook her head. "At least he didn't bring Rosco in here to be euthanized. We've got to give him credit for that, you know."

Rosco looked like he was about to relieve himself on Cynthia's desk. I pulled gently on the leash, and we headed down the hall to the kennel.

At ten o'clock, Vivian Porter stormed in the front door. I was leading our first client of the morning, a young woman with two small boys and a six-month-old beagle named Snoopy, into Room 1. Cynthia had taken a boarder back to the kennel, and Dr. Augustin was finishing up in surgery.

"Where is Dr. Augustin?" Vivian demanded. "I have an emergency."

She wore a pale blue, crisply pressed pinafore over a wheat blouse and tan slacks. There were ruffles along the shoulders of the pinafore that would have looked cute on Shirley Temple. A name tag pinned to the pinafore read, "St. Luke's Hospital. Vivian Porter, Volunteer." Her left arm had a smudge of what looked like mud and grease extending from her elbow to her wrist.

I quickly shepherded the Harris family into the exam room, told Mrs. Harris Dr. Augustin might be a few minutes, and closed the door. Then I returned to the reception room.

"What's the matter?" I asked Vivian. "Is something wrong with Dresden?"

"No, it isn't Dresden," she said. "It's a cat. I'm afraid I hit it with my car." She was red-faced and out of breath. "Is Dr. Augustin *here*?" The end of her sentence was punctuated with a downward stroke of her right index finger.

I nodded, and she dashed out to her car, the bow on her

pinafore bouncing and jouncing on her generous derriere like a squirrel's tail.

Cynthia walked into the reception room just as I was about to call Dr. Augustin on the intercom.

"Vivian Porter hit a cat with her car," I said quickly. "I'll go tell Dr. Augustin. Stick her in Room Two." I left.

Dr. Augustin was still in surgery, staring into a recovery cage at Booboo. The poodle's few remaining teeth were in a small jar on the counter.

"Vivian Porter is out front," I told him, "with a cat she says she hit with her car."

Dr. Augustin looked at me and vigorously chewed his bubble gum. "Well?"

I stared back.

"Give me some information, Samantha. Is the cat conscious? Is it breathing? Is it hemorrhaging?" He began opening drawers and cabinets. Suddenly, he stopped and turned around. "Well, where is it?"

I ran out of the surgery, down the hall, and into Room 2. Vivian was standing by the exam table peering into a pale blue cardboard storage box with an index card taped to the side. The card said, "Goodwill." Vivian's eyebrows were pulled together, and she was frowning.

I went over to her and looked in the box. Nestled in the center of a stack of clothes was a large black and white cat. Not only was it breathing and conscious, but it was also extremely displeased. Its ears were glued to the back of its head, its pupils were dilated, and a low rumble, interrupted periodically by quick gulps of air, emanated from its throat. The sound reminded me of a poorly tuned car misfiring. Suddenly, the cat opened its mouth and hissed. All of its teeth appeared to be intact.

Vivian put her hand on my shoulder. "Don't get too close," she said. "He wasn't like this when I picked him up off the road." She watched him, moving her head back and forth as if studying a piece of abstract sculpture. "Do you think he's . . . *rabid?*"

"Samantha!" It was Dr. Augustin.

I put my arms around the box while holding my face to one

side, in case the cat decided to lash out at me, and lifted. "Please wait here," I said to Vivian.

She seemed happy to comply, because she immediately sat down and began inspecting the grease on her arm.

Dr. Augustin met me in the hallway. "The whole point of triage, Samantha," he said through clenched teeth, "is to act quickly." He looked in the box, then jerked his head away, as the cat spit at him. The low rumble increased a few decibels and rose half an octave. Now it sounded like a swarm of angry bees.

I held my tongue and carried the vibrating container into the surgery. I placed it on the table and stood back.

Dr. Augustin had come to work that day in a rotten mood, the joys of hiking in the wilderness obviously as short-lived as the Alaskan summer. I knew he had attended the Brightwater Beach City Commission meeting the night before. I just didn't know what had transpired there. To Dr. Augustin, politics is an aerobic exercise, a game of verbal handball, and he rarely misses a meeting. He spends a couple of hours twice monthly studying the agenda and preparing his remarks. He apparently feels that without his help, Brightwater Beach would fall into chaos.

"Get the gloves," he said, as he reached for a syringe. "Left femur is broken, that's pretty obvious. Let's get a chest and abdomen and a left ML view of that leg," he said. "And we'll get a blood sample so you can run a feline leukemia and FIV test. No point in trying to patch up a stray just so it can die later after infecting the whole neighborhood."

"Mrs. Harris is waiting," I said.

To leave the poor woman and her charges confined for half an hour to a tiny, windowless room with only a giant plastic model of a cat's internal organs for entertainment would be inhumane to say the least.

Dr. Augustin swore, then looked at his watch. "At least let's sedate him," he said, taking a bottle of tranquilizer off the shelf.

When he was ready, I quickly pressed down on the cat's shoulders and back, careful not to touch the broken leg. The animal growled and hissed and attempted to bite me, but was unsuccessful. Dr. Augustin injected the tranquilizer into a back muscle, and we both stepped away. I took off the gloves.

"Go tell Mrs. Harris I'm on my way. I'll put this creature in a cage, as soon as he calms down." He went over to one of the recovery cages and opened the door.

I hurried down the hall, taking a detour into the reception room, when I heard Mrs. Harris yell at Snoopy.

"I thought the Harrises might be more comfortable in here with me," said Cynthia. "Vivian had to go to work. She said she'll pick up her box of clothes later." She waved a check at me. "She left a deposit."

Mrs. Harris was in the process of gathering up several dozen paper drinking cups that lay strewn on the floor around the watercooler like miniature dunce's caps. Evidently, her children had discovered how much fun it was to push the little button and get a drink of ice water. Snoopy obviously enjoyed chewing on the cups.

The phone rang as our 10:30 client drove up. I threw Cynthia a kiss and led Snoopy and the Harris family back into Room 1. I was pulling the door closed, when Cynthia stuck her head around the corner.

"It's Michael," she said.

I picked up the hall extension. "Hi, Michael, what's happening?"

"Hello, Samantha." He paused. "The paper is sending me to Ft. Lauderdale to cover that big rape trial. The first few days, anyway. Jury selection." Again, he paused.

"Gee, that sounds exciting," I said, attempting a laugh.

"I leave this afternoon."

"Oh."

"Can I have a rain check on the dinner date? I'll let you know the minute I'm back in town."

"Sure, Michael. Anytime."

"I'm sorry, Samantha. I was looking forward to it. By the way, I picked up a little something for you in St. Thomas. I'll bring it over before I leave."

"You didn't have to do that, you know."

"I wanted to. Listen, I'll call in a few days. Be good."

He hung up, leaving me to wonder why he hadn't sounded particularly disappointed, and why I was.

The blood test for feline leukemia and FIV was negative, so Dr. Augustin repaired the cat's leg during lunch. He also neutered the animal. It was quite a gamble, since we didn't know whether or not the cat actually belonged to someone. But Dr. Augustin is a big advocate of spaying and neutering, particularly for animals allowed to roam free, so he saw his chance and took it.

The postoperative radiograph of the cat's leg showed a very clean job, the pin pulling the two halves of the left femur into perfect alignment. Dr. Augustin had loosened up a little toward the end of the surgery, so I risked asking him about the City Commission meeting.

"Did your buddies on the commission miss you while you were away?" I knew the answer already. The commission rejoiced whenever Dr. Augustin was unable to attend a meeting.

He glared at me. "Fortunately, they had to put off their discussion of a tax hike to pay for the sewage treatment plant until last night. I think I convinced them to go ahead with it. There was the usual opposition from those old farts on Main Street who don't want to pay for anything."

I held the cat's leg while Dr. Augustin applied a final layer of cast padding and covered it with elastic adhesive tape.

"I suppose you have a date tonight with Mr. Halsey," he said. He made no attempt to hide his disapproval, but he wouldn't look at me.

"I did, but something came up, and he had to go out of town for a few days." I wasn't sure why I was telling him this. What I did with my free time was my business. He didn't own me.

"So, you're free?"

I looked up. He was smiling now, waiting for me to say something. I was still holding the cat's leg, even though Dr. Augustin had long since finished bandaging it. I let go of the leg and made a pretext of cleaning up the bits and pieces of cotton and tape.

Dr. Augustin laughed. "I just thought we might check out the Paper Moon. See if we can discover anything useful about

Arnie Silor." He ran his fingers slowly over his beard and watched me, his eyes so dark and shiny, I imagined I could see myself in them.

"Sure," I said, "why not." The Paper Moon wasn't one of Michael's favorite places, and I had become, quite truthfully, a little tired of piano bars and hotel lounges.

"Great," he said. He glanced at his watch. "Jeez, look at the time."

Together, we moved the cat into a recovery cage. Then Dr. Augustin dashed off for a quick bite at his favorite greasy spoon. I tried not to think about food while I cleaned up the surgery and got ready for our two o'clock appointment.

Cynthia called me on the intercom at five. I was in the middle of cleaning and medicating a weimaraner's ears. I pushed the talk button.

"I can't come up there, Cynthia. What do you need?"

The weimaraner suddenly shook his head, sending a flurry of gooey oil droplets containing earwax and God knows what else all over my uniform and the wall behind me.

"Great!" I exclaimed.

"Michael is here, Sam. He has something for you."

I reached for the button, this time hanging onto one of the dog's ears to prevent him from shaking.

"Can he wait? I'll only be a few minutes more."

"He says no, but he'll call you."

I was actually relieved. Not only was I tired, but now I was filthy, as well.

"Thanks a lot, chum," I said to the dog.

He licked my face, and I thought how much easier it was to deal with dogs and cats than with people.

After I put the dog back in his cage, I went up to the reception room. Cynthia handed me a small, velvet-covered box. She was grinning expectantly. Fortunately, the box was too big to be a ring box. I hesitated, anyway.

"Well," she said, "aren't you going to open it?"

I took a deep breath and snapped open the lid. Inside, nestled in a satin bed like lovers, was a pair of coral earrings.

They were exquisite. Suddenly, I thought about the fragile reef that had been violated so Michael could impress me.

"They're beautiful!" Cynthia gasped. Then she held up a similar box, containing two mother-of-pearl clip-ons. "Isn't Mike the most thoughtful man?"

Before I could hide my present, Dr. Augustin appeared in the doorway to his office. He looked at the coral earrings. "Very nice," he said. "I thought that collecting coral for commercial purposes was illegal. Something about endangered species, I believe." He smiled benignly.

I snapped the box closed and glared at him. "Michael probably doesn't know that. And I am not going to tell him, either. It was nice of him to think of me, and I refuse to spoil it."

Dr. Augustin shrugged, but didn't say anything more. I slipped the box in my pocket and headed for the kennel to finish up with treatments.

CHAPTER 7

•

Dr. Augustin told me to wear something appropriate. He wasn't specific, but I gathered he meant something inconspicuous. Of course, at most beach bars, inconspicuous means nearly nude, particularly in Brightwater Beach, where T-backs are still legal.

I decided on shorts and a baggy shirt over my one and only tube top. The shorts had wide cuffed leg openings, which helped to make my thighs look slimmer than they really were. If it had been up to me, I'd have worn a floor-length mumu.

When I got into Dr. Augustin's Jeep, he glanced at my legs, then smiled faintly. He didn't say anything, but I couldn't have felt more embarrassed if I *had* been naked. He wore his usual. Jeans and a T-shirt. The front of the shirt sported a manatee munching on a sprig of water hyacinth.

The Paper Moon is an upscale beer and wings establishment about fifty yards from the surf. "Upscale" on the beach means the place is air-conditioned and there is usually toilet paper in the ladies' room.

The Moon, as it is called by its regulars, is noted for its weekend beach volleyball games and the annual championship it sponsors. Olympian Karch Kiraly is said to have played there, as a warm-up for the Jose Cuervo Gold Crown competition held each year at the Hilton down the road. I have my doubts. The Moon is also popular with runners, because the owner had enough business sense to install an outside shower on the north end of the building. I've noticed that runners, especially long-distance runners, are big beer drinkers, and that shower is a great draw for the place.

We arrived close to eight. Jeffrey had been right about the sunset. The sky was a deep salmon overlaid with feathery lavender brush strokes. Thin gold rays fanned out from the horizon, where the sun, now a fuzzy orange ball, was slowly melting into the sea.

The beach race was coming to a close. A few stragglers, red-faced and dripping, were still shuffling through the sand toward the finish line a hundred yards south of the Moon. Most of the participants, however, were already enjoying liquid refreshment and reliving every muscle-pulling, tendon-straining moment, like the pain was, in itself, a reward. They sat on towels around the picnic tables that lined the two volleyball courts. A few apparently had recovered sufficiently to start up a game. I looked for Jeffrey, but didn't see him.

Dr. Augustin led me inside. Amazingly, there were two seats open at the bar, so we took them. I sat down facing the crowd and continued to look for Jeffrey.

The Paper Moon is an interesting place. The walls are divided in half by a chair rail. The bottom half is paneled in some kind of dark wood that has become scratched and stained through the years. The top half is completely covered with dollar bills—hundreds of them, stapled onto the underlying plasterboard in more or less straight rows. Not all of the bills are from the U.S. At least a quarter are Canadian and a few hail from faraway places like Australia and Germany. Hanging from the chair rail at various locations around the room are staplers. Patrons are encouraged by small signs here and there to write a message or indicate their city of origin on the bill before attaching it to the wall. Some of the messages clearly were written by individuals who would need a taxi to get home. Others were scrawled by wanna-be poets and stand-up comics.

I was watching a middle-aged woman staple a bill to the wall outside the restrooms, when I heard Dr. Augustin tell the bartender to bring us a couple of beers. The bartender asked if we wanted bottled or draft. I turned around.

The guy was so beautiful, I had to look away briefly to keep from swooning. He was an Adonis clone, at least six three, with shoulders broad enough for two people, but not so muscle-bound that his neck looked like it had been swallowed up by his deltoids. He had naturally blond hair, enhanced by the sun (at least, I wanted it to be the sun) and cut in a very preppie style, and a nice even tan that glistened as if he had rubbed himself all over with Pledge. The hairs on his arms were white, and he wore one of those little woven bracelets teenagers give each other, although he looked closer to my age. He had on a Paper Moon T-shirt, size 2X, and jeans.

I realized he was looking at me, and a lot of involuntary muscle contractions nearly took my breath away. I glanced furtively over at Dr. Augustin, but he hadn't noticed. The bartender winked, like he knew he had this effect on practically every female not prepubescent or blind, and went for our beers.

When the bartender came back, Dr. Augustin asked him to start a tab for us. Then he very casually mentioned Arnie.

"Too bad about Arnold Silor," he said. " He was an all right guy." He took a healthy swig of beer, then put his glass down and reached for the bowl of corn nuts. "Did you know him well?"

The bartender shook his head. "Didn't know him at all. Read about him in the paper, though." He smiled at me. His teeth were like expensive faux pearls, smooth and satiny and perfectly aligned. His parents had paid a fortune for those teeth. "Of course, I'm only here on weekends," he said. "Friday and Saturday from four-thirty until one." It was a pointed invitation presumably aimed at me.

Dr. Augustin moved around on his chair. " I guess his son's illness took a lot of his time and money."

"I wouldn't know," the bartender said. He winked at me, again, then left to serve a couple of girls at the opposite end of the bar.

I watched him smile at them and lean his elbow on the cherry veneer. I could almost hear the girls gasp and giggle. One of them was wearing a tiny shocking pink bikini top and matching short shorts. She was a healthy girl, well endowed, and I feared her swimsuit was on the verge of overflowing.

Her companion was a tall, skinny thing, wearing a blue and green sundress.

"He wasn't much help, was he?" I asked, turning back to Dr. Augustin.

He was watching the girl in the bikini top. "Nope." He picked up his glass and drained it. Then he pointed to my still full glass. "What's wrong, Samantha? I've never known you to turn down a free beer."

I took a drink. "It takes me a while to get going."

The bartender sauntered our way, and I couldn't help but notice how nicely his jeans fit.

"Two more?" he asked, picking up Dr. Augustin's glass.

"Just one for now," said Dr. Augustin. When his refill came, he asked, "Is the owner in?"

The bartender inclined his head toward the back of the room. "That's him in the green tee. Bill O'Shea."

His eyes fell on me, and I sucked in my stomach and straightened up. It was a reflex. Then the bartender moved off toward the cash register.

Dr. Augustin picked up his beer. "Let's go see what Mr. O'Shea knows."

When I looked at him, he was grinning. "What's so damn funny?" I asked.

"You are," he said. He tossed a five and two ones on the bar.

I slid off my stool, then remembered my beer and retrieved it. "So the guy is cute, okay? Like you never flirt with any of your female clients?" I realized I was embarrassed.

"He may be 'cute,' as you put it, but I'm surprised his vital organs are still functioning considering all the anabolics he takes." He glanced over his shoulder. "In fact, he does look a little yellow, doesn't he?"

"You don't know he uses steroids," I said.

"No? He's at the gym every time I go in there. Pumping iron like that's the only thing he lives for."

"So what? You work out."

The bartender came over to us, so Dr. Augustin grabbed my elbow and aimed me toward the back of the room. The place was really rocking by that time. We had to squeeze past a large group of runners crowded around a table intended for two. I recognized Mick Peters and waved, but he didn't see me.

Bill O'Shea was sitting by himself, operating a small electric adding machine. It was plugged into the wall behind him. A long streamer of paper curled across the table and hung over the edge. A nearly spent cigar rested between the first and second fingers of the man's left hand.

"Can I help you?" he asked, smiling.

He was in his sixties, but trim, with wavy salt-and-pepper hair and skin tanned to a nice caramel color. He was wearing a T-shirt that read "Cleanliness is Next to Godliness: Let's Clean Up City Hall."

Dr. Augustin and this guy should get along famously, I thought.

Dr. Augustin stuck out his hand. "I'm Lou Augustin," he said. "A friend of Arnie Silor. I'm trying to locate his son."

O'Shea hesitated a fraction of a second, then slowly extended his hand. "We'll all miss Arnie. He was a regular fixture around here. Loved the volleyball games." He didn't invite us to sit down.

Dr. Augustin was persistent. "I'd like to extend my condolences to Arnie's son. I heard he was ill. Is he at St. Luke's?"

O'Shea took a puff on his cigar and studied Dr. Augustin. He was still smiling, but I was beginning to think it was some kind of nerve disorder that made his lips turn up. His eyes certainly didn't look very congenial.

"Ralph is extremely ill," O'Shea said. "His father's death only made things worse, and I don't think a sympathy card from a stranger is the best thing for him right now." He turned the adding machine off and reached for a half empty coffee mug. He looked at the mug's contents, then signaled the bartender.

I knew Dr. Augustin's approach wasn't working, and I could tell he knew it, too.

"Haven't I seen you at one or two commission meetings, Bill?" he asked, attempting a different angle. "I try to attend regularly. Just to keep the bastards honest." He forced a laugh.

O'Shea stared at Dr. Augustin. Then the smile broadened, and this time it appeared genuine.

"Augustin! Of course," he said. "I didn't recognize you at first. The beard." He stuck the cigar into the lip of a small red plastic ashtray. Then he leaned over and pulled out the chair next to his. "Have a seat."

Dr. Augustin was just getting settled when a cute woman in her twenties came to the table carrying a tray containing a coffeepot, an empty mug, a small pitcher of cream, and a clean ashtray.

She had long brown hair and equally long fingernails painted fluorescent pink. She was dressed in black satin microshorts, panty hose, and an undersized crop top that had "Paper Moon" emblazoned on it. The word "Moon" was strategically placed over her breasts.

She put the mug and the pitcher on the table, filled the mug with coffee, and reached for the dirty ashtray. She stopped and stared at the cigar like it was a cockroach or a cat turd. Bill O'Shea reached over and picked up the butt.

"Thank you, Patty," he said. He winked at her.

She batted her eyelashes and made the "Moon" on her T-shirt dance around a bit. Then she grabbed the dirty ashtray.

As she undulated back to the bar, Dr. Augustin studied her like he was playing a game of "How many can you remember" and would have to recount all of her various features later. The belief Dr. Augustin apparently held—that only men can openly admire members of the opposite sex—irritated me. Besides, it was pretty obvious I was along solely as window dressing, and that really ticked me off.

"I'm going to get another beer," I said.

Dr. Augustin looked at me as if I had just arrived unexpectedly and sprang to his feet.

"This is Samantha Holt, Bill. She works for me at the clinic. And does a mighty fine job, too."

O'Shea smiled and indicated the empty chair across from Dr. Augustin. "Join us, please."

"That's okay," I said. "I'll let you guys talk politics for a while. Anyway, I need a refill."

Dr. Augustin sat down again, and I began to thread my way through the crowd.

All of the stools at the bar were occupied, so I went over to the waitress stand. The bartender spotted me and, pretty soon, was there radiating anabolic steroids and various other hormones. I was having trouble remembering why I had sworn off men. Why blond hair, big muscles, and a gorgeous smile had landed me nearly two thousand miles away from my family and friends.

"Need another beer?" he asked. His breath smelled like cinnamon.

"I certainly do," I said, handing him my glass.

When he returned, he pulled up the hinged panel over the waitress stand and came out.

"Want to join me?" he asked, pointing to a small table against the wall. A sign on the table said RESERVED. "I'm taking my break."

"Sure." I followed him to the table, and we sat down.

"I usually go outside to get away from the cigarettes," he said, "but it isn't too bad in here tonight."

"The air-conditioning must be working overtime," I said, for lack of anything better to say. I clutched my beer glass.

He was so casual in his manner, so confident, I felt certain I wasn't the first woman he had tried to pick up, and I wouldn't be the last. In college, we referred to his kind as "use it or lose it" men. Just sitting in close proximity to one was supposed to activate warning lights and sirens.

"My name is Toby," he said. "I haven't seen you in here before, have I? I'm sure I would have remembered."

His face was illuminated by an assortment of neon beer signs hanging on the wall above us. The light reflecting off his head made his hair look like a laurel wreath spray-painted gold.

"I'm Samantha," I said. "Everybody just calls me Sam." I took a drink of my beer. "I was here a few months ago for the volleyball tournament. A friend and I stopped in to watch."

He turned his head toward the table occupied by O'Shea and Dr. Augustin. "The guy with the beard?" he asked.

"No. Someone else. A neighbor." I pointed to Dr. Augustin. "He's my boss."

"Umm," he said.

"You told us you only work weekends. What do you do the rest of the week?"

"I'm a fitness instructor at Durante's Gym. I'm not crazy about the pay or the hours, but it'll have to do for now. Until I finish building my own health club."

"Will it be coed?" I asked. "With aerobics classes and stuff?"

He nodded. "Aerobics, sauna, juice bar, the works! I've already got the plans drawn up."

"That sounds great. And when can we expect this new health club to open?"

He frowned. "Not too long now, I hope." He checked his watch, then pushed back his chair. "I have to get back. Listen, why don't you drop by tomorrow around two? We can watch the volleyball game over lunch."

"Oh," I said, "I can't. I don't get off work until six. Maybe I'll come by afterwards for a beer."

"Sounds good. See you then." He went back behind the bar.

I started to pull my wallet out of my purse, but he waved me away.

"On the house."

"Thanks," I said, smiling.

When I came out of the ladies' room, Dr. Augustin was waiting for me.

"Ready?" he asked.

I nodded. "You find out anything good?"

He grinned, but kept quiet until we were in his Jeep headed for home.

"Ralph is in intensive care at St. Luke's," he said. "Room B625. Bill didn't seem to want to talk about him. Or Arnie for that matter. But I did manage to find out Bill and Arnie worked together up in D.C. Civil service job of some kind. They came to Florida after they retired." He paused, then continued.

"Bill is Ralph's godfather. He didn't say as much, but I gathered he's divorced or a widower, like Arnie was. But with no children of his own. He sees Ralph as his responsibility now that Arnie is dead. He's very protective."

"Do you think he knew about the counterfeit money?"

"Hard to say. I *do* know that Bill O'Shea would never do anything to hurt Ralph, and that includes murdering his father."

Suddenly, Dr. Augustin slammed on the brakes, and I saw a black and white cat dart across the road.

"That reminds me," Dr. Augustin said. "Did you call Vivian Porter to tell her how that stray is doing?"

"Cynthia called her."

"Did Cynthia tell her how long we'll need to keep the cat?"

"I don't know. Probably not. By the way, Vivian left us a deposit. A check for two hundred and fifty dollars."

"Good," he said. He was silent after that. For about six blocks. Then he cleared his throat.

"So, what did you and Hulk Hogan talk about?" he asked.

"He's not the 'all brawn and no brains' you think he is," I said, rather testily. "He *works* at Durante's. And he's building a health club. He seems quite savvy, actually." Steroids notwithstanding.

Dr. Augustin turned down Sabal Palm Court and pulled up in front of my apartment building.

"We need to find out what Ralph knows," he said, changing the subject. "You've got to get in to see him."

Lights began flashing, and sirens began sounding, but it wasn't because of Toby.

"*Me*?"

"Of course, *you*, Samantha. How far do you think *I'd* get masquerading as a candy striper?"

CHAPTER 8

•

Saturday, July 11

"Why didn't you tell me that money was counterfeit?" asked Cynthia. She was obviously offended.

My eyes darted over to Dr. Augustin's door, and the pout on Cynthia's face vanished. She lowered her voice, probably without thinking, as we often do at the clinic. Dr. Augustin has the ears of a cat.

"Oh," she said.

We were between clients, and Dr. Augustin was helping Frank with a particularly nasty German shepherd who hated water almost as much as cats do.

"So, how did you find out?" I asked.

"The bank called to remind me we were three hundred dollars short. When I told the woman I had no idea what she was talking about, she said the Secret Service had confiscated those twenties I deposited Monday. Believe you me, I felt pretty silly." She shook her head disapprovingly. "Dr. Augustin wrote a check from his personal account to cover it, but I wish someone had warned me."

I felt I had betrayed our friendship, so I updated her on nearly everything—Sarah Milton, Arnie's son, and Bill O'Shea. I left out any reference to Toby, because I wasn't ready to start looking at china patterns. Not by a long shot.

"Why do you think Dr. Augustin is so interested in who murdered Arnold Silor?" Cynthia asked. "He wasn't in here more than once or twice a year, and, as far as I know, he and Dr. Augustin weren't acquainted socially."

"I figured it's because of that three hundred dollars," I said. "He's probably mad because somebody tried to put one over on him. It's a macho thing."

I heard a car approaching, and when I looked up, I saw Mick Peters's van, with its M-P Computer Services logo on the side, pull into the parking lot.

"I'll go tell Dr. Augustin Mick is here for Jonesy," I said.

Cynthia nodded and began pecking away at the computer terminal.

I put Mick in an exam room and brought him his dog. Jonesy wagged his tail and strained against the leash. That started the dog coughing, and Mick frowned.

"He's okay, isn't he? I mean, I don't want to take him home if he's sick."

"The collar choked him," I said. "He's fine. Really."

It was pretty obvious that Mick loved Jonesy. Dr. Augustin's fear that the animal wouldn't get the attention it needed over the next several weeks was unfounded, in my opinion.

Mick took the leash from me and scratched Jonesy behind the ears. "Is there anything I should do? Anything I need to watch out for?"

"Dr. Augustin will be in soon to explain everything," I said. "By the way, how did you do last night?"

He looked at me blankly.

"The beach race. I saw you in the Moon afterwards. I waved, but you were otherwise occupied. Some woman was practically sitting in your lap."

He blushed. "I only started jogging a few months ago. To get in shape. I thought it might help me with the girls." He looked down at the floor.

"It must be working, then," I said.

"I gave up cigarettes, too. Cold turkey. It was the hardest thing I ever did, but I guess smoking would have killed me eventually. One way or another." He looked up at me, and a kind of sadness moved over his face, like a cloud passing in front of the sun. Then he smiled.

"Well, I think that's wonderful, Mick."

Dr. Augustin joined us, and, after saying good-bye to Jonesy, I went back to the front desk to get our next client.

When I passed by Isolation on my way to the kennel, Dr. Augustin was examining Randy. It was 5:30, and I wanted to go home. I had been thinking about Toby all afternoon, and now I wanted to see him. I stopped in the doorway.

"What's wrong?" I asked, fearful Randy had developed some problem that couldn't be fixed, even by Dr. Augustin.

"Nothing," he said. He put Randy back in his cage and closed the door. "We need to find out who has that fourth kitten. Assuming it's still alive, that is." He moved over to the next cage and scratched Pearl's chin through the bars.

I was relieved he had apparently given up trying to see Ralph. "Do you want me to start calling around?" I asked. There were nearly two dozen veterinary clinics in Brightwater Beach alone. It was a seemingly endless task.

Dr. Augustin shook his head. "Whoever has that kitten could have taken it anywhere. Besides, how are you going to explain our interest in the animal without someone—the guilty party, for instance—getting suspicious? No, I was thinking more along the lines of nosing around at Tuesday's BAVMA meeting. Casually inquire if anyone has contacted Dr. Farmington recently about repairing a cleft palate in a young kitten."

Dr. Augustin rarely attends the monthly meetings of the Bay Area Veterinary Medical Association. He considers them a waste of time. Not because they are, necessarily, but I assume because he feels above that sort of thing. And he almost never asks a colleague for help. Heaven forbid. This sudden change in character is hardly going to seem casual or innocent, I thought, trying not to smile.

"Why don't you come along, Samantha?" he asked. "Who knows, you might learn something."

I wasn't sure if he meant veterinary medicine or investigative technique, but I certainly wasn't going to miss the show. "I'll look forward to it," I said.

The Moon was crowded, this time with members of two local volleyball teams and their respective supporters. It was a rowdy bunch. The room was filled with loud music, equally loud laughter, and the choking acrid haze of too many cigarettes. These sports fans were more used to running for a sandwich at halftime than running a marathon.

Toby wasn't behind the bar. I checked the table with the "Reserved" sign. He wasn't there either. Instead, Mick Peters was sitting on one side, and a woman with a knockout figure was sitting across the table, her back to me. She had dark brown hair gathered up in a ponytail and tied with a bright red ribbon. The ponytail bounced up and down with each movement. And there was a lot of movement. Mick and the woman were arguing, their body language clearly conveying what their lowered voices failed to. Poor Mick, I thought. Girl trouble, money trouble. His dog is sick. The guy just can't seem to win.

I shook my head and started for the bar, intending to ask whoever was there if Toby was around. I didn't need to, because I suddenly spotted him in back switching a beer keg. Pretty soon, he came around to the tap and began pouring foam into a glass. Before I could get Toby's attention, one of the more rowdy volleyball players got up from a nearby table and came over to the bar. He smacked an empty pitcher down and called Toby's name.

Toby dumped the beer foam in the sink and turned around. He and I locked eyes briefly, but I saw no indication that he recognized me. Then the man with the pitcher rapped his knuckles on the bar and repeated Toby's name. Toby went over to him, got the pitcher, and refilled it. Having done that, he returned to pumping foam out of the new keg.

Angry and disappointed, I escaped through the rear exit. He really isn't my type, anyway, I told myself in a typical sour grapes fashion. All brawn and no brain. Well, maybe a little brain. Then, in my mind, I saw the grin on Dr. Augustin's face broaden, and I punched the accelerator, spitting sand and gravel out behind me.

"Damn him, anyway!"

CHAPTER 9

•

Tuesday, July 14

Our surgery schedule that morning was booked to overflowing—three spays, two declaws (on two of the spays, fortunately), and a tooth extraction. Without consulting Cynthia, Dr. Augustin had penciled in the two spay/declaws the previous afternoon. The owner, a woman, was a new client, probably referred to Dr. Augustin by Glynnis Winter, although she didn't say as much. She and Glynnis did live in the same condo, however. Probably had the same hairdresser.

With only me to do all the lab work *and* assist Dr. Augustin, I felt it prudent to get to the clinic early. I arrived just after seven and found that Frank was already there. His band usually has Monday night off and, as a result, Frank frequently comes in well before seven Tuesday, so he can leave early to practice. I had forgotten this fact and was irritated by his presence.

"I made coffee, Sam," he said proudly.

I put my lunch in the lab refrigerator and turned to look at him. He was standing in the doorway, holding a stack of old newspapers. His long, stringy hair was still damp from his shower, and he was wearing a pale blue knit shirt with a collar and relatively new denim jeans, instead of his usual vagrant attire.

"Thanks," I said. I smiled at him and regretted it instantly.

His eyes lit up. "I'll get the rooms ready for the morning appointments, if you like," he said, practically drooling. "I know you're going to be busy with surgery and everything."

He was like the little cartoon terrier who prances along after his big bulldog hero, Spike. I was Spike, always kicking the dog around, treating him like, well, doggie doodoo.

"Sure, Frank," I said gently. "That would be great. You'll need to get a fresh vial of rabies vaccine out of the treatment room refrigerator. I noticed yesterday we were running low in Room Two."

"No problem," he said. "I'll take care of it." He trotted off.

As soon as she arrived, Cynthia telephoned the spay/declaw client and asked her if she could drop off her cats early. The woman obliged. By 8:30 I had finished the blood work on all but the tooth extraction, and it could wait.

I called Dr. Augustin on the intercom, and a few minutes later he ambled in, reading a thin greyish-colored pamphlet bearing an oversized facsimile of a hundred-dollar bill on its cover. Ben Franklin, enlarged nearly twofold, looked extremely cherubic. He seemed more suited to bouncing grandchildren on his knee by the fire than to running around in a thunderstorm trailing a kite.

"What's that?" I asked. I was holding our first patient, a six-month-old Himalayan. The kitten was more interested in my name tag than in what was about to happen.

"It's called *Know Your Money*." He closed the pamphlet and tossed it onto the counter next to the sink. "Agent Nelson sent it to me. You and Cynthia need to study it. Tells you how to spot counterfeit currency. Very enlightening."

He quickly and efficiently anesthetized the kitten, then went to the sink to scrub. I took the clippers off the wall and began shaving the kitten's belly.

"Over the weekend the cops found another batch of funny money," he said. "And another body."

I stared at his back.

"It was in yesterday's paper. I'm surprised Cynthia didn't say something about it. I notice she usually manages to read the paper front to back every day."

It was an undeserved jab, but I kept my mouth shut.

"The guy's name was Howard Nichols. Director of Purchasing at St. Luke's. And get this—he suffered from emphysema. Carried around an oxygen bottle. And he was claustrophobic. Died of heart failure when the elevator he was in got stuck.

Someone apparently rigged it to stop between floors, so the cops are calling the death a homicide."

He dried his hands, then pulled on his gown. I tied it closed in back and opened his glove pack for him.

"I'd be willing to bet he was the one Sarah Milton heard over at Arnie's. Severe emphysema can cause a person to wheeze and gurgle like an old steam engine."

"Steam engine?"

"I presume that's what Sarah meant when she said he sounded like an old steam engine."

"Oh," I said. "Did the article mention anyone else? Anything about Arnie?"

"No, just the usual 'Investigation is continuing' line." He opened the spay pack's inner drape and arranged his instruments. "I'll bet Howard or someone who associated with him left us those kittens."

"Why?"

Dr. Augustin paused briefly and looked at me over his mask. "The notepaper you found in the basket was an ad for Theo-Dur brand of theophylline, a bronchodilator. Emphysema patients take theophylline. Howard probably took it. And the handwriting could have been Howard's. The paper said he was sixty-three. An older man, taught proper penmanship back in the thirties, might write that way."

"Or it was a woman's handwriting," I said quietly.

"Or it was a woman's." His tone was condescending. "At any rate, we need to pay Ralph a visit. See if his father knew Howard Nichols. And find out who else Arnie might have been friendly with."

"Maybe Ralph doesn't know about the counterfeit money. Isn't it possible Arnie wasn't involved?"

"Possible, but not very probable. Arnie was desperate. The impression I got from Bill O'Shea was Arnie would have done almost anything to save Ralph's life." He paused. "It *is* possible he didn't tell Ralph about it, though. To spare the kid any guilt."

He finished the spay and began closing the incision. "Who do we have next?" he asked, glancing up at the clock on the wall.

"You still have to declaw this one."

"Great!" he muttered. "Who scheduled all these surgeries?"

"You did," I said, keeping my eyes on the anesthesia machine's flow meter.

He sighed heavily and reached for one of the kitten's paws. "I know for a fact, I did not schedule that tooth extraction," he said.

At 11:30 a taxi drove up and stopped in front of the clinic. The driver, a scrawny, black, college-age kid in shorts, T-shirt, and worn high-tops, got out and opened the left rear door. He reached in and pulled out a cat carrier. Then he offered the passenger his hand. When it was refused, he stepped aside and waited. I couldn't see his face, but his stance suggested patient amusement.

In Florida, most of the people who hire taxis in the daytime are elderly men and women who know better than to drive or whose licenses have been revoked for one reason or another. A lot of them resent the fact that they must rely on others to get around. Who can blame them, really?

The young man's fare finally emerged and snatched the carrier from him. She was wearing red clam diggers and a plain white shirt. I blinked a couple of times, then laughed.

"It's Sarah Milton," I said to Cynthia. "Arnie's neighbor. The one with all the cats."

"She's not in the appointment book," Cynthia said with obvious irritation. "Our eleven-thirty is supposed to be Mick Peters. A recheck on Jonesy. He's late." Cynthia hates to see her carefully orchestrated schedule upset. And with good reason.

I watched Sarah hand the taxi driver his money, then opened the door. "Good morning, Sarah," I said. I went out to help her, but she clutched her purse and the carrier like they contained all her worldly possessions.

"What's so good about it?" she snapped. "The money that driver charged me, I should have had a limousine and champagne." She made her way slowly into the clinic and over to Cynthia's desk. "I'm here with Angel to see the doctor," she said. She looked around the room suspiciously, then put the carrier on the floor. "And I don't have all day."

Cynthia, her mouth open slightly, stared at Sarah. I hurried over to the desk.

"I'm sure Dr. Augustin will be happy to see Angel right away, won't he, Cynthia?" I was directly behind Sarah, and I nodded at Cynthia and winked.

Cynthia finally got the message. "Of course, Mrs . . . ?"

"*Ms.* Milton," Sarah said firmly.

Cynthia took out a new client form and began writing.

"Why don't I show *Ms.* Milton and Angel into a room?" I said, leaning over to pick up the cat carrier. "We can fill in the details later." I smiled.

Sarah pushed my hand aside and lifted the carrier herself. I could see she was having some difficulty, since Angel was no lightweight, but I didn't try to intervene.

We went into Room 2, which has pictures of cats decorating pale rose-colored walls. Room 1 is covered with doggie wallpaper—cute little beagles and cocker spaniels romping across a field of cornflowers. I figured the less we upset Sarah, the better.

"Dr. Augustin will be right in, Sarah," I said and quickly exited the room.

I found Dr. Augustin in Isolation. He was inspecting the stray Vivian Porter had hit with her car. The cat had turned out to be pretty friendly, once the fear and pain had subsided. And he was a finicky eater, which meant he was definitely someone's pet. Stray cats usually don't hold out for expensive canned food.

Dr. Augustin looked up when I came in the room. "Mick here yet?"

I shook my head. "No, but your favorite lady friend is waiting for you in Room Two." I tried to keep a straight face.

"What is Frosty's problem this time?" he asked. "Too much beef Wellington?"

"It isn't Mrs. Winter," I said. "It's Sarah Milton. She came in a taxi with Angel. And I must say, she's as pleasant and cheerful as ever."

He put the Porter stray back in its cage and closed the door. Then he went into the treatment room and began washing his hands.

"I wonder if she read about Howard Nichols," I said.

Dr. Augustin dried his hands and tossed the used paper towel into the trash can under the sink. "We'll see, won't we? I'm sure Sarah and I can work out a little trade. My services for another morsel of information." He chuckled. "She's something, that old lady."

I followed him down the hall to the exam room. He stopped at the door.

"Why don't you help Frank in the kennel," he said. "Or, better yet, do the lab work on that fox terrier, so I can yank those baby teeth during lunch." He didn't wait for me to respond. He plastered a big smile on his hairy face, puffed out his chest like Foghorn Leghorn, and went into the exam room, closing the door behind him.

Mick Peters never made an appearance. Despite my earlier confidence in his ability to properly care for Jonesy, I was becoming concerned. After Sarah Milton left, Cynthia called Mick at home and at work, but in each case got a recording.

It was almost one o'clock. Dr. Augustin and I were in the surgery with the fox terrier.

"If we don't get hold of Mick this afternoon," I said, as Dr. Augustin fumbled around in the dental drawer for his instruments, which were already waiting for him on the table, "I'll go over to his house on my way home and see what's up."

The terrier suddenly moved one of his front legs. Dr. Augustin had given the dog a quick-acting anesthetic that I knew would wear off just as quickly, and I wanted him to get on with it. All he had to do was pull out a couple of deciduous incisor teeth that had failed to drop out when the dog's permanent teeth came in. So why is he roaming around the room like a lost puppy? I asked myself.

"Sure, Samantha, whatever."

I stared at him. "Are you okay?" I asked.

He turned around, spotted the instruments on the table, and came over. "Of course, I'm okay," he said, a tad defensively. He reached for the forceps.

"What did Sarah have to say?" I asked.

"Absolutely nothing. Angel's paw isn't responding, so I

switched antibiotic." He freed up a tooth and pulled it out. "I asked her about Howard Nichols—told her I thought his voice might have been the one she heard at Arnie's—that he suffered from emphysema and probably wheezed when he talked. She acted like she didn't have the faintest idea what I was talking about."

"So I take it she didn't shed any light on the source of the counterfeit money."

"Nope."

"She's pretty old," I said. "Maybe she's getting a little senile."

Dr. Augustin extracted another tooth. "Sarah Milton is about as senile as my three-year-old niece."

Vivian Porter dropped by at 4:30. She wanted to pay the rest of her bill and discuss the "final disposition" of the cat she'd hit. She made it sound like the animal had died and its body needed to be dealt with.

I told her Dr. Augustin couldn't let it loose on its own until its leg had healed and the pin was out, which would take another few weeks, and he wouldn't give the cat to Animal Control, because they would probably euthanize it. It was an adult and injured, and that made for a hard-to-adopt cat. I didn't tell Vivian Dr. Augustin was more likely afraid the cat's owners would be looking for it and give him hell for neutering their precious kitty.

"Why don't you take it home, Miss Porter?" I asked. "He's very friendly, and Dr. Augustin neutered him for free, so he won't be inclined to spray or run off."

Vivian gasped. "Oh, gracious no," she said, shaking her head vigorously. "Dresden would kill the poor thing the first chance he got." She pulled down on her pinafore and straightened her little name tag. "Besides, I am not really a cat person, you know."

Dr. Augustin came out of Room 1 and saw Vivian.

"Afternoon," he said. "That cat of yours is doing very well. He should be as good as new in a few weeks."

"Well," she said, "it really isn't my cat, now, is it?" As if suddenly realizing who she was talking to, she blushed and softened her tone of voice. "However, I *am* responsible for its predicament. And very grateful to *you*, Dr. Augustin."

She was worrying the handle on her purse—a nice little number, something L. L. Bean might carry—and smiling broadly.

Dr. Augustin was eyeing her uniform. "You do volunteer work at the hospital? I think that's wonderful. Very admirable." He glanced over at me, then back at Vivian.

Vivian let go of her handbag. "Yes, four days a week. I help with admissions. Or I take files from one floor to another, if a patient is being transferred or sent up for tests. Sometimes I deliver flowers and cards to the rooms."

"More of us should be as service-oriented as you are, Vivian," said Dr. Augustin, mostly for my benefit, I feared.

The client in Room 1, her children and dalmatian puppy more or less under control, came out to the reception desk to pay. Dr. Augustin put his hand on Vivian's ruffled shoulder. She blushed.

"Why don't we step into my office, Vivian," he said, "and talk about your cat."

After they were out of earshot, and the client with the puppy had left, I leaned against Cynthia's desk and sighed heavily.

"Dr. Augustin wants me to volunteer at St. Luke's," I said, my voice low. "Not because he's so all fired civic-minded, but because he wants me to snoop around. Talk to Arnie's son. Ralph is in intensive care at St. Luke's, according to Dr. Augustin, and isn't allowed visitors. Except immediate family, of course, which he doesn't have any of now that Arnie is dead." I frowned. "One of these days, I am going to say no to Dr. Augustin, I swear."

Cynthia inclined her head toward Dr. Augustin's office. "Instead of St. Luke's," she whispered, "he ought to be snooping around over at Vivian's house." She drew her lips together.

"Oh, why is that?"

"Don't you think it's a little odd that someone who doesn't have a cat and doesn't want one would be inquiring about the price of cat food?"

"Vivian?" I asked.

Cynthia nodded. "Before you came up, she wanted to know how much a case of Feline Growth was. I told her Feline Growth was for kittens, that she probably meant Feline Maintenance. I assumed it was for the stray. That she'd decided to keep him. But she said she wanted to know about Feline Growth. She said a friend had asked her to check on it, but I think she was lying. Maybe she has that fourth kitten." Cynthia looked really pleased with herself as she waited for me to say something.

I couldn't believe my ears. The sleuthing virus had spread even to Cynthia. Next thing you know, I thought, Dr. Augustin will have Frank staking out people's houses.

Unfortunately, our conversation was cut short by the arrival of the next client. I picked up the woman's file and led her and her cocker spaniel into Room 2.

CHAPTER 10

•

I didn't tell Dr. Augustin about Vivian and the kitten food. I'm not sure why, exactly. Probably because I refused to look for the worst in everyone like he always does, refused to think like a paranoic all the time. But just in case, I decided to pay Vivian a little visit the next morning. Dr. Augustin had given me the perfect excuse—I needed to ask her about volunteering at the hospital.

On my way home Tuesday night to change, I cruised by Mick's place. He lived only a few blocks from me, and I had almost half an hour before Dr. Augustin was supposed to pick me up.

Mick lived in the left third of a nice little blue and white triplex, with carefully tended shrubbery and grass and a joint-use patio out back, where someone always seemed to be barbecuing something. This time, an overweight middle-aged man was grilling hamburgers. He had a beer in one hand and a spatula in the other. He looked up when I came across the lawn.

"Hi," I said cheerily. "Do you know if Mick is home? I don't see his van."

The man flipped over one of the burgers and flattened it with the spatula. A loud sizzling sound emanated from the grill, and my stomach began to gnaw on itself.

"He left yesterday. Him and that kid. And I ain't seen him since," the man said. His voice was deep and raspy. "He took that dog with him, thank God. Me and Martha was gettin' tired of listenin' to it bark and whine all the time." He took a swig of beer and burped lightly. "If it was up to me, which it ain't, there wouldn't be no pets allowed here." He put down the beer and the spatula and took out a pack of Camel cigarettes. He extracted one, stuck it in his mouth, and put the pack away. "He had a suitcase with him," he added.

He struck a match, lit the cigarette, and took a long drag on it. Almost immediately, he began to cough, a gurgling, drowning kind of cough that soon grew so fierce, the man's face became red, and he had to bend over. I thought he was in the throes of death or possibly about to throw up, but after a minute or so, he recovered and picked up the spatula.

I tried to smile. "Well, thank you. I guess I'd better get going. If you see Mick, please tell him that Samantha Holt stopped by." I started back toward my car.

"You're a new one," the man called after me.

I turned around. He was grinning. The look on his face gave me the willies.

"And a lot better-lookin' than the other one, by my way of thinkin'."

"Other one?" I asked.

He laughed. "So you guys don't know about each other, eh?"

"I guess not," I said. I laughed. "Well, you know Mick, quite the lady's man."

The guy really howled that time. "Lady's man, you say? I must be going blind, then."

Suddenly, a woman wearing a yellow terrycloth bathrobe, her hair done up in pink foam curlers, stuck her head out of the middle apartment. She glared at the man. "Luther! My hamburger had better be pink in the middle like I ordered it, you hear?" She gave me a dirty look, then slammed the door.

Luther finished his beer, gave each burger a final flattening, then transferred all four of them to a plate. He tossed his empty bottle into the shrubbery.

"To each his own, I guess," he said, still grinning, and went inside with his dinner.

I walked back to my car. It didn't make any difference to me who Mick Peters entertained. All I cared about was

Jonesy. At least the dog was with him and not locked up in the house or tied up outside in the heat.

When Dr. Augustin and I finally arrived for the BAVMA meeting at Jeremy T's House of Beef, the social hour was coming to a close. Everyone in the private dining room was wandering about looking for a place to land. Five tables, each seating six, were scattered around a room designed for twice that. I felt sorry for the speaker, whoever he or she was. No matter how many people showed up, it would still look like a poor turnout.

A podium stood off to the left like a naughty child, and a buffet line ran along the right wall. Tiny blue flames licked at the bottoms of three huge covered pans. I could only guess at their contents. A crystal bowl, brimming with what looked like tossed salad, promised to be satisfying, at least. Jeremy T's is known for its steak and ribs, not its chicken à la king.

Dr. Augustin purchased a Coke for me and a beer for himself from the bartender, who was packing up her stuff. Then he led me to a table already occupied by two men and by a woman I recognized from a local veterinary technician meeting. She and I smiled briefly at one another. Her expression indicated she really didn't want to be there.

"Hello, Gary," said Dr. Augustin.

The older man nodded. His name tag read "Gary Farmington, DVM, Veterinary Referral Associates." "Greetings, Lou," he said. "I want you to meet Dick Shaw, my new partner. Got his board certification in January. Internal medicine. Dick, this is Lou Augustin, Paradise Cay Animal Hospital."

The younger man shook hands with Dr. Augustin. "Glad to meet you," he said. Then he smiled at me. "And you are . . . ?"

"Samantha Holt," I said, offering him my hand. "Dr. Augustin's technician."

He was short and muscular, with curly red hair and the kind of stare that makes a girl check to see if her blouse is unbuttoned. Out of the corner of my eye, I noticed the woman, Tracey Nevins, cringe when Dr. Shaw took my hand in his.

Suddenly, a fork rapped against a glass somewhere to our

left, and instructions for dinner were announced. Our table was designated last in line for the buffet, so we stayed put.

Dr. Augustin and Dr. Shaw, both graduates of UC Davis it turned out, talked about everything from their least favorite professors to football. Tracey and I politely sipped our Cokes and then our water until, finally, I had to hit the ladies' room. Tracey joined me.

"God, I hate these meetings," she said from the stall next to mine.

"How many have you been to?" I asked.

"More than I care to admit. It's Dr. Farmington. He feels all of the staff should attend whenever we can. Unfortunately, I'm the only single technician he's got and the only one who doesn't have a valid excuse for not coming."

"You need to get more creative," I said, as we both primped in front of the mirror.

Tracey laughed. She was somewhere in her early to mid-twenties, not terribly attractive, with a long, angular face and very dark brown hair cut much too short for my taste. She had really pretty eyes, though, a nice deep blue, and long eyelashes, the kind the average woman would kill for. She was wearing a bulky knit sweater and jeans.

"It would be different if I learned something," she said, applying a coat of lip gloss. Her face was bare, except for a light dusting of blusher. "But most of the speakers they get talk about how to make the practice more efficient or how to improve communication between the doctors and the staff. Or how to relieve stress." She shook her head. "Sometimes I think Dr. Farmington sleeps through the presentations, because we never get any more efficient, and the stress level never seems to go down."

"At least we get a free meal out of it," I offered.

Tracey grimaced. "Yuk," she said, with considerable feeling. "The food here is awful. They should have these things at Mario's. Then we could order cheese ravioli or pizza. Mario's makes the best pizza crust in the world. Well, outside of New York, I suppose."

I looked at her reflection in the mirror. She was obviously competent, or Dr. Farmington would never have hired her.

And she was used to the unpredictable, often chaotic life at a veterinary clinic. But, best of all, she liked pizza.

"How long have you been with Farmington?" I asked.

"Two years," she said.

"Do you like it? I mean, does he pay well?"

She hesitated. "It's okay. We get a lot of cases the average clinic never sees, which is nice. I do lab work, primarily. Most of it for Dr. Shaw, now." Her face became hard and brittle. Then her mouth cracked into a faint smile. "We have another technician who assists Dr. Farmington in surgery. And a third tech who helps in the rooms and doubles as a receptionist."

"We're looking for a lab tech right now," I said. "If you hear of anyone who'd like to change clinics, let me know." I handed her one of my cards. "It probably isn't any less stressful than other clinics, but there are side benefits." I grinned. "We eat a lot of pizza, on the house." I almost said "from Mario's," which was true, but I decided that would be a little like gilding the lily.

Tracey took the card and put it in her purse. "Thanks. I'll pass the word along."

When we got back to the room, our table was already halfway through the buffet line. Tracey and I threw our purses on our chairs and hurried over to the salad bowl, which was still brimming. Male veterinarians, especially the older ones, seem to be big meat and potatoes fans. Probably all that cow college influence.

The salad was really nice, so I skipped the stuff in the chafing dishes. It was difficult to tell what it was, anyway.

Tracey and I ate in silence, while our bosses talked about the latest in surgical equipment and laboratory tests and how to deal with anesthetic complications. I found it all rather fascinating. Dr. Augustin even managed to bring up the subject of cleft palates, without mentioning Randy or his siblings directly.

"I usually like to see a kitten at around three to four months of age," said Dr. Farmington. He stirred a heaping teaspoon of sugar into his coffee. "As you know, it's a better anesthetic risk after twelve weeks, plus we have more room to work. We can sometimes cover the defect temporarily with an acrylic prosthesis until the animal is old enough for surgery."

"How many do you get a year on average?" Dr. Augustin asked, as casually as possible for him. He made a big show of collecting all of his plates and cutlery into a neat pile for the waitress, who was cruising around the room with a pot of coffee.

"One or two. Rarely more. Most are euthanized shortly after birth. I'm sure you're aware, that's the traditional approach. However, many of the less severe clefts can easily be repaired."

And then he lost me in a very detailed description of the procedure. I could tell Dr. Augustin was mentally taking notes.

"I'd love to watch you do one," said Dr. Augustin. "Seeing what you consider salvageable might help me counsel my clients."

"Glad to have you observe. I'll give you a call the next time I get one in. Dog or cat."

I looked over at Dr. Augustin, and he shrugged ever so slightly. I was as disappointed as he obviously was. Apparently, no one had contacted Dr. Farmington yet.

The guy with the glass and spoon started in again, and then the BAVMA president walked over to the podium to announce the speaker. It turned out to be a sales rep who talked about Lyme disease and how it was spreading into Florida. He had color transparencies of maps and pictures of people with the characteristic tick bite rash, that he projected onto the wall over the buffet line. Unfortunately, whoever remembered to bring the projector forgot the screen, and the speaker's subjects took on a strange blue cast from the wall paint.

After the speaker finished and the business portion of the meeting was over, Dr. Augustin left me in the hotel lobby so he could chat briefly with a couple of his friends. Tracey came by and suggested we go into the lounge for a drink, but I declined, so she flopped down beside me on the sofa.

"What's Dr. Augustin like?" she asked. "To work for, I mean."

"He's stubborn, opinionated, hyperactive, and a perfectionist," I said, smiling. "He's also the best veterinarian I've ever worked for, particularly in surgery, and underneath all that machismo lies a very soft heart." I didn't add the fact that he tended to stick his nose where it didn't belong and lately it seemed the clinic was doubling as a private detective agency.

"He's also quite a hunk," Tracey said, as Dr. Augustin and three other veterinarians wandered out of the meeting room. She was watching him with what I interpreted as more than casual interest.

I didn't say anything and, fortunately, Dr. Augustin signaled me that he was ready to leave.

"I've got to go, Tracey," I said. "It was nice seeing you again."

She nodded. "Same here. Listen, I'll give you a call sometime." She lowered her voice. "Who knows, maybe about that job opening." Then she winked and headed for the door.

As I crossed the parking lot with Dr. Augustin, I was mentally kicking myself for telling Tracey about the job. She really wasn't what we were looking for, after all. Too young. Not dedicated enough. What we really need is someone with a family, I thought. Someone more responsible. Older. Married.

Maybe she wouldn't call.

CHAPTER 11

•

Wednesday, July 15

It took me thirty minutes to find Vivian Porter's house. She only lived eight miles east of the clinic, but her address was 176 1/2 Oak Street, which put her in the old section of downtown, where the two-story woodframe houses are jammed together like library books and you can't get to any of them without going down an alley or two. Most of the alley entrances are camouflaged with garbage cans and discarded furniture, and none of the addresses are off the main roads. I have often thought it is a defensive ploy designed to confuse salesmen and out-of-town relatives.

After five trips around the block, I finally spotted Oak Street and parallel-parked behind an old Ford station wagon. At least it looked old. It had those fake wooden side panels that cost extra, then fade and peel a year after you buy the car.

There was no way to tell if Vivian was home. She had a detached two-car garage, and both doors were down. I got out of my car. A four-foot chain-link fence ran all the way around Vivian's tiny lot. A gate near the garage was latched but not locked. A large red sign proclaiming BAD DOG in luminous gold letters hung from it.

Since I knew Dresden and had never seen even a hint of aggression from him, I proceeded nonchalantly up the walk, past a side door I presumed opened into the kitchen. If Vivian Porter was keeping a cat, the kitchen was the most obvious place to look for evidence of it, but I continued around the house to the front door. There was no point in attracting attention by peeking in the windows. Somehow, I would talk my way into the kitchen—ask for a glass of water or her recipe for meat loaf.

The front of Vivian's house was typical of the homes built in Florida in the twenties and thirties. It had a wide wrap-around porch and big French doors that could be opened up to allow for flow-through ventilation in the summer. Of course, Vivian, like most second- and third-time owners of these houses, undoubtedly had added central air and heat.

There were two white wicker chairs, a settee, and a matching glass-topped table on the porch, along with several hanging baskets containing what I guessed were orchids. The flowers looked like they ought to be in the center of a bridal bouquet or, at the very least, gracing the bosom of the bride's mother.

I hadn't pictured Vivian as being inclined toward the green thumb type, although it did sort of fit with the bird-watching image. I walked up the steps to the front door and knocked. There was no answer, and I was about to knock again when Dresden came around the corner.

If there is such a thing as a Dr. Jekyll and Mr. Hyde persona in dogs, Dresden would certainly qualify. His body seemed fatter and taller, his head larger than I remembered. His ears still hung down like a basset hound's, but his eyes, rather than soulful, were like tiny acetylene torches. He didn't bark or growl, but his lips were drawn back from his teeth, which seemed abnormally long and startlingly white. Saliva dripped from his chin, and I tried to remember when he'd last had a rabies shot.

"Hello, Dresden," I said softly. "You know me, don't you?" I'm the one who sticks you with needles and pokes thermometers up your butt.

Dresden stopped a few feet short of the porch and snapped his jaws together a couple of times just for practice. I could feel the sweat pop out on my face and arms, and it wasn't from the heat.

Never make eye contact with a strange dog, the woman who taught our animal behavior class warned. It is interpreted as a challenge. Squat down to their level and extend your hand in greeting. Sure, I thought, but make it your left one, if you are right-handed.

Very slowly, I bent my knees and lowered myself to a squatting position. There was no way I was going to take my eyes off of him, but I aimed my face at the ground and watched him through my lashes.

Suddenly, a neighbor's dog barked, which started several other unseen dogs barking from various points around Vivian's house. I feared I was about to become dinner for a pack of wolves. Fortunately, the diversion caused Dresden to close his mouth and turn his head toward the street. Realizing I might not get another chance, I stood up, leaped off the porch, nearly breaking my ankle in the process, and limped for the gate.

Dresden, now barking ferociously, ran after me. He flung himself against the gate a second after I closed and latched it. He then proceeded to wrap his canines around a section of the chain-link. Little specs of foam and blood appeared on his lower jaw. I let out a deep sigh and wondered how I was going to feign sympathy when Vivian brought her dog to the clinic with a couple of broken teeth and torn gums.

I was breathing hard, and my ankle was throbbing, but I tried to look casual as I hobbled to my car. I didn't see anyone watching me from behind parted curtains, which seemed odd, since most of the residents in that part of town are nearly as old as the houses and long since retired.

I got in my car and started the engine. I still didn't know if Vivian had Pearl's remaining kitten. I was thankful I hadn't said anything to Dr. Augustin about Cynthia's suspicions. Now I wouldn't have to listen to him tell me what an idiot I was for ignoring Vivian's red and gold warning. Like *he* would have. Ha!

CHAPTER 12

•

I arrived at the hospital at 2:30. St. Luke's recently renovated parking lot encompasses over eight city blocks, not including the covered staff parking located next to the McNealy Children's Center. It is so immense, the aisles are given names and numbers like at Disney World, in the hopes that visitors won't take to sleeping in the hospital corridors because they can't locate their cars. I parked in Pinellas 32. Goofy 32 would have been more appropriate.

My ankle was beginning to swell under my slacks, but it didn't hurt as much as I had anticipated, despite the quarter mile hike from my car. I was glad I could walk around without being mistaken for a patient.

The main entrance and reception area were in one of the newer add-ons, and the decor was a sterile yet pleasing blend of pastels and parchment. Large, comfortable chairs and love seats, most of them occupied, were scattered here and there, along with end tables piled high with the requisite copies of *People, Sports Illustrated, Southern Living*, and *Newsweek*. The vast expanse of wall space was broken up by framed watercolors depicting children at the zoo holding balloons and people picnicking at the beach or canoeing down some serene blackwater river. A gift shop and a florist were situated just inside the front doors.

An information desk, located like a wheel hub at the intersection of three main hallways, was manned by a middle-aged woman dressed in the same pinafore I had seen on Vivian

Porter. She was glued to a small television set that occupied one corner of the desk. From her expression, I gathered the program was a soap opera where the dashingly handsome male lead was dying of some obscure tropical disease.

"Excuse me," I said to the woman.

She looked up, obviously miffed at having been interrupted. Her name tag said "Kathleen Bower, Volunteer."

"I'm interested in doing volunteer work here at the hospital," I said.

"What department?" she asked, one eye on the TV.

Over her head, a myriad of brass sign plates pointed east, west, and northwest to Radiology, Outpatient Surgery, Maternity, Admissions, Physical Therapy, and Administration. All of the truly exciting places like the Morgue and Intensive Care were obviously inaccessible from the hospital's main entrance.

"I'm not sure," I told her.

Without moving her head, she pointed northwest. "Down the hall. Follow the yellow line to the elevator."

I thanked her, although I doubt she heard me, and headed off, feeling more than a little like Dorothy in search of the reclusive wizard.

The floors, I discovered once I left the reception area, were painted with green, blue, red, yellow, and white stripes. Each stripe apparently was intended to help dazed and fearful patients (or visitors) find their respective destinations. There were plenty of signs, but if you missed one of them, you could wander aimlessly around for hours, possibly days. Hence the trail markers.

Because of all the wing additions over the years, the floor dipped and rose like a tiny roller coaster. Each time I encountered a new fork in the road, I would lose one of the stripes. Finally, the yellow and blue stripes ended at a set of elevators. When I entered an empty car, I found a sign directing those seeking Physical Therapy to press 3. Those wishing Administration were to press 1. We were on 2, evidently.

I was trying to decide where to go, when a nice-looking young man in navy surgical scrubs got on. He smiled and pressed 3.

"What floor?" he asked me.

"I'm not sure," I said. I was beginning to sound like a broken record. "I'm interested in doing some volunteer work here at St. Luke's, and the woman at the information desk wasn't very helpful."

I smiled innocently and tried not to appear too obvious, as I studied the ID badge he had clipped to the pocket of his smock. The word "Volunteer" was printed in large red letters below a passport-style picture of the man. His identification number was printed below that.

"You need to go down to Administration," he said. "First floor. Ask for Betty."

He was tall, with wavy auburn hair and green eyes. His chin and nose were marred by the remnants of adolescent acne. He was about nineteen or twenty.

"I'm a volunteer," he said proudly. "Physical Therapy. I'm a PT student at the university. I come here one day a week for credit."

The elevator stopped, and the doors opened.

"Where do you work?" I asked. "I mean, are your patients ambulatory, or do you go to their rooms?"

"Some of them come to us, but we usually go to the rooms. Orthopedics, one of the intensive care units, the Children's Center." He acted like he really enjoyed it.

"Well," I said, as he stepped off the elevator, "maybe I'll see you around."

He grinned boyishly. "My name is Derek," he said. He stuck his foot out to keep the doors from closing. "What's yours?"

"Samantha. Sam, for short. Thanks for the information, Derek." I pressed the button for Administration.

Derek removed his foot, and the doors began to close. "Bye, 'Sam for short,' " he said, laughing.

Now why couldn't he be twenty years older? I asked myself.

It wasn't difficult to find Betty, once I got off the elevator. Administration occupied most of the first floor, and Volunteer Services was the first door on the right. Betty Bayonne, Volunteer Coordinator, according to the sign on her desk, was seated at a large metal, government-issue-style monstrosity located just inside the door. The desk top was nearly obscured by overflow from her in-box, two framed photographs that faced away from me, a philodendron badly in need of water, sunlight, or both, a coffee mug that was doubling as a pencil holder, and a half-eaten sandwich. Tuna on whole wheat, by the look and smell of it.

Betty, a slightly overweight, middle-aged peroxide blonde with a pleasing albeit overly made-up face, was on the phone. She motioned for me to come in and sit.

I took the remaining chair. Two people, an elderly man and a college-aged girl who looked like she'd partied hearty the night before, were already waiting. The man smiled. The girl had her eyes shut. She was wearing a uniform. The top was peach with a white collar, and her pants were wrinkled white. She had on nurse's shoes, white hose, and a name tag I couldn't read.

Betty hung up and turned to the girl. "They're expecting you in Nursing, Miss Thomas. Room 153, down the hall." She pointed to her right.

The girl abruptly opened her eyes, struggled to her feet, and mumbled, "Thanks," as she left the office. Betty shook her head, then smiled at the elderly man.

"We'll have your paperwork shortly, Mr. Agee. You'll enjoy Admissions. Mrs. Porter will show you the ropes." She looked at me. "How may I help you, Miss . . . ?"

"Holt," I said. "I'm interested in volunteering a couple of days a week. Wednesdays and Sundays. In Physical Therapy."

"Is this for class credit?" she asked. "Are you a student?"

"I'm considering a career move," I said, which lately wasn't altogether untrue.

"Physical therapy is a very lucrative as well as rewarding field of endeavor," she said. She sounded like an official from the local Economic Development Council.

She opened a drawer and extracted several sheets of paper, which she attached to a clipboard, then took a pen out of the coffee mug/pencil holder on her desk. She handed both items to me.

"Just fill out this application, if you would."

I got up and took the offering, then sat down again. The phone rang, and Betty answered it. The call was obviously from one of her children because, very shortly, she became involved in a heated discussion regarding a weekend trip to Epcot Center and why hadn't he (or she) thought to save his (or her) allowance to pay for it.

I stared at the form. It appeared to be a routine application for employment at St. Luke's Hospital. In addition to the usual spaces for education, past employment, and felony convictions, there were several dozen questions about the prospective employee's health. "Have you or any member of your family ever had" type questions. Did I suffer from night sweats, low-grade fever, recurrent yeast infections, bleeding gums, chronic cough, sore throat, back trouble, painful joints, difficulty breathing, urinating, etc.? Had I ever been treated for mental illness? Hospitalized? Had I ever considered suicide (how about now?)? Was I a homicidal maniac?

I resisted the temptation to answer "Yes" to several of the more exciting maladies, just to see what would happen.

The elderly man chuckled, and I looked up.

"They're pretty nosy, aren't they?" he asked, grinning. "At my age, if you don't have bleeding gums, painful joints, and difficulty urinating, you're probably dead."

I laughed. He reminded me of my grandfather.

I finished filling out the form and took it over to Betty's desk. She was still on the phone, this time with someone from the hospital who had evidently called to complain about one of the volunteers. Betty told the caller she would look into it and hung up. She clucked her tongue a couple of times, wrote herself a note, then turned her attention to my application.

"It will take a few days to process this," she said.

I couldn't tell her I didn't have a few days.

"But I can give you a temporary ID badge, so you can go up to Physical Therapy and talk to Irma Shoaf, the Director. A very nice woman. And we'll need a passport-sized photo. You can drop that by anytime."

She opened another drawer and pulled out a plastic badge that was identical to the one Derek had been wearing, minus the picture and ID number. She handed it to me. Then she took a manila envelope out of the same drawer.

"This packet contains information about St. Luke's, its

various services and programs, including the volunteer program, and a map to help you find your way around. The areas marked in red are restricted to authorized personnel only. Wear your ID badge whenever you are on a floor other than one or two. The cafeteria, located on the second floor, is open from five A.M. to midnight. The Snack Shop is open twenty-four hours a day. The dress code varies according to the department you are in."

She rattled this off so quickly and with such precision, I expected her to end with "Thank you for flying with us. Have a nice day."

"I appreciate this," I said, taking the envelope.

The phone rang.

"I'll give you a call in three or four days," Betty said and picked up the receiver.

I clipped the ID badge to my collar, picked up my purse, and winked at the old man, who winked back. Then I left.

When I got to the elevator, I punched 2. Since I had no intention of going to Physical Therapy then or in the future, I decided to visit the cafeteria for a sandwich and a chance to study the map. Derek had mentioned he routinely traveled around the hospital, even venturing into Intensive Care, so I presumed my ID badge could get me there, as well.

The cafeteria was nearly deserted. The kitchen help were busy cleaning up the lunch stuff in preparation for dinner. I managed to talk them out of the last tuna on whole wheat and a glass of skim milk. Although $6.50 seemed like a lot of money for a sandwich and a glass of milk, I was hungry and needed to sit down. My ankle was beginning to throb.

I opened the manila envelope and pulled out the map. It was a threefold, 11 x 14 schematic undoubtedly drawn by some medical student moonlighting as an architect. Color-coded corridors wound through the various hospital wings like the arteries and veins in my cat cadaver in comparative anatomy lab. It was so complicated, I expected to find a AAA office or, at the very least, a traffic control cop standing guard at each elevator.

There appeared to be an intensive care unit on virtually every floor. They were, thankfully, yellow areas rather than the dreaded red. According to Dr. Augustin, Ralph Silor was in Room B625. I assumed that meant he was in the B wing, which was nowhere near the main entrance.

I swallowed two aspirins with the rest of my milk, gathered up my papers and my purse, and, with the map in hand, headed for the elevator. I needed to go up four levels and across three hallways to reach the sixth floor of the B wing.

As I was leaving the cafeteria, I glanced at the dinner menu posted on the wall by the cash register. Like it or not, there was a good possibility I might still be around for the evening meal. Unfortunately, the special of the day was liver and onions, which seemed fitting, somehow.

CHAPTER 13

•

When I got off the elevator on the sixth floor, I was beginning to limp noticeably. Two nurses and a doctor asked if I needed help. One of them went so far as to direct an orderly to get me a wheelchair. When I explained I had twisted my ankle walking on the second floor roller coaster, I instantly became a legal leper, and they left me alone.

There were no watercolors depicting children at the zoo this far from the main entrance, no pastel chairs or love seats, just sterile white walls and spotless linoleum. The hallways were cluttered with multitiered dollies laden with the remains of lunch and drug carts that looked like catering trays, their tiny white nut cups arranged in neat little stacks. Doctors, nurses, orderlies, and a few bathrobe-clad patients trudged along, all with the same general glazed expression. They reminded me of early morning commuters sorely in need of a cup of coffee.

The intensive care unit was clearly marked with a sign that said LIMITED ACCESS: ALL VISITORS MUST REGISTER AT THE NURSES STATION. I ducked into the restroom and stared at myself in the mirror. I had been relieved to see that every room was a private room and, although the outer wall was glass, a curtain could be drawn around each patient's bed, providing privacy. Since Ralph Silor probably didn't need a physical therapist, explaining my presence in his room wasn't going to be easy, unless I could conceal myself somehow.

I propped my packet of papers (and my map) on the top of the tampon dispenser, tucked my purse into the bend of the sink's drainpipe, and straightened my Volunteer ID badge. Temporary or not, it was all I had.

I tried not to limp as I walked purposefully up to the nurses station. Because it was an ICU station, it was well manned and busy, which was probably a blessing. It took a minute or two for someone to even notice me standing there.

"Yes?" asked one of the women in white. She was in her fifties and looked extremely competent. She also looked extremely harried at that particular moment and acted like I was the proverbial straw about to break the camel's back.

"I'm from Physical Therapy. I was told Derek was up here, and I need to speak with him about a patient on four." I hoped there were patients on four.

"Derek?"

"Tall, cute PT student." I tried to remember what he'd been wearing. "Navy scrubs."

"Oh, yes. I haven't seen him for a while, but that doesn't mean he isn't up here. Try 620." She glanced at my badge and hesitated. Then the phone rang and, while she answered it, I took off down the hall. I did not look back.

Room 612, Edwards, R. was to my right, and 613, Richter, L. was to my left. I walked as fast as I could, considering my ankle, past 620, and turned the corner. At the far end of the corridor, the individual glass-walled rooms gave way to an open, congregate area with beds arranged in a large semicircle around an enormous nurses station. There was enough high-tech equipment on the wall behind the station to monitor environmental conditions in the space shuttle. And there were a lot more doctors wandering around than at the entrance to the intensive care unit. To make matters worse, none of them looked bored.

I silently prayed that Ralph was in one of the few remaining private fishbowls. I was pretty sure I wouldn't get very far if I ventured into the critical care area.

Room 625 was next to the last on the left. The little name card inserted in a slot by the door said SILOR, R. I stopped, gave thanks, and knocked lightly. A male voice from behind the curtain told me to enter, so I pushed open the door and went inside.

I had never met Ralph, so I wouldn't have known him even if he had been healthy. But the way he looked then—skin the color of mustard, cheeks sunken, his hair badly in need of washing—his own mother would have had trouble recognizing him. Illness had added years to his features.

"Ralph?" I asked. I tried to keep my face from showing how I felt.

"Yes?" he said. He had an IV line taped to his hand, and he was hooked up to a heart monitor that silently traced his heartbeat on an oscilloscope to his right. A urinary catheter ran from beneath the covers to a bag hanging below him on the bed frame.

"My name is Samantha Holt. I work for Dr. Augustin, your father's veterinarian."

Despite his obvious pain and nausea, he chuckled. "I knew my doctors were running out of ideas," he said, "but I'm not sure a veterinarian is what I need right now."

I smiled and pulled up one of the tiny room's two chairs, careful to conceal it and myself behind the curtain. "May I?"

Ralph nodded. "I hope Pearl is okay," he said. "Dad really doted on that cat." He looked like he was about to cry.

"She is," I said quickly. "We have her at the clinic. Along with one of her kittens. I've named him Randy. He looks just like Pearl." I avoided mentioning the demise of his two siblings. "I probably don't have much time," I said. "I'm really not supposed to be here, but I wanted to talk to you." I paused, unsure about how to go on.

Ralph watched me, his face passive.

"Someone left Randy and two of his littermates on our doorstep," I said, "along with three hundred dollars and a note asking us to care for them. Dr. Augustin is trying to find out who that person was. We think there was a fourth kitten, and Dr. Augustin is fairly certain whoever left the three hundred dollars has it. The kittens have a medical problem that needs specialized treatment. That's why Dr. Augustin wants to locate the fourth kitten."

"It was probably someone from the Paper Moon," Ralph said. "It's a bar Dad and I used to hang out at. The owner, Bill O'Shea, is my godfather. He's been raising money all along to help with my medical expenses. A couple of weeks ago, he held a volleyball tournament there at the Moon, with the proceeds going to me and my father. Dad said they were able to collect almost a thousand dollars." He winced suddenly and took a deep breath. "Anyway, someone from the bar probably took the kittens off of Dad's hands and donated three hundred dollars for their care. Maybe the fourth kitten died. I've been in here forever, it seems like, and didn't even know Pearl was pregnant."

He struggled to sit up, and I went over to help him.

"Thanks," he said weakly, as if his day's ration of energy was nearly spent. "Have you talked to Bill about the money? Maybe he left it, along with the kittens. It sounds like something he'd do. You know, not take credit for a good deed."

At that moment, the door opened, and someone with crepe soles walked in. Suddenly, the curtain was whisked aside, and I was face-to-face with a young nurse, who looked extremely surprised to see me sitting there at Ralph's side. She was carrying a small tray containing a pitcher of water and one of the small nut cups I'd seen earlier. She put the tray down on Ralph's bedside table.

"Who are you?" she asked suspiciously.

"This is a friend of my father's," said Ralph. "Samantha Holt, this is Ramona James, my nurse."

The way he said her name and the look on his face when he said it made me think of Lt. Henry and Catherine Barkley in *A Farewell to Arms*. Ralph was obviously in love with the girl, which wasn't surprising, considering the circumstances.

I smiled at her. "How do you do?"

She had olive skin and dark brown eyes that reminded me of Dr. Augustin's eyes. Her figure, enhanced by the snug-fitting, contoured uniform, was the kind that attracts men like raw meat attracts flies. Her shoulder-length hair was dark brown and very straight. She wore bangs that touched her eyebrows.

"Visitors to the ICU are restricted to family members, Miss Holt," she said. She continued to eye me and my temporary ID badge suspiciously.

"I know," I said. "And I hope I haven't caused Ralph any

undue stress. But I wanted to let him know Pearl, his father's cat, is being well cared for."

I felt like I had at age ten, when the guy at the convenience store caught me shoplifting. Any second, Ramona would press the little red button over Ralph's head, and an army of hospital security people would storm in and cart me away. I could almost hear Betty Bayonne, Volunteer Coordinator, clucking her tongue.

"Well, I'm sure Ralph appreciates that, Miss Holt," said Ramona, "but I'm also sure you'll understand if I ask you to leave now. Ralph needs to rest." She plumped up his pillow and pulled the covers up under his armpits.

Ralph stared up at her with the adoring eyes of a faithful dog. I was obviously intruding. I headed for the door.

"Get better, Ralph," I said. "Pearl and Randy are waiting to go home."

Ralph glanced over at me and smiled wanly. "There's nothing I'd like better," he said.

I made a hasty retreat into the ladies' room to collect my things. I was glad no one had swiped my map, since I was not at all sure I could find my way back to the parking lot without it.

I had just stepped into the hall when Vivian Porter whizzed by, pinafore bow strings flapping. She was carrying an arm load of files and never saw me. Mr. Agee, the man from the Volunteer Services office, was trying to keep up with her. He glanced over at me and winked, then hurried after Vivian, who was already heading around the corner toward the high-tech area.

CHAPTER 14

•

Thursday, July 16

"Were you successful yesterday?" Dr. Augustin asked me, without looking up and without so much as a how-de-do.

Dr. Augustin is not big on small talk. Besides, I knew he was ticked off at me for coming in twenty minutes late. But the pain in my ankle made getting ready for work difficult and, on top of that, I hadn't slept well. I kept seeing Ralph's tortured expression and yellow eyes.

I limped over to the treatment table and wrapped my arms around the head and shoulders of a miniature dachshund Dr. Augustin was attempting to examine, for some reason without the benefit of a muzzle. The little dog had a herniated disc in its lumbar spine and wasn't too keen on being poked and prodded. From the look of Dr. Augustin's left hand, I concluded the dog had already nailed him once or twice that morning.

"Did you get in to see Ralph?"

"Yes," I said.

At that, Dr. Augustin looked up and smiled. "Well, good for you. See, I told you it would be a snap."

Yeah, a snap, I said to myself.

Dr. Augustin very carefully lifted the dachshund off the table and carried it to its cage. He came back to the table, made a few notes in the animal's file, then closed it.

"So what did Ralph have to say?" he asked. He ran water over the small but still oozing bite wounds on his hand.

"He doesn't know anything about the fake money *or* Pearl's kittens," I said. "He told me Arnie and Bill O'Shea had raised nearly a thousand dollars toward his medical bills shortly before Arnie was killed. It sure doesn't sound like Arnie was involved in any counterfeiting operation."

"What about Arnie's murder? Did Ralph have any idea who might have wanted to kill his father?"

He dabbed a cotton ball soaked in alcohol over his hand. I watched him, but he didn't flinch. After he was finished anointing himself, he went into Isolation and opened the door to Pearl's cage, reached in, and picked her up. She looked terrified. The smell of alcohol wasn't helping, either. She began to smack her lips and squint.

"No," I said. "They found me in his room and threw me out before I could ask him. Besides, Ralph is too sick to tolerate much interrogation right now, anyway."

Dr. Augustin snorted. "I guess we'll have to investigate other possibilities, won't we?"

What's this "we" stuff, I wanted to ask him, but I didn't. Instead, I stuck my fingers through the bars on the door to Randy's cage and wiggled them. Randy pounced, then proceeded to chew on my thumb.

"I think Pearl can be moved into the kennel," said Dr. Augustin. "Find an empty cage on the top row." He handed her to me. "I'll spay her when I get the chance."

He went into the next room, gathered up the files from the morning's treatments, and headed for his office.

At 9:30 Cynthia called me up to the reception room. I wanted it to be Michael Halsey, back from his sojourn to the east coast. Cynthia's voice had sounded mildly excited over the intercom, but she wasn't breathing hard, so I knew it couldn't be Michael. I wasn't expecting Tracey Nevins, however, and to say I was disappointed would be a gigantic understatement.

"Hi, Sam," Tracey said. "I decided to drop by and check out that job opening. Today is my day off, and I didn't have any plans."

She was wearing a longish denim skirt with a wide ruffle around the hem, a long-sleeved white cotton blouse with turquoise and silver buttons, and suede boots with fringe down the back. Her earrings were big porcelain ovals with an artistic rendering of the desert Southwest painted on them. Turquoise and black, like her buttons. All that was missing was a Stetson to go with the boots. Or maybe a pony. I wanted to tell her Billy Bob's was a few hundred miles west, but I controlled myself.

"Gee," I said finally, "this is a surprise."

I indicated a chair next to the watercooler, then sat down beside it. Tracey sashayed across the room and joined me. Her purse looked expensive. It was made of soft fawn-colored leather and had tiny wolf faces and eagles stitched on the flap, the kind you usually see carved on totem poles.

Cynthia cleared her throat. I looked over at her.

"Cynthia," I said hastily, "this is Tracey Nevins, a technician at Dr. Farmington's clinic." I looked back at Tracey. "This is our receptionist, Cynthia Caswell."

"Hi, Cynthia," Tracey said, her tone a little too chummy to suit me. Like she already had the job.

"I know Samantha would like to see Dr. Augustin hire another technician as soon as possible," Cynthia said, smiling sweetly. "She's running herself ragged trying to be in two places at once, aren't you, Samantha?"

I glared at her. For some reason, she was acting downright traitorous. Couldn't she tell from Tracey's getup that the girl simply would not fit in?

Before I could think of something appropriate to say, Dr. Augustin opened the door to his office.

"I thought I heard your voice, Tracey," he said. He leaned against the door frame. "Come to check out the job opening?"

His eyes weren't burning holes through Tracey's skull, like I knew they could if he wanted them to, but Tracey popped up like a jack-in-the-box anyway and sailed over to him, her boots barely touching the floor, or so it seemed.

"Samantha told me about the lab tech position and suggested I stop in for a chat."

I felt my mouth drop open. I most certainly had not suggested anything of the kind. "I though she might know of someone who wanted a change of scenery," I said quickly.

Dr. Augustin stepped back into his office and pointed at the chair by his desk. "Come on in then, and let's talk about it," he said.

Tracey glanced back at me and grinned, then followed Dr. Augustin into his office. She pulled the door closed behind her.

"Couldn't even wait for the body to get cold," I muttered.

"What was that?" asked Cynthia.

"Oh, nothing," I said and hobbled off down the hall.

Tracey left at ten, when our first client of the morning arrived with a litter of springer spaniel puppies.

Dr. Augustin and I were so busy docking tails and removing dewclaws, I forgot to ask him if he'd hired Tracey. As it turned out, I didn't have to.

"Tracey starts Monday," he said to me and Cynthia, as the woman with the puppies was leaving.

"I think that's just wonderful," Cynthia said enthusiastically. "Sam, I'll bet you're pleased."

"Pleased as Punch," I said.

Dr. Augustin gave me a quizzical look, then went into Room 2.

Mick Peters came in with Jonesy at 11:30. He didn't have an appointment. We were running half an hour late as it was, but Dr. Augustin told Cynthia to put him in a room anyway, which didn't sit too well with the two clients already waiting in the reception area. One of them, a man with a moth-eaten tomcat who'd evidently been in a fight, got up and left. He said he would take his cat to someone who was professional enough to keep on schedule.

Dr. Augustin said, "Good riddance," under his breath. Then he flashed a smile at the remaining client, a woman by the name of Leitel, who was probably Glynnis Winter's sorority sister, by the look of her, and told me to bring the two Himalayan declaws up to an exam room.

I started to leave, then looked back at the woman. She was thin but not overly so, dressed in snug-fitting designer jeans and a maroon silk blouse you could see through, only because behind her the sun was bouncing off the chrome on the cars parked in front of the clinic. Her bra was one of those tiny lace jobs, in black or navy. She had on very little jewelry, but what there was contained a lot of nice sparkly stones I felt certain were genuine. Her strawberry blond hair was feathered on top and left long at the sides and back. The color looked natural but probably wasn't. I couldn't see her eyes because she was wearing sunglasses. Her fingernails were acrylic, light mauve, and her left ring finger was bare. All in all, she was very attractive. Probably fifty or so, rich, and, like Glynnis Winter, bored.

I left for the kennel and the woman's cats, feeling strangely depressed. I thought about my cats, Tina and Miss Priss, who I loved dearly but who I hoped wouldn't be my sole sleeping companions twenty years hence.

While Dr. Augustin was drooling all over Ms. Leitel and practicing his lady-killer routine on her, I went in to see Mick and Jonesy.

Mick looked tired. He had dark circles under his eyes, and his hands shook. It wasn't like he was hung over or anything, more like he had drunk too much coffee and had too little sleep. He was wearing slacks and a new sport shirt, which was a shock. And he apparently had started smoking again. I could see a pack of cigarettes in his shirt pocket.

"We missed you Tuesday," I said. I decided if Luther what's-his-name hadn't mentioned it, I wouldn't tell Mick I had dropped by his apartment.

"I had to go out of town unexpectedly," he said. "On business."

"We were concerned about Jonesy."

I scratched the dog's head. He seemed healthy enough. He wasn't coughing or breathing hard, and his doggie smell wasn't overpowering, as if he'd recently had a bath.

"I know," said Mick. "But I was careful not to get him too excited or hot and made sure he rested the whole time I was . . . busy."

"You look tired yourself, Mick. Are you all right? And where is Cindy?"

Mick didn't say anything at first. He let go of Jonesy's leash and went over to the chair in the corner and sat down. He looked up at me and smiled. It was forced.

"She's staying with . . . relatives for a while. I've been working a lot of hours lately. Trying to expand the business. I'm thinking about moving up north somewhere. Maybe Atlanta."

"Seems like a good choice for someone in the computer business," I said. "But we'll miss you and Cindy. And Jonesy."

The dog perked up its ears and came over to me, trailing the leash.

"Thanks, Samantha, we'll miss you."

Dr. Augustin opened the door and came in. He examined Jonesy, listening to his heart and lungs, prodding his liver, all the while watching Mick out of the corner of his eye. He took a blood sample from the dog and asked me to run a CBC ASAP, so I left them and went into the lab. When I was finished, Mick and Jonesy were gone.

"Someone or something has Mick scared half to death," said Dr. Augustin from the doorway between the lab and his office.

I handed him the results of the blood work, and he studied them.

"I noticed he was smoking again," I said. "And his hands shook pretty bad. I just figured he was worried about his business. And now Jonesy. He said he was thinking about moving to Atlanta."

"Oh, really?" Dr. Augustin came into the room and put the lab sheet down on the counter.

"What are you thinking?" I asked him, afraid of what he might say, but too curious not to ask.

"I'm thinking we should find out if Mick ever did any business with St. Luke's. Specifically the purchasing department."

He plucked a tissue out of the dispenser next to the microscope and began polishing the eyepieces. Considering how often he does this, I am amazed there is any glass left to polish.

"Purchasing department? You don't mean he was involved with Howard Nichols and Arnie, do you? That's ridiculous."

Dr. Augustin whipped his head around so violently, I feared he might suffer a cervical dislocation.

"Don't be so sure, Samantha," he said, focusing his deadly photon torpedoes on my forehead. "If you had read that Treasury Department brochure like I asked you to, you'd know that several years back, office color copiers forced the government to make a few changes in the way U.S. currency is manufactured." He continued to glower at me.

"But Mick sells computers, not copiers, right?"

"Ever hear of laser scanners? He could have come up with some computerized process that's even better than a copier."

I had to agree, the theory had merit. Mick *was* a genius when it came to computers. A nerdy genius, but a genius nonetheless. "Yes, well maybe he's manufacturing funny money," I conceded, "but Mick could never *kill* anyone, and you know it."

Dr. Augustin turned his head and stared, unseeing, at the urinalysis chart on the wall behind the microscope.

"I'm a little uncomfortable about that part, myself," he said.

CHAPTER 15

•

I thought about Mick off and on the rest of the day. It didn't do much for my already ailing mood. By the time 4:30 rolled around, I was practically in tears and probably would have broken down altogether if we'd had to euthanize anyone. Fortunately, another litter of puppies came in at five for their first shots, and that cheered me up considerably.

Miss Priss and Tina were, as usual, plastered to the living room window when I reached the landing at a quarter to six. It is amazing how friendly and loving cats can be when they are hungry. Ten minutes after they eat, you can't find them anywhere.

I took off my shoes, dumped my purse in the chair by the TV, and went into the kitchen. Priss and Tina followed me, practically tripping over each other in their haste to be the first to the cabinet where I keep their food. Their mixed purring and meowing reminded me of a rusty sign squeaking in the wind. I poured food in their bowls, and the sound changed abruptly to one of boots scrunching through the snow.

I opened the refrigerator. I was starving. A carton of fat-free cottage cheese, a box of fat-free saltines, and a questionable chicken thigh stared back at me. For some reason, Michael Halsey came to mind.

I continued to think about him as I changed my clothes. The box containing the earrings sat on my dresser, a constant reminder that I hadn't heard from him in almost a week. He had promised to call, but his exceedingly uncharacteristic lack of sincerity when he'd said it worried me. Had he found someone else? Someone closer to his own age and less standoffish than, admittedly, I was most of the time? If I found out where he was staying in Ft. Lauderdale and called his hotel room, would a woman answer?

I went back into the kitchen and poured myself a glass of wine. Why did I care? *That* was the real question. I wasn't in love with Michael, at least not passionately, not the way I had been with David. I found him comfortable. Was that enough reason to marry someone? Of course, Michael wouldn't ditch me on my wedding day for a bimbo with big tits, either. At least, I didn't think so. "You never know, though," I said aloud. Men are unpredictable. As long as they have hormones circulating in their systems, they cannot be trusted.

I was about to switch on the TV when the phone rang. Tina ran out of the kitchen, still chewing. Tiny pieces of food fell to the floor as she went, creating a bread crumb-like trail into the bedroom.

I picked up the receiver, expecting it to be Michael, as if telepathy wasn't just in the minds of science fiction writers.

"Hello," I said. I put the wineglass down on the end table.

"Hi, Sam, it's Toby," the rich, steroid-modulated voice said.

I felt my pulse quicken and sat down. "Hi, Toby. How on earth did you find my number? Not that I'm sorry you did, of course."

"There's only one S. Holt in the phone book," he said.

"Right. I forgot."

"Listen," he said, "what are you doing tomorrow after work? And I remember you said your boss usually keeps you until six. I mean later. Around seven."

"I don't have any plans yet. But I thought you tended bar from four-thirty until one."

I watched Priss emerge from the kitchen. She spotted the trail of crumbs and began to vacuum them up.

"I've already asked a friend to cover for me," he said. Then he paused, and I could hear him take a drink of something. "How about dinner?"

"Dinner would be nice," I said.

"Great. Where do you live?"

I told him.

"I'll pick you up at seven. I promise I won't be late." He laughed nervously. "Gotta run. Bye." And he hung up.

I put the receiver back in its cradle. Despite a long and trying day at the clinic, I felt positively exhilarated. Instead of staying at home, I wanted to do something—go dancing or swimming. I certainly wasn't hungry anymore.

That's another thing about Michael, I thought. When I'm in love, I can't eat, and Michael has no effect on my appetite. If anything, all his fancy restaurants and before dinner imbibing have caused me to gain six pounds in the last five months.

I poured the remains of my wine down the drain and went out onto the landing. The sun, still an hour and a half from setting, was intense. I leaned against the railing and squinted across the street at a man walking his dog. The man was middle-aged and overweight, and his dog, an Irish terrier, was straining against the leash. When they reached the fire hydrant at the corner, the dog stopped to investigate. The man took out a handkerchief and wiped his face. I could tell he was winded.

How does Michael manage to stay in shape? I asked myself. Then I thought about Toby, whose shape made me giddy, and Michael was forgotten.

CHAPTER 16

•

Friday, July 17

Frank was waiting at the door when I arrived for work. "Pearl is missing," he said. "I've looked everywhere."

I thought I detected a hint of guilt in his voice. We walked down the hall to the kennel.

"Her cage door was unlatched when I got in, and I swear, Samantha, I closed it last night after I fed her." He pointed to Pearl's empty cage and the empty cage next to hers. "Charlie was out, too, but I found him asleep on Cynthia's desk. I think Charlie let Pearl out." He slammed both cage doors closed. "As usual, I'm going to catch hell for it."

Several months earlier, Charlie had discovered that by sticking his paw through the bars and pushing up on the door latch he could open his cage. Unfortunately, he practiced this newfound talent on various other cages throughout the clinic, usually after hours, including several whose occupants were supposed to be kept confined for one reason or another. Charlie figured out that if he let the prisoners loose, he could help himself to any leftover food. He wasn't picky. Dog food, cat food, special diets, even bland, high-fiber stuff was acceptable.

After a particularly exciting incident involving a two-hundred-pound mastiff named Mad Max, Dr. Augustin instructed Frank to padlock Charlie's cage every night. Unfortunately, Frank tends to get a little sloppy about details when he is in a hurry to leave, and now and then forgets about the padlock. This was obviously one of those times.

"It's partly my fault," I said. "I should have put her in a top cage like Dr. Augustin told me to, not down here next to Charlie, where he can reach her door latch." Against my better judgment, I put my hand on his shoulder. "We'll locate her, Frank. Cynthia can help." I smiled. "Dr. Augustin doesn't need to find out about this."

He looked up at me, but all I saw in his eyes was gratitude. "Thanks, Sam," he said. "I'll show you where I've already checked."

Pearl was still missing at nine, when Dr. Augustin drove up. Cynthia had spent the better part of an hour searching through cabinets, the storage room behind her desk, and any other cubbyhole likely to harbor an eight-pound cat determined to disappear. No luck. We were fairly certain Pearl couldn't get out of the clinic, but Frank called her name every time he went out to the dumpster, just in case. I warned him Dr. Augustin might get suspicious if he heard us calling her, but Frank just lowered his voice and went right on calling. Frank may dress like a deadbeat, but he really is very responsible most of the time.

At noon, Cynthia went to the dry cleaners, and I took my turn at the front desk. Several clients came by for dog food or flea shampoo, so I didn't see Michael Halsey's car pull into the parking lot. It was only after Mrs. Harris and her two boys left with a case of puppy food and enough flea products to treat a seven-thousand-square-foot house that I noticed Michael sitting in the corner reading the latest copy of *Consumer Reports*.

"Michael!" I exclaimed. "You're home."

He got up, put the magazine back in the rack by his chair, and came over to the reception desk. "For a few days, at least," he said.

He looked like he had just stepped out of an ad for razor blades—"The Best a Man Can Get"—with his perfect shave, perfect hair, perfect clothes. He was wearing a pale grey linen suit, with a white shirt and tasteful grey and maroon striped tie. His black Florsheims were like glass.

"I'm sorry I didn't call, but the trial has been hectic, and I've been somewhat preoccupied. I thought I'd make it up to you by taking you to Tuttles for dinner. Would seven be too early?" He leaned against the desk and exhaled the remains of a Wint-O-Green Lifesaver.

Tuttles is a posh, expensive seafood restaurant on the beach. Michael took me there on our first date, and we've been a few times since, mostly when he hasn't seen me for a while. He knows I like the food and the atmosphere. I guessed it was his way of apologizing.

I frowned. "I can't tonight, Michael. I have plans." Afraid he might take this as another put-off, I added hastily, "But I'm free tomorrow night."

Michael shook his head. "I'm committed to a gathering of newspaper people Saturday night. You'd have a terrible time, trust me."

The phone rang. While I took the call, Michael continued to stand by the reception desk, watching me. I'm never sure what he's thinking when he looks at me. I *am* sure I remind him of his wife, Mary, who died a couple of years back. The fact that he may actually see *her* rather than *me* is troubling, to say the least. I have considered the possibility that he doesn't ask me to business-related functions because he doesn't want his coworkers to notice the similarity. Or maybe he doesn't want them to notice the difference in our ages.

I hung up the phone.

"How about brunch Sunday?" Michael asked. "At the Sea Breeze. Not too early. Say, one o'clock."

Brunch meant tons of food, probably accompanied by Bloody Marys or champagne, if I knew Mr. Halsey. Good for at least a pound or two.

"I'd love it."

He beamed. "I'll pick you up at twelve-thirty."

"Sounds good," I said. I cleared my throat. "Not to change the subject, but I have a little problem I'd like some help with."

Michael sat down in the chair closest to the desk, unbuttoned his suit jacket, and crossed his legs. His socks were the same shade of grey as the suit.

"Whatever I can do, Samantha," he said. "You know that." He meant it.

I hesitated a few seconds, then lowered my voice, more out

of habit than anything else, since Dr. Augustin was gone until two. "Remember that guy who was murdered a couple of weeks ago? The one they found in the canal with his hands chopped off?"

Michael nodded. "Silor, wasn't it? Arnold Silor?"

"That's the one," I said. "Anyway, Dr. Augustin thinks Arnie's murder and the murder of Howard Nichols—the Director of Purchasing at St. Luke's—are related. You remember the cops found counterfeit money on Mr. Nichols? Well, someone left us three hundred dollars in counterfeit twenties the day they found Arnie's body. The money was in a basket with three kittens. Arnie Silor's cat, Pearl, is the mother of those kittens."

Michael's expression didn't change appreciably, but I knew from experience he was hanging on my every word. Like a good reporter should. Voluntarily talking to the press is akin to mutiny, as far as Dr. Augustin is concerned. But Michael is an honest, respectable reporter, and I have grown to trust him. If you tell him something is off the record, he won't write about it, no matter how juicy. Besides, even Dr. Augustin has to admit, Michael is a great source of information.

"I know this is probably a stupid question," he began, "but has Dr. Augustin contacted the police about his suspicions?"

I looked down my nose at him. "You've *got* to be kidding. Of course he hasn't gone to the police. He wants to find the person or persons responsible himself. If you want my opinion, he's PO'd because someone tried to pass funny money off at our clinic as the real thing. They almost got away with it, too."

I told him about Agent Nelson's visit. Then about Sarah Milton and the "steam engine voice" she heard and our quest for the missing kitten. I recounted Wednesday's harrowing experience. Michael showed genuine concern for my ankle, something Dr. Augustin had yet to notice.

"So how can I help with this investigation?" Michael asked, after I'd assured him that my ankle was on the mend.

"Dr. Augustin believes another one of our clients, a Mick Peters, is somehow connected with the counterfeit money and . . ." I paused. ". . . and the murders." It was as if saying it aloud might actually make it true, and I felt like I'd ratted on a friend.

"He sells computers and software," I continued. "His company's name is M-P Computer Services. Dr. Augustin contends he is smart enough to have rigged up some laser scanner/printer combination that can produce good fake currency. Better than a copy machine."

"I suppose it's possible. They wouldn't have the clear polyester strip with the matching denomination printed on it, but most people probably wouldn't notice, if the bill looked and felt real enough."

I stared at him. He leaned forward, pulled his wallet out of his back left pocket, and opened it. He searched through the bills until he found a twenty, then handed it to me.

"Hold it up to the light," he said.

"I did as I was told. The letters clearly visible on the narrow see-through plastic thread imbedded in the paper read, "USA TWENTY USA TWENTY USA TWENTY." I handed the bill back to him.

"Amazing," I said. "I feel really dumb asking this, but how long has that strip been there?"

"Since 1990, I believe." He grinned. "I'm surprised your esteemed boss hasn't suggested you and Cynthia learn to spot counterfeit currency."

I didn't say anything, and Michael stood up.

"You want me to see what I can find out about this Peters fellow?" he asked.

"If you wouldn't mind," I said. "Maybe see if he did any business with St. Luke's purchasing department."

Cynthia's car pulled into the parking lot. As she got out, she looked over at Michael's BMW, with its "Press" decal on the driver's side window, then hurried across the pavement to the door.

"Michael!" she exclaimed, as she came inside.

Michael buttoned his jacket and stood patiently as Cynthia gave him a hug and planted a dainty kiss on his cheek.

"We're so glad you're home," she said, out of breath and flushed after this latest attack of cardiac reflex that Michael seemed to bring about in her. "Aren't we, Samantha?"

I suddenly had the urge to say something ugly and caustic to

Cynthia. Lately, she and Dr. Augustin seemed compelled to make decisions for me, even speak for me, as if I was three years old or, worse, suffering from dementia or senility. But I held my tongue and simply nodded in agreement.

Michael glanced at the clock on the wall behind me, then at his watch. "Well, ladies," he said, "I've got to be going." He paused, looked over at me, and winked. "Pick you up Sunday at twelve-thirty?"

I couldn't help but notice Cynthia's elated expression, and it took some of the fun out of Michael's invitation. I sighed. "I'll be ready," I said.

When I left at 6:10, Frank was back in the kennel. Normally, he would have been long gone, especially on a Friday night, but we still hadn't located Pearl. Frank said he wanted to put out a dish or two of food for her but couldn't until Dr. Augustin went home. Miraculously, our "esteemed boss," as Michael put it, hadn't realized Pearl was missing. That surprised me, since very little of a veterinary nature gets by him. I could dye my hair red, and it would probably take Dr. Augustin a week to notice, but if a cat sneezes anywhere in the clinic, he hears it and investigates.

I wished Frank luck and raced to my car. I still hadn't decided what I was going to wear. Mrs. Winter could get away with jeans, at a hundred bucks plus a pair, at almost any of the moderate-priced restaurants on the beach. Unfortunately, all I owned were Levi's. On the other hand, a dress and heels might seem a bit much for McDonald's. The more I thought about my date with Toby, the more nervous I got. And the more I wished for a quiet, comfortable evening with good ol' Michael.

CHAPTER 17

•

At 7:30, I quit pacing around my living room and turned on the TV. Toby hadn't called, and I figured he had decided not to show. It wouldn't be the first time I had been stood up by a guy who liked looking at himself in the mirror more than he liked looking at me. You'd think I'd learn after a while.

At 7:40, I went into my bedroom to change from the cotton print dress and sandals I was wearing to shorts and a T-shirt. I was in my closet when the doorbell rang. I slipped the sandals back on and raced for the door.

Toby stood on the landing holding a bunch of daisy chrysanthemums. He was dressed in olive safari shorts, a beige and olive striped shirt, and Berkenstocks. He handed me the flowers.

"Sorry I'm late," he said. "The guy who was supposed to fill in for me at the Moon didn't show, and I had to start my shift at four-thirty, until another friend got off work and could take over."

"That's okay," I said.

I stepped aside so he could come in. His cologne was like a citrus grove in full bloom.

"Nice place," he said, looking around. He spotted Miss Priss. "Oh. I see you have a cat." His tone indicated he would rather visit someone with a pet alligator. Then he saw a photo of me taken at the conclusion of a 5K race held earlier in the year. I was standing next to Jeffrey, who had placed second in his age group and was holding up a little bronze medallion. His roommate had taken the picture.

"I see you run," said Toby. "That's great, Sam. I try to get a few miles in every couple of days, but I don't compete. Too much muscle mass, I guess."

It was probably my imagination, but I thought he flexed his pecs and biceps, just to show me how much was too much.

"I don't compete, either," I said. "I've only run in a couple of races, and only because the guy next door coerced me. I'm not very fast. I just do it for the exercise."

"Same here," he said. "Listen, we'd better get going. The place I'm taking you to closes at nine."

I put the flowers in the kitchen sink, turned off the TV, and got my purse. On the landing, Toby waited while I locked my door.

"Have you lived here long?" he asked.

"A couple of years," I said. "It's close to where I work, and the neighborhood is nice. Mostly, I stay because the rent is reasonable." It sounded like an excuse, and I wondered why I had said it, since it wasn't true.

We went down the stairs to his car, an early model Pontiac Firebird. Black. It looked to be in pretty good condition.

"Buckle up," he said, after I'd eased myself into the leather bucket seat and pulled the door closed. The car's interior smelled like Armorall and vanilla.

I secured the lap belt, and Toby started the engine and backed out of the parking lot. Then he headed, not for the beach, but across the bayou to the mainland.

Without asking if I minded, he turned on the radio. The station was one of the few remaining classical stations in the area. I was surprised. Somehow I had imagined Toby as more the fuzzy dice type.

Toby tapped on the steering wheel in time with the music, a rollicking Irish ballad played on a dulcimer, and hummed along, as if I wasn't there. I confess I could have struck up a conversation if I'd wanted to. But he seemed a little ill at ease and not particularly interested in talking, so I leaned back in my seat and stared out the window.

Eventually, we passed the alley that ran behind Vivian

Porter's house. I wondered how Dresden was doing. If Vivian really did have Pearl's remaining kitten, I fervently hoped the dog hadn't wrapped his jaws around it like he had tried to do to me.

"Here we are," said Toby.

He slowed the car down and turned into a long, narrow parking lot fronting a commercial strip center. Several small neighborhood businesses, including a restaurant called the Hearts of Palm, were crammed into a short city block between Duncan and Soroa streets.

"You're going to love the food here, Samantha," Toby said.

He stopped the car and got out. Without thinking, I waited for him to come around and open my door, like Michael always did, but opened it myself when I realized he was headed for the restaurant. I caught up to him.

A young woman in black leggings and a stark white cotton tunic greeted us. She smiled at Toby and blushed. Her skin was nearly as white as her tunic, and the flash of color in her cheeks made her look, at the same time, both vibrant and feverish. But the color faded as quickly as it had appeared.

She took us to a small table against the wall and placed an open menu in front of each chair.

"Christopher will be your server," she said. "Enjoy your meal." She smiled and blushed again, then left.

I looked around. Despite the late hour, half the tables were occupied. Most of the patrons appeared to be in their twenties, but there were two couples with grey hair. Everyone looked slender and fit.

The decor in the Hearts of Palm was early Americana, with lots of plain wood furniture, made-to-look-old gingham tablecloths and seat cushions, and mismatched handmade pottery. The paper napkin holders were formed from grapevines. Someone had painted a mural on the far wall. A barn, several tiny cracker houses in a clearing bordered by pine and cabbage palm, and a winding dirt road, all in a primitive style, gave diners the feeling they were part of the scenery. The effect was lovely.

As if trying to hurry me along, Toby pointed to the list of

entrées in my menu. "The spinach lasagna is delicious," he said. "Or the asparagus quiche."

I glanced down. There were six dinner entrées, ranging from the lasagna and quiche to mushroom feuillete and ratatouille. I was impressed. Most little eateries nestled between laundromats and hair salons are glorified diners or expanded Greek delis.

According to the fine print at the top of the menu, each selection included a choice of tomato or carrot juice, mixed green vegetables, garlic bread, and tropical fruit cup. The carrot juice was the tip-off. No self-respecting diner would serve carrot juice. Tomato juice, maybe, especially with a little vodka in it, if the establishment was fortunate enough to have a liquor license. No, the Hearts of Palm looked suspiciously like a vegetarian restaurant. I searched through the menu but couldn't find a single item that contained meat or fish of any kind. Only eggs and cheese.

I looked up at Toby. He was watching me, apparently waiting for my reaction. I smiled.

"The lasagna sounds wonderful," I said.

Toby closed his menu and nodded at a young man leaning against the cutlery and condiment table. The man nodded back, straightened up, and came over.

He was young, tall, with very short dark hair and light blue eyes. His skin was the same translucent white—like a seashell rubbed smooth by the surf—as the girl who had greeted us. Sunshine is loaded with nasty ultraviolet radiation, I reminded myself. It is also difficult to avoid when you live in Florida, and I wondered how anyone not confined during the day to a coffin managed to keep from getting just a tiny bit tanned.

"Have you folks decided?" Christopher asked. He held a small pad of paper and a pencil, ready to take our orders. He looked tired, but attentive.

"I think we'll both have the lasagna," Toby said.

"Carrot or tomato?" our server asked.

"Tomato for me," said Toby.

"I'll have the carrot juice," I said, like I needed to prove something. I'm not sure what. "And a glass of water."

Christopher took this down, gathered up our menus, and

headed for the kitchen. In less than a minute, he was back with our juice and two glasses of water.

Toby looked grateful for the chance to occupy his hands and immediately picked up his glass of juice. I tasted mine and made a face before I could stop myself.

Toby grinned. "It's made fresh every day, but I have to admit, they should put a little salt in it." He reached for the shaker of sea salt and sprinkled a liberal dose of crystals into his glass.

"Toby," I said. "That's short for Tobias, isn't it?"

He nodded and frowned. "Pretty awful, isn't it? My mother felt beholden to some great-uncle of hers and named me after him. Tobias Lancaster Reynolds. My father left town before I was born, so he obviously didn't care."

"Toby Reynolds has a nice ring to it," I said.

"Thanks." He downed his juice, then wiped his mouth on a paper napkin. "So. Where do you work?"

"I'm a veterinary technician at Paradise Cay Animal Hospital," I said. "My boss, the man you saw me with at the Moon, is Dr. Augustin. He owns the clinic."

I stared at my carrot juice. Salt was not going to help it. Nothing would. I couldn't decide if Toby was worth risking throwing up for.

"I'll bet you see a lot of interesting animals," Toby continued. "Ever get any raccoons?"

"No, we handle dogs and cats, mostly. A few birds."

I switched my gaze to the girl in the black leggings. She was sitting behind the cash register reading a book. I couldn't see the title.

"I'd be afraid of rabies, myself." Toby said this like he wouldn't be afraid at all. Like it would be fun. "But I guess Animal Control gets all the strays." He was attempting to fold his napkin into a paper airplane.

"Most of them. We get a few from time to time. Brought to us by kindhearted animal lovers. In fact, we've got a cat right now who was hit by a car. But don't worry, I've never actually seen a case of rabies at our clinic."

Toby put the napkin down and picked up the pepper shaker—a little wooden cube painted sky-blue. "What's he like? Dr. Augustin, I mean. He doesn't look like a veterinarian." He laughed. "More like a lumberjack."

Christopher came out of the kitchen balancing a large platter on his shoulder. He grabbed a tray stand and set it up next to our table, then lowered the platter onto it. He carefully arranged the dishes in front of us, making certain the plate containing the lasagna was turned so the decorative circle of Bibb lettuce leaves and cherry tomato halves was displayed properly, then took the tray and tray stand and left.

"This looks delicious," I said.

The lasagna was oozing with cheese and exuding wonderfully fragrant steam. I tasted the sauce. It was loaded with garlic and lacked salt, but was very good otherwise.

"You were telling me about Dr. Augustin," Toby said. He popped a cherry tomato half into his mouth.

"There's not much to tell," I said. "He's an excellent veterinarian. His clients love him." I grinned. "Especially the women." I took a bite of lasagna.

"What does he do in his spare time?" asked Toby.

I found it strange that Toby hadn't asked me what *I* did in my spare time. "He likes local politics," I said. I paused, then laughed. "I think he would enjoy being a city commissioner, but I'll deny I ever said that if he asks."

Toby stared at me. "A city commissioner? Whatever for?"

"I don't know, to tell the truth. It's not like he's power hungry. Maybe you should ask your boss, Mr. O'Shea, what the attraction is. He and Dr. Augustin are regulars at the commission meetings. I guess it gives them something to do. Not that Dr. Augustin needs anything more to do."

The girl in the white tunic flipped over the "Closed" sign in the window and turned off the outside lights. I watched Christopher and a busboy from the kitchen collect up the condiment jars from the vacant tables. It was pretty obvious the help wanted to clean up and go home.

"What do *you* do in your spare time?" I asked. "Other than work out, of course."

Toby chewed thoughtfully. "Not much. I've been working on the plans for my health club, mostly." He scraped up the remains of his lasagna with a piece of bread.

"Tell me about it," I prodded. "Where are you hoping to locate? Do you have the land already?"

He shook his head. "Not yet."

The conversation was going nowhere fast. I started to ask him how long he had lived in Florida and where his family was located, but it seemed like more trouble than it was worth. So I finished eating in silence, which seemed fine with Toby. Pretty soon, Christopher came by with our fruit cups and cleared away our dirty dishes, leaving my carrot juice. He came back and placed the bill next to Toby's water glass.

"I'll take that up when you're ready, Toby," he said.

I wondered where "up" was, since the cash register was behind Toby, next to the kitchen. I also wondered if Toby brought all of his dates to the Hearts of Palm. He was obviously on a first-name basis with the employees, particularly our waiter.

Toby took a twenty out of his wallet and handed it and the bill to Christopher. "I guess we'd better shove off," he said, standing up.

I wasn't finished with my dessert, but I put my spoon down, took a last gulp of water, and pushed back my chair.

Once in the car, Toby turned on the radio, and we listened to Tchaikovsky's *Romeo and Juliet*. I didn't dare open my mouth for fear of disturbing Toby's contemplation, although I was dying to ask him about his choice of music. There is something incongruous about listening to classical music in a Pontiac Firebird. And with a bodybuilder, no less.

After we were back on the island, Toby went north a couple of blocks and pulled up to the curb in front of Durante's Gym. He turned off the engine and took the key out of the ignition.

"I hope you don't mind, but I need to pick up my paycheck. I'll only be a minute."

I watched him go inside. He really is incredibly handsome, I thought. But whatever physical attraction I'd had for Toby back at the Moon had stayed at the Moon. I hadn't enjoyed myself that evening and, clearly, neither had he.

It was as if the dinner had been a test. As if Toby took everyone he was interested in to the Hearts of Palm to see if they were worth continued pursuit. I apparently had failed that test. If only I had choked down that carrot juice, I thought. And I chuckled, because I really wasn't all that taken with him, anyway. He had a strange personality. No, I told myself, he has *no* personality.

Ten minutes passed, and I was thinking about browsing through Toby's glove compartment, when he finally came back outside. He had a white envelope in his hand, which he tossed up on the dash.

"Thanks for waiting," he said.

Toby dropped me off at my apartment. I asked him if he'd like to come up for a glass of wine. It was only fair, since he'd bought me dinner, but he said he needed to relieve his friend at the bar.

He didn't even wait for me to climb the stairs before pulling out of the parking lot. Like he'd just attended my bon voyage party and was heeding the last "All ashore who's going ashore" call.

"I'll phone you," he shouted, as he drove off.

But I knew he wouldn't.

CHAPTER 18

•

Saturday, July 18

I had not slept well. A huge clove of garlic and a vampire in black leggings kept waking me up. At six, I called it quits and went jogging.

Frank still hadn't arrived when I got to the clinic at 7:50. An empty food dish sat in the middle of the reception room floor.

"Pearl?" I called. "Here kitty, kitty."

A rustling sound started in the supply closet but stopped when I turned on the light. I looked behind the stacks of canned cat food, in the half-full cases of flea shampoo, and on top of the mountain of dog food bags, but didn't see anything. Not even a mammoth cockroach stirred between the layers of corrugated cardboard.

Suddenly, out of the corner of my eye, I saw a ceiling tile over Cynthia's desk bend down, then up. A second tile bowed, then a third.

"Pearl!" I shouted.

I followed, as the bending and retracting continued in a more or less straight line, until I lost the culprit over the lab.

Now how did she get up there? I asked myself.

I heard Cynthia come in the front door and went back to the reception room. I bent over and picked up the empty food dish.

"Pearl is in the ceiling," I said, pointing over my head. "She's somewhere over the lab right now."

"How in heaven's name did she get there?" asked Cynthia.

"Who knows. If Frank ever bothers to come to work, he can

look for a loose tile. Pearl probably jumped up on a cabinet and found a way to push the tiles apart."

The dogs in the kennel started to bark and rattle their food bowls, so I knew Frank had come in the back door. He tries to sneak into the clinic on the days he is late, but our built-in alarm system makes sneaking essentially impossible.

"I'll go tell him," I said.

Edna Carlyle arrived at 8:30 with Rosco. She didn't have her Tupperware container with her. Of course, she also didn't have an appointment.

"We wondered what happened to you yesterday, Edna," I said, taking Rosco's leash.

Appointment or not, Frank would have to squeeze Rosco in. We couldn't let Edna catch hell from Dr. Friedman because, God forbid, his dog smelled less than daisy-fresh. No matter whose fault it was.

Edna shook her head. "It was Dr. Friedman's doing. He decided at six o'clock yesterday morning to have a dinner party last night for some people from the Cystic Fibrosis Foundation. And with Mrs. Friedman out of town until Monday." She tut-tutted. "Gave me a shopping list long as my arm and told me to polish the silver. I had to start cooking before the sun was up."

"And I'll bet everything was perfect, too," said Cynthia.

"He didn't complain, if that's what you mean. But poor Rosco was banished to the doghouse out by the garage."

The dog turned his head away from the invisible spot he'd been snuffling over and looked up at Edna. He wagged his tail.

Edna snickered. "You're not going to believe who was there. Mrs. Friedman Number Two. Sondra." She said the woman's name like Sondra was royalty or some movie star or other, then put her hand over her heart and rolled her eyes. "Bless my soul, it was like old times."

Two more baths arrived. Edna promised to bring us something special later in the day and left.

I took Rosco and a grey and white stripped tabby back to the kennel. Frank was busy cleaning cages. I told him about Pearl, and he said he would investigate as soon as he could.

He looked like he'd had a hard night, so I decided to look for Pearl myself during lunch.

Saturdays are generally busy but not overly stressful. We don't schedule any routine surgeries, and most of our appointments are vaccinations and other nonemergencies. Things the average working person can put off until the weekend. Best of all, Dr. Augustin is usually in a pretty good mood. As a result, I tend to relax, let my guard down. Of course, this is never a wise move in a combat situation, as I determined later on that day.

Our ten o'clock appointment was a new client by the name of Ken Williston. His dog, a four-month-old yellow Labrador mix, had shown up at his place of business earlier that week with an empty belly and a coat full of fleas. According to Cynthia, no one had reported the dog missing, so Williston decided to keep her. He had named the dog Sunny. They were waiting for us when Dr. Augustin and I emerged from the treatment room.

Sunny was lying on the exam table, panting contentedly. She'd obviously had a bath and was sporting a new, bright red collar and matching leash.

"Greetings," said Dr. Augustin, as we went into the room.

Williston had been sitting in the corner reading a brochure entitled *Your New Puppy*. He got up and extended his hand.

"Hello, Doctor," he said.

He was tall, several inches taller than Dr. Augustin, and nicely constructed. He had curly brown hair and green eyes. He wasn't breathtakingly handsome—his nose was a little too long, his eyes a little too close together—but he was decent-looking. He was wearing tan Dockers and a Banana Republic cotton shirt, freshly ironed, depicting wildlife on the Serengeti. I guessed his age at mid to late thirties.

"I'm Dr. Augustin's technician," I said, "Samantha Holt."

He shook hands with me, too, then gave his dog a pat on the head. "Sunny needs the works, I guess. We have to assume she hasn't had any shots." He directed this at me, as if Dr. Augustin wasn't even present.

Dr. Augustin took careful note. I saw his mouth twitch up at the corners, and he looked over at Williston briefly before beginning his exam. After listening to Sunny's heart and lungs, gazing into the depths of her eyes and ears and down her throat, and poking and prodding practically everywhere else, Dr. Augustin turned around and opened a drawer. He took out a 3cc. syringe.

"Sunny's color is good, but I'd like to check her blood count anyway," he said over his shoulder. "Fleas can make a puppy anemic in very short order."

He turned back around. I was holding Sunny, and Mr. Williston was standing at the end of the table, watching me. It was obvious he hadn't heard a thing Dr. Augustin had said.

Dr. Augustin cleared his throat loudly. "We should also check Sunny's blood for evidence of heartworms," he said. "She needs to be on some type of preventative medication. I recommend the once-a-month tablets. They'll protect her against hookworms, as well."

Williston finally heard Dr. Augustin and reluctantly switched his attention to his dog. "Whatever you think is best is fine with me," he said.

He seemed ill at ease. I wasn't sure why. I didn't think it was because girls made him nervous. I was mildly curious to see how Cynthia's "groom-o-meter" had rated him.

Dr. Augustin drew a blood sample, put it in a collection tube, and handed the tube to me. Williston hadn't fainted or turned green, which added points to his total score. Not that I was keeping track.

As I headed for the lab, I heard Dr. Augustin start his little spiel about obedience training. If I hadn't known better, I would have assumed he was referring to Mr. Williston, rather than Sunny, when he said, "Discipline is a cornerstone in any successful relationship."

Sunny's blood was fine. No anemia, no heartworms. Dr. Augustin gave the dog her first shot and told Mr. Williston to make an appointment for her second one.

"I certainly will," he said. His enthusiasm was admirable.

I walked Williston and his dog out to the reception room. I noticed that Cynthia wasn't panting or grinning or browsing through bride magazines. Strange, I thought.

When I turned to go, Mr. Williston said, "Dr. Augustin suggested obedience training for Sunny. Is there a particular school or class you recommend?"

I took one of the clinic's business cards out of the holder on Cynthia's desk, picked up a pen, and jotted down a number I knew by heart.

"This woman regularly has evening classes for puppies. She also has a class that meets in the City Hall parking lot each Saturday morning." I handed him the card. "Why don't you give her a call?"

Williston pocketed the card. He thanked me profusely for everything and did his best to show me all of his nice white teeth. His smile was a bit like that of a dog caught between a snarl and a sneeze. It didn't make you want to run and hide, but it made you start looking around for a suitable location. I excused myself and went to clean the exam room.

Dr. Augustin spent the rest of the morning rationing his words like they were Godiva chocolates. If there was any free time between clients, he vanished into his office and closed the door.

At noon, he left, which gave the rest of us a chance to search for loose ceiling tiles. Frank found what we'd been looking for in Dr. Augustin's office.

"Here it is, Sam, a hole in the ceiling over Dr. Augustin's bookshelf."

He was standing on a chair he had pulled in from the reception room, trying to reach up into the darkness above the bookcase.

"Get a ladder, Frank, and stick a bowl of food up there. Tuna fish is nice and smelly. Let's see if she's hungry enough to venture over. Then, hopefully, we can grab her. Preferably before Dr. Augustin gets back at two."

While Cynthia was at the grocery store purchasing a can of tuna and a box of cheap, tasty cat treats, I sat up front and read the paper. I had brought yogurt for lunch, but the garlic was still with me (as Cynthia had so kindly pointed out), and I wasn't even remotely hungry.

My appetite was further diminished by a headline in the

local section of the paper that read, FOOD POISONING SUSPECTED FROM UNDERDONE HAMBURGER. I scanned the article and reread the first paragraph just to make sure I hadn't imagined it.

According to the *Times*, Luther Tyndall and his wife, Martha, of 850 Sabal Palm Court, had been admitted to St. Luke's Hospital late Thursday night complaining of severe stomach pains and vomiting. Mr. Tyndall died early Friday of respiratory failure. Mrs. Tyndall remained in critical condition. A late supper of grilled hamburgers, prepared by Mr. Tyndall, was suspected of being the cause of the illness. Mrs. Tyndall admitted liking her hamburgers rare, and doctors at St. Luke's were investigating the possibility that bacterial contamination of the beef used in the hamburgers indirectly resulted in Mr. Tyndall's death. Mr. Tyndall had a heart condition.

I frowned. The guy was a jerk, I said to myself, but no one deserves to die from eating a hamburger. Then I wondered where Martha had done her grocery shopping. Suddenly, carrot juice and veggie burgers didn't seem like such a bad idea.

After Cynthia returned with the tuna, Frank and I positioned ourselves on either side of the hole in Dr. Augustin's ceiling and waited. I knew Pearl was close by, undoubtedly curious about the food and all the commotion, because there was a sag in the ceiling tiles off to our left that hadn't been there earlier. Pretty soon, the sag began to inch forward. Frank lifted his right hand toward the hole, and I grabbed his arm. I put my finger to my lips. Just let her start eating, I thought. Let her nose and taste buds get the better of her other senses.

"What the hell are you two doing?" bellowed Dr. Augustin from the doorway between his office and the lab.

Frank jumped to the floor and pressed himself snugly against the wall. He looked like he'd just been caught in the girls' locker room.

I glanced up as Pearl sped away, her movements across the tiles creating a sort of wave motion reminiscent of that produced by sandworms in the movie *Dune*.

"It's Pearl," I said, climbing down the ladder. I refused to hurry or in any way act like I was guilty of anything. "She's up in the ceiling. We were trying to coax her out with some tuna. Now you've scared her away." I glared at him but concentrated on his nose for fear his eyes might turn me to stone.

He drummed his fingers on the door frame. It reminded me of a rattlesnake shaking its tail.

"Maybe she'll come back later," I said, mentally heeding the warning.

"If you had padlocked Charlie's cage like you were supposed to, we wouldn't be having this conversation," said Dr. Augustin to the wall on my right.

I'd forgotten about Frank, who was doing his best to become part of the room's decor. Frank shrugged his shoulders but didn't say anything.

"Never mind," said the snake. "Just get that fish smell out of my office." He walked over to his desk and sat down. "Pearl will come out of there when she's good and ready." He looked up. "In the meantime, Frank, you still have two dogs and a Persian to bathe. I suggest you hop to it."

Frank hurried up the ladder, retrieved the food dish, and jumped to the floor. He looked at me briefly, winked, then raced down the hall to the security of the kennel.

I continued to stand next to the ladder.

"Don't you have something to do, Samantha?" Dr. Augustin asked.

"It wasn't entirely Frank's fault," I said.

"It never is around here." He began idly flipping through a magazine, not looking at me.

"So, how long are you going to stay mad at us?" I asked, taking a couple of steps back toward the lab.

He kept flipping pages, although I suspected he wasn't seeing what was on them. "I'm not mad, Samantha, just disappointed."

When he didn't elaborate, I figured he was finished, and I turned to go.

"Mostly with you," he said.

"Why? What have *I* done?"

He abandoned the magazine and stared at the photograph he had taped to the wall. "I thought you had more sense than to fall for every Tom, Dick, and Harry who comes along."

I was momentarily confused. I hadn't told anybody about

my date with Toby. Not even Cynthia. Especially not Cynthia. There was no way Dr. Augustin could have known about it.

"And what is that supposed to mean?"

Dr. Augustin turned around and drew his eyebrows together. With all the hair on his face, he looked like a giant schnauzer.

"Ken Williston. I saw you give him your phone number. Samantha, you don't know anything about him. He could be the next Ted Bundy for all you know." He folded his arms over his chest.

I could feel my nails biting into my palms. It was none of his business who I "fell for." The fact that I hadn't given anyone my number, at least not recently, made absolutely no difference.

I stuck my hands in the pockets of my uniform top and focused on the brightly colored balls in Dr. Augustin's bubble gum machine. If I don't look directly at him, I said to myself, he can't intimidate me or force me to give in. I want an apology and I'm not leaving until I get one. My feet are glued to this spot.

Dr. Augustin was back to flipping pages in his magazine. It was a brief but uncomfortable silence.

Suddenly, Pearl stuck her head through the hole in the ceiling and looked around. Then, like thick syrup, she slowly and deliberately eased herself down onto the bookshelf, one paw at a time, not making a sound, not disturbing a single item on the shelf. She crouched there for a few seconds and stared, unblinking, at Dr. Augustin. Then she sprang, ballerina fashion, to the ladder and nonchalantly made her way to the floor. She paused to lick an imaginary speck of dirt from her left foreleg.

"Well, hello, Pearl," Dr. Augustin said quietly.

The cat ignored him, gave her leg a final lick, extended her tail into the air, and marched out of the room.

"I suggest that you put her in a top cage this time," said Dr. Augustin.

He drew in a deep breath. I thought he was going to say something else, but the intercom crackled, and Cynthia announced our two o'clock appointment.

CHAPTER 19

•

Sunday, July 19

At 12:30 sharp, Michael rang my doorbell. Punctuality is one of his obsessions. That and sticking to a schedule. Dr. Augustin could learn a lot from him.

I opened the door. "Hi," I said. I let him in.

He was wearing a white shirt, open at the neck, with a navy blazer, dark grey slacks, and penny loafers. He smiled, and I saw him look at my earrings—the ostensibly contraband ones he'd brought me from St. Thomas.

"Afternoon," he said. "You look wonderful." He kissed me. He'd changed his after-shave. This one was sharp and aromatic.

I had on a black and white linen sundress, a short white linen jacket, and white pumps. The earrings went perfectly.

"Thank you," I said, closing the door. "And thank you for the earrings. I think I forgot to say that when you were at the clinic Thursday."

He leaned over to scratch Miss Priss, who was napping on the sofa. "I've decided to get a cat, Samantha. I need someone to keep me company."

He glanced up at me, but only briefly. It was clear he didn't really mean a cat, but I pretended not to understand.

"I thought you said you spent too much time away on assignment to have a pet." I sat down on the sofa, but got up again when Michael continued to stand.

That time he looked directly at me. His blue eyes were intense, but they would never have the piercing quality of Dr. Augustin's eyes.

"I've been promoted to Assistant Editor of the City and State section. I'll be spending most of my time here at the office." He continued to look at me.

"Congratulations!" I said. "It's about time they took you off the streets."

I laughed, then made a production of picking up my purse, slinging it over my shoulder, and turning off the lamp. I took out my keys, pointedly jingling them. Anything to redirect his attention. God help me, I thought. Don't let Michael propose over the eggs Benedict.

Michael sighed heavily, then appeared to recover. He looked at his watch. "We're going to be late if we don't hurry."

He ushered me out of the apartment and waited while I locked the door.

"Have you ever been to the Sea Breeze, Samantha?" he asked, as we went down the steps to his car.

"No. I'm not even sure where it is."

"Well . . ." he began, opening my door for me, "you are in for a real treat."

Great, I thought. I just love surprises.

Michael and I talked about St. Thomas over the sounds of Kenny G, playing quietly but elegantly on the car's surround-sound CD player. I was starting to relax. Michael, as usual, kept the conversation going with his easy, folksy style. I often wonder if he developed this friendly manner to get information out of people, or if it's really just the way he is.

We headed south along the Gulf. The traffic, both vehicular and pedestrian, was awful. Elderly people creeping along after church, sightseeing, or young families from somewhere in the Midwest headed for the beach, their fish-belly white skin lathered with sunscreen.

Michael turned off the main road onto a long, narrow spit of land bordered on both sides by mangroves. A great blue heron rose up suddenly out of the vegetation to our left. It squawked and honked its protest as it glided effortlessly through the air to another growth of mangroves some distance behind us. The sun was almost directly overhead, and the glare off the water was blinding. I had to squint, despite my dark glasses and the BMW's tinted windows.

At the end of the road was a large octagonal stilt house. It was white, with big smoked glass windows. A boardwalk circled the building, then extended out into the bayou about a hundred feet. A burnished wood sign at the turnoff had read SEA BREEZE.

"I never knew this was here," I said. "I'm always so intent on not running over some tourist, I miss a lot, I guess."

"I'm glad," said Michael. "How am I going to keep impressing you, if you've already been to all the really good restaurants in the area?"

He pulled up to the entrance, and a young man in cuffed white shorts and a shirt covered with colorful tropical birds opened my door. I got out and waited for Michael at the curb. The young man handed Michael a ticket stub and got in the car. He whipped Michael's BMW quickly and efficiently off to an adjacent parking lot. Another young man, also attired in bird plumage, opened the door for us.

The interior walls and ceiling of the Sea Breeze were snow-white, with large dark green palm fronds painted on them. I half-expected bird droppings or coconuts to rain down on us from overhead.

The tables and chairs were white, the tablecloths and napkins dark green. Several live parrots watched the patrons from inside two Plexiglas cages, located on either side of the front door. One of the birds, a scarlet macaw, nibbled at a piece of broccoli. Another was eating a grape. The cages were very clean, and the birds appeared to be healthy.

The buffet was to the right of the main entrance. In addition to an enormous island crammed with baskets of bread and pastries, bowls of salad, boiled shrimp, and fresh fruit, and an awe-inspiring variety of breakfast meats and potato concoctions kept warm over pans of hot water, there were three smaller islands. These were each manned by a smiling chef in a spotless, starched uniform, ready to prepare the perfect omelet, Belgian waffle, or crepe.

Patrons, most of them carrying plates laden with food, moved around the room like a sluggish stream. Here and there a waiter appeared to pour coffee or orange juice. I was surprised by the lack of background music. A tape of sea gulls crying or waves rolling across a beach or a waterfall would have been nice. One of those tranquil nature recordings that have become so popular lately. But all I could hear was quiet conversation and the muted clatter of dishes and cutlery.

Michael checked in at the reception desk. A woman wearing a dark green skirt, white blouse, and dark green bow tie verified our reservation and led us to a table for two next to one of the windows.

I saw Michael look at his watch. "They should be opening the champagne about now," he said.

It wasn't long before a waiter came to our table carrying a pitcher of orange juice and a bottle of champagne. He filled our glasses with some of each, asked if we would like coffee, then, when we declined, directed us to a stack of plates on the main food island.

"Is this a regular restaurant during the week?" I asked Michael, as we started around the buffet.

"Yes," he said. "They specialize in seafood, as you can probably guess, but what they're really known for is their Sunday buffet."

"I can see why," I said, scooping up a serving of eggs Benedict. I started to put the spatula down, then shrugged and lifted a second egg-topped muffin to my plate. What the heck, I said to myself, I'll have a banana for dinner.

We made a complete round of the buffet. Michael paused at the omelet station, while the chef, a woman, prepared a western omelet for him. I watched her technique, trying to see how she folded the omelet without tearing the egg or letting any of the filling escape.

Back at our table, I picked up my champagne glass and held it out. "To you, Michael. Congratulations, again, on your promotion."

Michael touched his glass to mine, and we each took a sip. Then Michael reached into his pocket.

The mind is capable of operating at incredible speeds when

it has to, I am told. They say your entire life flashes before your eyes in an instant just before you die. At *that* instant, I saw a tiny velvet-covered box emerge from Michael's pocket. It had the letters *JT* stamped in gold on the lid. Jameson Tucker, Fine Jewelry, Hartford, Connecticut. And I saw, not Michael, but David, open the box to reveal a two and one-half carat, flawless diamond engagement ring, the most beautiful ring I had ever seen. The same ring that I later hurled across the dressing room at St. Stephen's Episcopal Church, because, at the last minute, David decided marriage was too mundane for the likes of him.

But when Michael withdrew his hand, he was holding an envelope, not a ring box, and I felt my face redden. I quickly fanned myself with my napkin.

"Are you all right, Samantha?" Michael asked. He picked up my water glass and handed it to me.

"I shouldn't drink champagne on an empty stomach," I said. "It goes straight to my head." I smiled. "But I'll be fine. Especially after I have some of this wonderful food." I picked up my knife and fork and sliced into one of the perfectly poached eggs.

Michael seemed relieved and opened the envelope. He placed a Xerox copy of a purchase order on the table. "I did some asking around and found out that Lane Mitchell 'Mick' Peters *did*, in fact, sell some computer equipment to St. Luke's Hospital in the spring. April, I think. Most of it went to Purchasing. The requisitions were signed by Howard Nichols." He ate a forkful of omelet, then pointed the tines at me. "Your Dr. Augustin is a clever man."

Our waiter passed by, pausing long enough to top off our champagne glasses.

"Yes," I said, lowering my voice. "But he's wrong about Mick murdering Howard Nichols. Mick Peters would never do anything like that."

Michael buttered a roll. He was grinning. His expression seemed, to me, to be a little patronizing.

"You have a trusting way about you that's endearing, Samantha," he said. Then a cloud passed over his normally sunny features, and he narrowed his eyes. "I don't mean to sound cynical, but you can never really know about someone, not even someone close to you."

Was he speaking from experience, I asked myself, or was he trying to warn me? And if so, who was he warning me about?

"You're right, Michael, you *do* sound cynical." I cut a slice of cantaloupe into small pieces. "No one who loves animals the way Mick loves his dog could possibly kill anyone. At least not on purpose."

Michael slowly shook his head. "According to the Brightwater Beach Police," he said, "Lane Peters was arrested in 1988 for resisting arrest and striking a police officer. Broke the fellow's nose. Apparently, Mr. Peters was attending a beach party that got out of hand. The police found marijuana, although they couldn't pin possession on Mr. Peters."

"He was young," I said. "Maybe he fell into the wrong crowd." I pointed a finger at Michael. "We've all done things at one time or another that we're not proud of."

Suddenly, I feared he might take the comment as an accusation. I stopped pointing and picked up my champagne glass.

"Yes," said Michael, "that's true. In the case of Mr. Peters, however, it demonstrates the potential for violence. Given the right set of circumstances, anyone with a short fuse and under the influence can lose control. Just remember that."

I didn't like this darker side of Michael's personality. Usually he was cheerful and optimistic, a strong contrast to Dr. Augustin's brooding pessimism. Truth was, however, what I knew about Michael Halsey you could fit inside a matchbook. In particular, the question of where he got all of his money continued to plague me.

"Do you know if the police found any counterfeit money at Arnold Silor's house? And do they think there's a connection between Arnie and Howard Nichols?"

"Apparently not," he said. Then he cleared his throat. "You realize Dr. Augustin is hampering their investigation by refusing to tell them about Arnold Silor's cat?"

"Yes," I said. "But there's absolutely nothing I can do about it. And don't *you* say anything to anyone, either."

Our waiter came by, again, to refill our champagne glasses. I put my hand over mine. "No thanks," I told the man.

Michael also declined a third glass. "How about some coffee, Samantha?" he asked, the twinkle back in his eyes. "And a trip to the dessert table for a slice of chocolate Amaretto cheesecake?"

I groaned.

CHAPTER 20

•

Monday, July 20

On the way to the clinic, I rehearsed what I was going to say to Tracey. I promised myself I wouldn't lose my temper when she came to work late, or make some snide remark about her thoroughly inappropriate clothes. I would act as mature and professional as possible. Dr. Augustin had hired her, after all, and I wanted him to see what a gargantuan mistake he had made. Acting like a brat in front of him wouldn't accomplish anything.

She was waiting at the door when I pulled into the parking lot at 7:40. Her uniform, a pale blue smock and white slacks, looked freshly pressed, and her white Reeboks were obviously new.

"I wasn't sure how long it would take me to get here during rush hour," she said, as I approached, "so I gave myself plenty of time."

She stepped aside while I unlocked the door. I absently wondered where Frank was.

"Most of the people out here are retirees or tourists," I said, aware that my tone was less than congenial. "They don't hit the road until eight at the earliest."

We went into the reception room. I flipped on the lights and the AC.

"You'll have to give me a key," said Tracey, "so I can open up and get the instruments turned on."

I stared at her, without saying anything.

She turned a little pink. "In case you're going to be late for some reason. Or have a doctor's appointment or take a day off." She was backpedaling fast and furiously.

"You'll have to check with Dr. Augustin. He hands out the keys."

I put my lunch in the refrigerator in the lab and my purse in the cabinet over the sink. I held the cabinet door open, so Tracey could put hers there, as well.

"Whoever gets here first makes coffee," I said, taking a packet of coffee and a paper filter out of one of the drawers. "And whoever is last to leave cleans out the pot and dumps the grounds." I showed her the trash can under the sink. "That includes Cynthia and Dr. Augustin. Frank empties the garbage every day and puts a new trash bag in each can."

"Who is Frank?"

"He's our kennel person," I said. "Actually, we call him the clinic's kennel manager, but he doesn't manage anyone except himself." I attempted a laugh. "He cleans the place, feeds the animals, bathes and dips, and lets me or Dr. Augustin know if one of the boarders has diarrhea or isn't eating." I uncovered the microscope.

"I must have missed him last week when I was here."

"You'd remember Frank, believe me," I said. "And I think I should warn you. Frank is a little strange. He's a drummer in a local rock band. And he can be a pest, particularly if he decides he likes you. But don't get me wrong, he does a good job."

"Thanks for the warning," said Tracey.

I showed her where all of the lab supplies were kept and how Dr. Augustin liked test results to be recorded. She was familiar with our instruments, she said, and didn't ask very many questions. When I suggested she watch me do routine analyses for a day or so, she told me she was pretty sure she could handle them on her own. I didn't argue with her, although I probably should have, just to be safe. The thought that she might blame me when Dr. Augustin caught her screwing up *did* occur to me. "I tried to get her to help me, but she just wouldn't," I could hear her saying.

"Cynthia posts the surgery and appointment schedules on the hall bulletin board each day," I told her. "We do surgery every morning except Saturday, so the blood work for those animals needs to be done as soon as the clients bring them in." I looked at my watch. "It's five till eight. We have two spays and a neuter scheduled. The neuter is already here, because he's boarding for a couple of days. I'll help you get a blood sample from him, if you like, or Frank can help you. Assuming he's here."

"I'll ask Frank," Tracey said. "I need to introduce myself, anyway, and I want to check this guy out." She raised her eyebrows a couple of times and grinned.

"Suit yourself," I said. I secretly hoped Frank would switch his attention to Tracey and leave me alone. It would serve her right, I told myself, although I wasn't sure why.

In the treatment room, I showed Tracey where the blood collection supplies were kept. Tracey was standing in the doorway between the treatment room and Isolation. She spotted Randy watching her from his cage in the corner. As usual, he had one paw stuck through the bars, hoping to snag some unsuspecting passerby.

"What an adorable kitten," she said. She went into Isolation and opened his cage. "What's he in for?" She picked him up, and he began to purr. I could hear it all the way across the room.

"He was a stray, left in a basket out back a couple of weeks ago. There were three kittens, originally. Dr. Augustin had to euthanize the other two."

"But he's so little," Tracey said, scratching Randy under the chin. "Who would leave tiny kittens alone outside?"

I started to tell her about Pearl and the fourth kitten, but a little voice in my head stopped me. A little voice that said, "Loose lips sink ships." A decidedly male voice.

"They all had cleft palates," I told her instead. "Randy's isn't too bad. I guess Dr. Augustin feels that Dr. Farmington will be able to repair it."

"Oh, I remember," said Tracey, wrinkling up her nose. "Last Tuesday's wonderful dinner conversation." She put Randy back in his cage. "Well, he sure is cute."

Cynthia had apparently arrived, and she called my name, so I left Tracey to deal with an ill-tempered male chow and Frank

Jennings. It was a toss-up as to which she would find the more unpleasant.

While Dr. Augustin did the neuter, I told him what Michael had discovered about Mick Peters.

"I still can't believe Mick is a murderer," I said quietly.

The door between Isolation and the surgery was closed. Even so I kept my voice down. Dr. Augustin, however, didn't seem to care if Tracey overheard us.

"One thing's for sure," he said, "Mick, if he *is* guilty, has a partner."

"How do you know that?"

"The kittens. That note you found in the basket with them wasn't written by Mick Peters. I've seen plenty of his handwriting in the past year, and he prints everything." He finished closing the incision, dabbed at some residual spots of blood on the dog's abdomen, then pulled off his gloves and dumped them on the instrument tray. He took off his mask.

"I thought you'd decided it was Howard Nichols's handwriting," I said.

"Possibly." He lifted the dog off the table and carried him to a recovery cage. "We need to get a look inside Mick's place."

I put the used instruments in the sink and began picking up the mess on the table. I should have known Dr. Augustin wouldn't be happy until he got to practice his burglary skills.

"Why can't we go there on some pretext involving computers and, while you're talking to Mick, I could look around? You know, pretend to browse through the games and books he has on those shelves next to his desk." I sprayed the table with disinfectant.

Dr. Augustin opened the cabinet over the autoclave and took out a fresh spay pack. "Not his office, Samantha, his apartment."

"And just when are *you* planning on doing this breaking and entering?"

My emphasis on the word *you* never registered.

"I thought we might go there Friday," he said. "Mick is usually at the Moon on Fridays."

Cynthia saved me from having to respond. "Call for you, Samantha," she said over the intercom. "Mick Peters."

I looked at Dr. Augustin, then went into the hall and picked up the extension.

"Hi, Mick, it's Samantha."

The noise on his end of the line was terrible. Lots of voices in the background, some of them quite animated, and what sounded like several radio talk shows blaring. I couldn't decide if he was at the Moon or not. There wasn't any music, and it was too early for the lunch crowd.

"I'm going to be tied up for a few days," he said. "I wasn't expecting this, and I didn't make any arrangements for Jonesy to be looked after." He sounded strung out, and I began to worry he was on drugs or something.

"Can you go over to my apartment building—it's on Sabal Palm Court—and get Jonesy? He's with my landlord right now, but I'd like you to board him there at the hospital. Just until I can get things sorted out here."

He began to argue with someone and covered the telephone receiver. When he came back on, he was obviously in a hurry. "I'd really appreciate it, Samantha. Just for a few days? Please?"

"Sure, Mick, I'll go get him after lunch."

"Thanks loads. Listen, I'll be in touch." He hung up.

I went back across the hall and told Dr. Augustin. His reaction was surprising.

"Good. That solves our problem, doesn't it? You can check out his apartment this afternoon, when you go get his dog."

In honor of Tracey's first day, Dr. Augustin had Cynthia order pizza from Mario's for lunch. We were waiting for the delivery boy to show up when Michael Halsey's BMW pulled into the parking lot.

"Oh, goody," Cynthia squealed. "It's Samantha's gentleman friend."

Tracey looked at me from her chair by the magazine rack and raised her eyebrows.

"Cynthia, *please*!" I said.

The pitch of my voice startled Randy, who was in my lap, playing with a length of gauze.

"Well, he is, isn't he?" she asked.

"Michael Halsey is a reporter," I told Tracey, dangling the gauze. "We've been out to dinner a couple of times, but that's *all.*"

Cynthia pretended not to hear me. She got up, went to the door, and opened it. "Hello, Michael, you're just in time for lunch," she said. "Mario's is delivering pizza, courtesy of Dr. Augustin."

Michael was wearing tan Dockers and a powder-blue, short-sleeved Oxford shirt. There was a little polo player embroidered on the pocket. "What's the occasion?" he asked.

"It's our new laboratory technician's first day on the job," Cynthia said. "Michael, this is Tracey Nevins. Tracey, meet Michael Halsey." She shot me a dark look, then added, "A very dear friend."

Tracey and Michael shook hands. Then Michael came across the room and sat down next to me. He reached over and stroked Randy's head. Randy proceeded to wrap his front paws around Michael's wrist and chomp on his hand.

"I need to talk to you, Samantha," Michael said. "It's about that matter we discussed Sunday. I have some new information." He pulled his hand free. There were tiny red tooth marks on his thumb.

I got up and tossed the gauze into the trash can next to the watercooler. Randy watched it fall and tried to wriggle out of my arms.

"Let's go into an exam room," I said.

"I think Dr. Augustin will want to hear this."

I hesitated a few seconds, then, with Cynthia and Tracey watching us intently, I ushered Michael into Dr. Augustin's office and pulled the door closed. I could only guess at what was being said out in the reception room. The thought of Cynthia filling Tracey in on my love life angered me more than it should have.

Dr. Augustin swiveled around in his chair. He saw Michael and put the book he'd been reading facedown on his desk. He smiled.

"Greetings," he said cheerfully. "Have a seat." He indicated the chair next to his desk.

I frowned. Now what's wrong with this picture? I asked myself.

Evidently, Michael was also momentarily perplexed by Dr. Augustin's pleasant manner, because he eyed him suspiciously. Then he shrugged and went over to the chair. I took Randy to the daybed and sat down.

"Mick Peters was arrested early this morning," Michael said. "First-degree murder."

Dr. Augustin didn't bat an eye.

"The results of the autopsy on Luther Tyndall were released last night," Michael continued. "The police must have put a rush on it. Anyway, he was poisoned. Nicotine. Their analyses showed traces of it in the hamburgers Tyndall and his wife ate. They were both heavy smokers. I guess that's why they didn't notice it. Nicotine has a fishy taste." He grimaced.

"What are the cops saying about the motive?" asked Dr. Augustin.

"Peters and Tyndall fought continuously, according to Mrs. Tyndall and the owner of the triplex. Mostly about Mr. Peters's dog. Mrs. Tyndall said it barked all the time and did its 'business' all over the yard. And Mick complained about smoke from the barbecue grill coming in his bedroom window. It seems that the Tyndalls cooked something on the grill nearly every night." He chuckled. "They must not have read the latest on the dangers of charbroiled meat."

I glanced over at Dr. Augustin, a big fan of Burger King, and smiled faintly.

"And the cops found a plastic bag filled with wet tobacco outside in Mick's garbage can," Michael said. "Apparently, he extracted the nicotine and poured the liquid on the hamburgers when Tyndall wasn't looking. That's the theory, anyway."

"Anything new about Howard Nichols?" asked Dr. Augustin, changing the subject.

"They aren't charging Peters with *his* murder, if that's what you mean. At least not yet, although I couldn't get anyone to tell me what they have so far on the Nichols homicide. The

Secret Service is involved, because of the counterfeit currency, and that complicates things."

Michael looked at his watch. "I'd love to stay for pizza, but I have an appointment at two in Sarasota, and I'm going to be late as it is." He stood up.

Dr. Augustin stuck out his hand. "Thanks, Mike, for the information. Keep us informed."

Michael shook Dr. Augustin's hand. "I'll let you know if I hear anything about Nichols or Arnold Silor. I understand from Samantha that you have evidence the two of them were connected in some manner to this counterfeiting operation."

Ordinarily, the fact that I had spoken to Michael at all, not to mention divulged "sensitive" information to him, would have infuriated Dr. Augustin. This time, however, rather than glower at me, he actually smiled.

"Yes, we do," he said. "Of course, all of this is 'off the record,' you understand. I'd like to collect a little more data before letting the police put all the blame on Mr. Peters."

"I understand." Michael opened the door, stopped, and looked down at me. "Think about what I said, Samantha. About wanting a . . . cat." His eyes darted over to Dr. Augustin, then back to me. He started to say something else but closed his mouth.

"Bye, Michael," I said quickly. "I'll talk to you later."

He smiled and left, leaving the door open. I heard him tell Cynthia and Tracey good-bye.

"Michael Halsey is all right," said Dr. Augustin. "For a reporter."

He grinned, then picked up his book.

When I got back from Mick's apartment at six, Cynthia and Tracey were already gone. I put Jonesy in a bottom cage in the kennel, got him a bowl of water and a dish of food, and scribbled, "Peters, Jonesy. Limited exercise" on a cage card.

"You weren't gone very long," I heard Dr. Augustin say from the surgery.

I went across the hall. He was working on a golden retriever who'd been brought to the clinic earlier that afternoon with an ear hematoma.

"I couldn't get into Mick's apartment," I said from the doorway. "The cops have strung yellow tape all over the place and sealed both Mick's and Luther Tyndall's apartments. I'm surprised they're letting the owner, Mr. Kline, stay in his unit." I almost added, "Of course yellow tape and big black letters warning everyone to keep out wouldn't have stopped you," but reconsidered when blood suddenly squirted onto Dr. Augustin's exam jacket.

Dr. Augustin threw his scalpel angrily onto the table and reached for a handful of gauze sponges. After a few seconds, he looked up. "What did Mick's landlord have to say?"

"Not a whole lot. He normally works weekdays and doesn't see much of Mick or Cindy. But he said Mick is neat and pays his rent on time. I got the impression that Luther Tyndall wasn't either of those things." I went over to the dog and checked its color and pulse. "I asked him if he had ever seen any of Mick's friends. He said no, that he didn't think Mick had many friends. He also said Mick wasn't home much in the evenings because of his job at the junior college. I guess Mick takes Cindy to a sitter somewhere. Kline did remember seeing a woman with Mick a couple of times. He said he was impressed, because he'd always pictured Mick as kind of a nerd, and the woman was very attractive."

Dr. Augustin clipped off a piece of suture material. "I wonder if they've sealed Mick's office," he said. Then, without looking up, he added, "How about you and me driving by there this evening?" He didn't wait for me to answer. "I'll finish here, then swing by your place around eight. Wear something dark."

I snapped to attention and saluted, but it was a wasted effort, because Dr. Augustin was concentrating on the dog's ear. I didn't have the nerve to say, "Aye, aye, Captain."

CHAPTER 21

•

Dr. Augustin picked me up at 8:10. He was like a little kid on Christmas day after being told, yes, although it was only four in the morning, he could open his presents. I sat next to him, staring sullenly out of the window. I already knew what *I* was getting, and it wasn't what I had asked Santa for.

"We'll go in from the alley," Dr. Augustin told me. "I watched Mick deactivate the alarm system from there once, and I think I remember how he did it."

"You *think*?"

"If we trigger the alarm, we'll leave," he said. Like a siren blaring suddenly in a quiet, mostly residential neighborhood wasn't going to give us instant celebrity status.

"What if the cops have sealed off the place?"

"They use yellow plastic ribbon, Samantha, not some high-tech force-field."

Right, I thought. How stupid of me.

When we reached the street Mick's shop was on, Dr. Augustin slowed to 15 mph. He drove past the little strip of stores that included M-P Computer Services and turned right at the first intersection.

"No suspicious-looking cars out front," he said gleefully. "No sign of anyone working late in the adjacent businesses."

He turned right again, down an alley behind the strip and drove slowly past each door, pausing at the one marked with a large 2.

"That's it," he said.

He picked up speed and drove to the end of the block, turned left onto Myrtle, then parked at the curb behind a red pickup truck.

"We'll walk back," he said, getting out. "We don't need someone to remember seeing a Jeep Cherokee parked behind Mick's shop, do we?"

It was a rhetorical question, so I didn't say, No, and we don't need someone to remember seeing Blue Beard and a blonde in a black leotard and black stirrup pants breaking into Mick's shop, either.

Dr. Augustin went around to the back of his Jeep and opened the rear door. He took out an enormous duffel bag that clanked slightly when he hefted it. Then he closed the door and started down the alley.

When we got to Mick's shop, Dr. Augustin hesitated, like his conscience had suddenly surfaced. But he shrugged, opened up his duffel bag, and took out a large pair of bolt cutters. I'd expected him to pick the lock with his trusty surgical instruments, but the door was secured with one of those locks you see people attempt to open on TV by shooting bullets at them. The direct approach was obviously in order here.

With very little effort, Dr. Augustin snapped the fat metal hook in two. The sound was like a huge piece of glacial ice breaking. It echoed down the alley, and I instantly prepared myself for flight. Dr. Augustin, on the other hand, merely glanced around before removing the lock from the latch ring. He put the lock and the bolt cutters in his duffel bag and extracted two pairs of surgical gloves, one of which he handed to me. I put the gloves on.

"Stay here," he whispered. "I've got about ten seconds after I open the door to locate the security panel and turn off the alarm. I'll come back and get you." He took a flashlight out of his bag, switched it on, and pushed open the door.

If the noise the bolt cutters had made wasn't enough to alert the people living on the other side of the alley, the screech of the door opening on tight, poorly lubricated hinges should have been. I was looking for a hole to jump in, when I heard a dog growl. I turned around very slowly and found myself staring down at a mongrel who was part chow, part German shepherd. It was jet black and mostly mouth. Its lips were curled back, exposing a full set of teeth, and it had a ridge of hair standing straight up along its back.

With absolutely no thought whatever as to how Dr. Augustin might react, I backed into Mick's shop, dragging the duffel bag after me. Then I pushed the squealing door shut as quickly as I could. The dog had obviously lunged at me, because I heard a dull thud against the exterior of the door.

Suddenly, a bright light momentarily blinded me, and I froze. The light went out, and I felt a hand on my shoulder.

"I thought I told you to wait," said Dr. Augustin's voice.

I rubbed my eyes, realized I had latex gloves on, and stopped. "A very large dog just tried to eat me out there," I said. Then I remembered the alarm. "Did you find the security panel?"

"The alarm wasn't on," he said. "Which is odd. Mick is a lot of things, but sloppy isn't one of them."

"Maybe the police didn't reset it, after they finished searching the place."

"It doesn't look like the police have been here. Everything is too neat." He sounded concerned, but didn't say why.

I watched the beam of his flashlight bounce across the room. Then I heard a click, and the overhead fluorescent fixture fluttered a couple of times before finally coming to life.

"Won't people see the light from the street?" I asked, feeling suddenly very naked.

"This is a storage area. The door to the front room is closed. Since Mick keeps his filing cabinet in here, I thought we'd start with it. If necessary, we can search the rest of the place later in the dark."

He put the flashlight back in his duffel bag and went over to a grey, four-drawer filing cabinet. He opened the top drawer.

"What are you hoping to find here?" I asked.

He flipped through the files. "I'm not sure. Bank statements, receipts indicating a large expenditure of some kind. Anything to show he'd recently come into a lot of cash. Especially in the form of a personal check from someone like Howard Nichols. Also, any connection to Arnold Silor. I suppose it would be asking too much to find a few counterfeit twenties." He pulled out a file folder and handed it to me. "Here, see what this has to offer."

The folder was marked "Tidewater Rental Agreement." I sat down on an empty wooden crate and studied the file's contents.

The first few pages spelled out Mick's lease for his portion of the building known as Parker Plaza. There didn't seem to be anything out of the ordinary in it. I *was* surprised to see how much Mick paid each month for nine hundred square feet. The rent, as well as the "Plaza" part of the development's name, seemed a little highfalutin to me.

I turned to the last page. It was an addendum stating that, as of September the first, Mick would be leasing Unit 3, in addition to Unit 2. A small drawing indicated the wall between units 2 and 3 was to be removed.

"I think I've found something," I said.

Dr. Augustin was leaning against the file cabinet, going through the file folders in the second drawer. He looked up.

"Mick was planning an expansion, starting September one. He was going to take over the unit next to this one. Sounds like a large expenditure to me." I got up and carried the file over to Dr. Augustin.

He scanned the page in question. "Well, that explains a great deal," he said. "Take a look at this." He picked up a file lying on top of the cabinet and handed it to me. It was labeled "Union Bank."

I opened the file and began thumbing through a stack of monthly statements and routine bank correspondence.

"The last two pages," said Dr. Augustin.

I pulled them out. The first was a copy of an application for a small business loan. The second page had been balled up, then smoothed out. It was a letter from the bank dated April 2 telling Mick his loan application had been denied. No explanation was given.

"I guess we know why Mick turned to counterfeiting, don't we?" said Dr. Augustin.

"This doesn't prove anything," I said. "And what about Luther Tyndall? Why would Mick kill him? He didn't have anything to do with the counterfeiting, surely."

Dr. Augustin took the folder from me and put it and the one labeled "Tidewater Rental Agreement" back in the file cabinet. He closed the drawer. "I don't think he killed Tyndall."

"What about the tobacco they found in Mick's garbage?"

Dr. Augustin picked up his flashlight. "Why didn't he just flush the tobacco down the toilet? Why leave it out for the cops to find? No, Mick is entirely too smart for that. Besides, the garbage can is outside. Anyone could have planted that tobacco there." He pointed at the door to the display and sales area. "Let's see if there's anything on Mick's desk out front."

He got his flashlight, turned it on, and flipped off the overhead light. He was about to open the connecting door, when a loud noise, like the sound a brick makes when it is thrown through a plate glass window, stopped him. That sound was followed by a lot of hooting and hollering and a couple of catcalls, then tires squealing on pavement.

We both stood motionless for several seconds. Then Dr. Augustin picked up his duffel bag and pushed me toward the door to the alley.

"Idle teenagers in search of entertainment, no doubt," said Dr. Augustin. "Let's get out of here, before the cops show up."

I was more than happy to oblige, but I let Dr. Augustin go first, in case the Tasmanian devil was waiting. Fortunately, the dog had given up and wandered off. With a few broken teeth from his encounter with the door, I hoped, most uncharitably.

Once in the alley, Dr. Augustin reached into his duffel bag and took out a new padlock, which he installed in place of the one he'd cut off. Then we headed for the Jeep.

"If Mick didn't kill Luther Tyndall, who do you suppose did?" I asked Dr. Augustin, after we were on the way back to my apartment.

"Maybe Tyndall's wife killed him. Maybe she intentionally poisoned herself just a little to divert suspicion. Maybe the landlord did it. And Mick was an easy and convenient frame. They fought all the time. Lots of people knew that."

"So now Mick is in jail for a murder he didn't commit, although you think he deserves to be in jail for murders he *did* commit. Is that it?"

Dr. Augustin didn't say anything. I wanted him to come out

and tell me in no uncertain terms that Mick Peters was a cold-blooded killer. But I knew from his silence he wasn't totally convinced himself.

Suddenly, he smacked the steering wheel. "We've *got* to find that fourth kitten," he said.

"What if it died?" I asked. "What if it was dead from the very beginning? I mean, those two you put down were so frail. Maybe the fourth kitten was already dead when 'whoever' dropped off the remaining kittens at the clinic."

He didn't say anything. He pulled up to my apartment building and stopped. "See you tomorrow," he said. His voice was flat.

"Bright and early," I said and got out.

I watched him drive away. He knows that kitten is dead, I told myself. And anyway, he was dreaming if he thought we could find it, even if it *was* still alive.

I started up the stairs. I felt sorry for Mick, but prayed Dr. Augustin would give the thing a rest. Let the cops do their job.

"Now look who's dreaming," I said aloud.

CHAPTER 22

•

Tuesday, July 21

"Who's the woman with Dr. Augustin?" Tracey asked. "The one in the photo on his wall?"

We were in the lab. I was filling a prescription, and Tracey was gazing through the microscope at a hookworm egg.

I hated to admit it, but she was doing a pretty good job, at least for the moment. She was thorough and neat and, more importantly, efficient. Surgery workups and routine lab tests were completed on schedule, sometimes ahead of schedule. One thing Dr. Augustin does not like to do is wait. I'll bet he was a gem when he was a child.

No, I couldn't complain about the job Tracey was doing. In fact, she was so good, I wondered why she left Dr. Farmington. Of course, I wasn't too impressed with her social skills. She was nosy, for one thing.

"I can't remember her name," I said. I did not intend to let on that Dr. Augustin had failed to mention the woman. Even Cynthia didn't know who she was. "He went camping with her last month," I continued.

"Is she his girlfriend, do you think?"

Quite obviously, Tracey wanted to know if Dr. Augustin was available.

"Could be."

"That's too bad," she said, dropping the slide she'd been studying into a tub on the counter by the sink. "What about Frank? Does he have a steady girlfriend?"

I smiled broadly. "No," I said, trying to control myself. "Frank doesn't have a girlfriend right now."

Vivian Porter stopped by at 1:30. Cynthia called me on the intercom, and I came up to the reception room, chewing the last of an apple. I'd been eating my lunch in one of the exam rooms.

Vivian still had her St. Luke's ID badge clipped to the ruffle of her pinafore.

"Samantha," she said, "Betty Bayonne asked me to drop by and check on the photo she requested. The one for your permanent ID badge." She crossed her arms. "And she said you never went by to see Irma Shoaf in Physical Therapy."

I could tell she was mentally tut-tutting. "I was feeling a little under the weather that day," I said. Then, as an afterthought, I added, "Female problems, you know." I certainly wasn't going to tell her I'd twisted my ankle diving off her front porch.

"I see. Well, you need to check in with Mrs. Shoaf, so she can put you on the schedule." She narrowed her eyes, and a furrow appeared between her eyebrows. "To be quite honest, I didn't know you were intending to change careers. Is Dr. Augustin aware of your plans?"

I thought I detected a note of suspicion in her voice. Then, her eyes relaxed, and she thrust her chin in the air.

"Of course, it isn't any of my business," she said, like it was every bit her business.

"Career change?" I asked. Then I remembered my conversation with Mrs. Bayonne. "Oh, yes. It isn't so much a career change as something to do in my spare time." I almost choked over the word *spare*. "An *avocation*, if you will." I smiled sweetly. "I've been so impressed, Ms. Porter, by all the volunteer work you do there at the hospital, I thought I'd give it a try."

It was obvious Cynthia was having difficulty keeping a straight face. I tried not to look at her.

Vivian beamed and puffed out her chest. "I'd be happy to show you around, Miss Holt. Introduce you to some of the other volunteers. When were you planning to start?"

She'd caught me totally unprepared. A good liar can improvise at will, but I was new at this.

"Samantha! We need you in surgery!" It was Dr. Augustin.

"I tell you what," I said. "Let me give you a call after I've spoken with . . . the woman in Physical Therapy." I hurried across the room to the hallway, then turned around. "How does that sound?"

Vivian looked a touch put out, but she nodded. "I guess so," she said.

I gave Cynthia a parting nod and left, intensely grateful for whatever emergency had saved me.

Dr. Augustin was leaning against the wall outside the kennel, drinking a Coke and chewing his gum. He grinned. "You sounded like you needed some assistance out there."

"Thanks," I said. "I'd forgotten all about that stupid application form I filled out. I guess I should call Irma What's-her-name and tell her I've changed my mind about volunteering."

"Don't be too hasty," he said. "We might need to see Ralph Silor again."

"What for? He doesn't know anything." I simply refused to go snooping around the sixth floor intensive care unit a second time.

"Maybe you didn't ask Ralph the right questions," he said. He went into Isolation and stuck his fingers through the bars on Randy's cage. "If only you could talk, little one," he said to the kitten.

Randy pounced on Dr. Augustin's finger and began to chew.

"Well, excuse me," I said. "Next time you can give me a script." Better yet, *you* go, I thought. You're a better liar than I am any day.

Dr. Augustin ignored the jab. "The key to all of this is at that hospital. Someone who worked with Howard Nichols or who deals with the Purchasing Department on a regular basis and has access to Ralph Silor."

I was having trouble following his logic, which was nothing new. Like, what was Ralph's involvement in all of this? Okay, so Ralph's father was involved or, at least, his cat was. But I was positive Ralph, himself, knew nothing about the counterfeit money. I was also positive if I asked Dr. Augustin to explain, he would roll his eyes and say, "Isn't it obvious?" Which, of course, it wasn't, or I wouldn't have asked. It was easier to just nod and act impressed that he could figure out something Brightwater Beach's entire police force had failed to figure out.

"Someone who wouldn't look suspicious wandering around the hospital," he continued.

Suddenly, an image of Vivian Porter sailing down the hall past Ralph's door with a stack of files in her arms flashed in my head, but I shook it aside. Vivian Porter was a busybody, sure, but what reason would she have to kill someone?

"A volunteer, perhaps?" I asked anyway.

"Perhaps," said Dr. Augustin. He took a file out of the holder on the wall. "By the way, how is Tracey working out?"

If Dr. Augustin's logic sometimes overwhelms me, his ability to change directions, mid-stride, simply blows me away.

At six o'clock, just as I was about to leave for the day, a white sedan pulled up and stopped. The car was driven by a woman, and she had a teenaged boy with her.

The woman got out and went around to the passenger side. She opened the door, and the boy struggled to his feet, cradling a nearly limp, bloody mixed-breed dog. I didn't recognize either the woman or the boy, but the dog looked familiar.

"We've got an emergency out front," I shouted through the door to Dr. Augustin's office. "Looks like a dog has been hit or chewed up."

I unlocked the door and let them in.

"We've been pet-sitting for a neighbor," said the woman. She seemed on the verge of hysteria. "The Sullivans. Benji, here, got out when my son went over to feed him. He was hit by a car right in front of our house."

The woman was somewhere around forty-five, with honey-colored hair and a figure a little past its prime. She wore jeans and a too-large Duke basketball T-shirt tucked into the jeans. The boy, about fifteen, had on denim cutoffs and a previously white singlet, now heavily stained with blood. His face was streaked with tears and had spots of blood on it. His arms were filthy. I noticed the woman had somehow managed to stay clean. There was a small orange smear just below the "D" in Duke, but it looked more like tomato sauce than blood.

Before I could say anything of a consoling nature, Dr. Augustin came out of his office, buttoning his exam jacket. He peered into one of the dog's eyes and checked its gums. Then he slid his arms under the dog and took it from the boy.

"Why don't you have a seat," he told the woman.

The woman started to say something, but Dr. Augustin was already on his way to the surgery. I put my hand on the boy's shoulder.

"If you'd rather wait at home, you can," I said. "Give us a call in a couple of hours." I smiled. "Benji is in good hands."

Then I raced down the hall, realizing too late that I hadn't gotten the woman's name or phone number. I prayed she was, indeed, a neighbor of the Sullivans and not the driver of the car that hit Benji. To say I would be in deep doodoo if I let them get away without paying some kind of deposit was putting it mildly.

Benji was beginning to stir at 8:15 when the phone rang. I left Dr. Augustin to finish bandaging the dog's leg and hurried out to the hall extension. After four rings, the answering machine cuts in, and I didn't want Mrs. Sullivan's neighbor to hear Cynthia's voice telling her to call back at eight in the morning.

"Hello," I said.

"Where's Dr. Augustin?" the voice on the other end demanded.

"I'm sorry," I said, "but who is this?" I'd heard the voice before, but I wanted to make certain it was who I thought it was.

"Sarah Milton. Put Dr. Augustin on."

"Dr. Augustin is in surgery, Ms. Milton. We had an emergency. Perhaps I can help you."

"Oh, all right," she said, disgust evident in her voice. Her attitude toward me, for whatever reason, clearly had not changed one iota. "There's someone sneaking around Arnie's house."

"What do you mean *sneaking*?"

"Just what I said. Someone is over there. I can see a light on in Arnie's bedroom."

"Have you called the police?" Before the question was out, I knew the answer.

"Why would I do that?" she snapped. "Police aren't going to do anything. They haven't found Arnie's killer, have they?"

I had to agree with her there. "Can you hold the phone a minute, Ms. Milton, while I speak to Dr. Augustin?"

"Go ahead." One thing was for sure, Sarah Milton did not waste any energy when speaking.

I pushed the hold button and went into the surgery. "It's Sarah Milton," I told Dr. Augustin. "She says someone is in Arnie's house. And, no, she hasn't called the police."

Dr. Augustin arranged Benji on a rack in one of the recovery cages and closed the door. When he turned around, I saw he was smiling. "Tell her we'll be there as soon as we can," he said.

I did as he asked and had just hung up the phone when it began ringing again. "Hello?" I said.

"I'm calling about Benji," the voice said. It sounded like the teenager.

"Benji is doing very well," I told the boy. "His leg was broken, but Dr. Augustin has repaired it. I know you were probably scared by all of the blood, but the wounds looked worse than they really were. Dr. Augustin sewed up Benji's shoulder and says he will be as good as new in no time. Why don't you come by tomorrow morning after ten and see for yourself."

The boy said he and his mother would stop by during lunch.

"Great. Let me have your name and phone number, and I'll have our receptionist pencil you in our appointment book."

He told me his name and number, and I wrote them down on the notepad attached to the wall by the phone. Then he thanked me and hung up. From the tone of his voice, I hadn't done much to mitigate the guilt he felt.

"Poor kid," I said aloud.

"In more ways than one," Dr. Augustin said from the doorway. He was drying his hands on a paper towel. "I have a feeling that kid is going to be responsible for my bill. I hope his summer job is paying him more than minimum wage."

He went back into the surgery, and I heard the trash can lid open and close. Then he appeared again in the doorway.

"Benji is awake," he said. "Let's go check out Sarah's prowler."

CHAPTER 23

•

Dr. Augustin cruised slowly by Arnie's house, pausing briefly so we could check the windows and yard. We didn't see any light inside or any other evidence of a prowler.

"Whoever was here is probably long gone by now," said Dr. Augustin.

He stopped the Jeep in front of Sarah's house and turned off the ignition.

Sarah's hearing was obviously better than that of most seventy-five-year-olds, because we hadn't even gotten out of the car before the porch light came on. Then Sarah opened her front door and stepped outside, closing the door behind her.

"About time," she said, as we approached. She was wearing a grey, short-sleeved sweatshirt and clam diggers. Black, rather than her usual red ones.

"We got here just as soon as we could, Sarah," Dr. Augustin told her, with uncharacteristic patience. "Did you see anyone?"

"Course not," she said tersely. "They probably came and went through the back door. You should go over and see if the lock's been busted."

"Thanks," Dr. Augustin said. "We'll do that." He turned around and started toward the street.

"While you're here, you might as well look at Angel," Sarah said. "And I've got a boy cat not eating."

Dr. Augustin paused. "All right, Sarah," he said over his

shoulder. "As soon as we check Arnie's house." He continued walking.

Sarah looked at me, her face devoid of expression. Then she went back inside her house. I caught up with Dr. Augustin at his Jeep. I waited while he opened the passenger door and took a flashlight out of the glove box.

"You think Sarah made up that prowler thing to get you here, so you could doctor her cats?"

He chuckled. "Could be. I fear I may have created a monster." He reached under the seat and pulled out a tire iron. "I doubt I'll need this," he said. "But it might come in handy."

We crossed the street and shuffled through the sand to the rear of the house. As we rounded the corner, Dr. Augustin stopped. He suddenly grabbed my arm and pulled me over to the north wall of the house.

"Stay here," he whispered. "And don't move." He put his finger to his lips, then pointed toward the alley.

I let my eyes follow his finger. Arnie's Dodge was parked in the driveway where it had been on our first visit. But now, another vehicle, a small foreign car, was situated right behind it. And I could hear the engine running. It was too dark to see who was inside the car, but the light in the alley clearly showed a figure in the driver's seat.

Dr. Augustin crouched low and made his way to the bungalow next to Arnie's. There didn't appear to be anyone home. When he reached the back door, he straightened up and walked casually down to the alley, like he was going to dump something in the big black garbage container located at the end of the driveway. Then he stopped.

Common sense told me to run back across the street to Sarah's house and call the police. Dr. Augustin's tire iron seemed piss-poor protection against an automatic weapon. Or any weapon for that matter.

I was about to leave when I saw Dr. Augustin start toward the car. This is it, I told myself. He's finally going to get himself killed. But I just stood there and watched him, unable to move.

When Dr. Augustin reached the rear of the vehicle, he paused. He switched on his flashlight and aimed it at the ground. Then he went quickly around to the driver's side and pointed the flashlight in at the figure behind the wheel.

"Samantha! Come here!"

I overcame my paralysis and ran down the driveway. Dr. Augustin was attempting to open the driver's side door. When he couldn't, he lifted the tire iron.

"Stand back," he said.

I did as he asked, and he struck the back window with the tire iron. The window shattered, but remained intact, so Dr. Augustin punched out a hole just large enough for his hand. He reached through to the front door lock and pulled it up. Then he opened the front door.

The figure behind the wheel, a man, fell partway out of the car. Dr. Augustin grabbed the man under the arms and pulled him all the way out, then dragged him several feet, before letting him down on the sand. The odor of exhaust fumes rolled out of the car in a nauseating wave.

I looked at the man's face and gasped. "Oh my God, it's Bill O'Shea!"

"He's unconscious," Dr. Augustin said quickly. "Go to Sarah's and call the paramedics." He straightened Bill out and felt for a pulse.

I didn't hang around to admire Dr. Augustin's technique. I ran around Arnie's house to the street, then up to Sarah's porch. I knocked loudly on her front door. "Sarah!" I called.

She opened the door a crack. "What do you want?"

"Please dial 911, Sarah. There's a man in Arnie's driveway. He's unconscious, and Dr. Augustin said for you to call the paramedics."

I was out of breath and scared, mostly for Bill, and in no mood to fight. But Sarah surprised me.

"I'll do it," she said. And then she shut the door.

I stood on her porch for several seconds, trying to think. Was Bill the intruder in Arnie's house? After all, he probably had a key. But what was he doing there?

My eyes drifted up to the little brass door knocker, tarnished and crooked and threatening to fall off its hook on the door. It had the words, "All are welcome here," engraved around its base plate. I hadn't noticed the message before and was suddenly afraid I'd been transported to someone else's porch. Then I heard Sarah yell at one of her cats.

What if she doesn't call the paramedics? I asked myself. Should I barge inside and check? But I was too much of a coward to face Sarah Milton's wrath alone, so I headed back across the street to see if there was anything I could do to help Dr. Augustin. We can always drive Bill to the fire station, I thought. It's only a mile or so down the road.

By the time I reached Arnie's driveway, I could hear sirens wailing faintly, off in the distance. The sound grew louder, and then the little white cottages on either side of the alley were awash with red, pulsing and wavering like the glow from a nearby fire, as a Fire Rescue truck barreled down the alley. The truck came to a stop behind Bill's car, and two men jumped out. One of them went around to the far side of the vehicle, while his partner went over to Dr. Augustin.

Bill O'Shea apparently was either stable or dead, because Dr. Augustin was sitting quietly next to him on the sand. I noticed that Bill's car wasn't running anymore.

"How is he?" I asked, squatting down beside Dr. Augustin.

"He's still unconscious," Dr. Augustin said. "But he's breathing." He shook his head. "It's hard to say how long he was in there."

The paramedics politely but firmly asked us to step aside, so Dr. Augustin and I went over to the steps up to Arnie's back porch and watched them administer oxygen and IV fluids to Bill. One of the men began talking into a two-way radio, but I couldn't hear what he was saying. Then the dispatcher said something back, but the words sounded garbled, and I couldn't understand them.

After a few minutes, an EMS van and a police car, both with their full complement of lights flashing, joined the Fire Rescue truck. There were so many colors bouncing off the houses and pavement, it lit up the sky like an aurora borealis. Needless to say, all of this attracted the attention of several of the neighbors, who began emerging from their houses up and down the alley. They reminded me of bears coming out of hibernation. Some of them were even dressed in their bedclothes, which made me check my watch. But it was only 9:30.

Pretty soon, the EMS technicians and the Fire Rescue guys loaded Bill onto a gurney and slid him into the back of the van. One of the paramedics, holding the IV bag aloft, and one of the EMS technicians climbed in with Bill. The other two men got into their respective vehicles and took off down the alley. At the intersection with the street, the sirens began their wailing. I listened as the sound grew dimmer, and then, except for an occasional hiccup from the police radio, the street was quiet again. One by one, the alley's residents began to disappear.

"What do you think happened to Bill?" I asked Dr. Augustin. "I smelled exhaust fumes. And what was he doing in Arnie's driveway, anyhow?"

Dr. Augustin seemed unusually subdued. At first, he just stood there, watching the cops. They were wandering around Bill's car, peering inside.

"It would seem that Bill O'Shea tried to commit suicide," he said. "A hose, connected to the car's tail pipe, ran under the floor and, presumably, up through a hole into the car."

"Suicide?" I drew in a quick breath, then let it out, noisily. "I knew he was upset about Arnie's death. But why would he abandon Ralph now, just when Ralph needs him the most?"

Dr. Augustin looked at me and half-smiled. "Good question," he said.

I thought about this for a minute. "You think someone tried to kill him, don't you?"

He didn't answer. One of the cops was approaching us. Dr. Augustin reached over and gave my arm a squeeze, then stepped forward.

"Evening," said the cop.

He was tall and wiry, top to bottom, with almost no discernible figure past his neck. It made the pistol on his hip seem larger and bulkier than it really was. I had trouble keeping my eyes off of it.

"Dr. Augustin, isn't it?" he asked. He didn't wait for an answer. "According to Officer Mitchell"—he inclined his head in the direction of his partner, who was still peering into Bill's car like there was a topless dancer sitting inside—"you said you were called here by a woman who lives across the street. Is that correct?"

"Yes," said Dr. Augustin. "Sarah Milton, one of my clients. She was concerned when she saw a light on in Arnold Silor's house. Mr. Silor, as you probably already know, was found murdered earlier this month."

I watched the officer take all of this down in a little spiral-bound notebook.

"And you found the victim unconscious and locked in his car?"

"Yes. I broke the rear window on the driver's side and unlocked the front door. Then I pulled Mr. O'Shea out of his car."

The officer looked up. "You know the victim?"

Dr. Augustin nodded. "He owns the Paper Moon, a bar down the street. I've been in there a couple of times."

"Did you happen to see anyone else on the premises, or any sign that someone had been in the house?"

"No."

The officer looked over at me.

"This is Samantha Holt," Dr. Augustin said. "She works for me and took the call from Sarah Milton."

Apparently satisfied, the officer closed his notebook and put it and the pen in his breast pocket. "Officer Mitchell has your telephone number, if we need to get in touch with you," he said. He looked across the street. "Could you point out the Milton home, please?"

Dr. Augustin smiled. "The one directly across from Mr. Silor's house. Three seven five, if I'm not mistaken."

"Thank you," the officer said.

He went back to his partner, who was talking on the radio. A car came up the alley and stopped at the end of Arnie's driveway. Two men in suits got out and went over to the cop who had spoken to Dr. Augustin.

"Let's get out of here," said Dr. Augustin. "Before this turns into a circus, with us the star attraction." He picked up his flashlight and the tire iron.

"What about Sarah?" I asked, as we headed for his Jeep.

"You said you'd look at Angel and her boy cat who isn't eating."

Dr. Augustin kept walking. "Maybe later, after the cops leave." Then he chuckled. "Although it sure would be fun to hear the conversation between Sarah and that patrolman, wouldn't it?"

"What if she tells them about Arnie? Or about Pearl and the kittens?"

This time Dr. Augustin laughed. "Are you kidding? They'll be lucky if she gives them her real name. The whole interview will probably be conducted on her porch."

He opened the passenger door, stowed the flashlight and tire iron, then waited while I got in. "I guarantee she won't let them inside with all those cats." He went around to the driver's side and slid behind the wheel. "Right now, I want to drop by the hospital and see how O'Shea is doing."

CHAPTER 24

•

There hadn't been any recent natural disasters or seventeen-car pileups on the interstate. It wasn't even a weekend. You wouldn't have known that, however, from all the activity at St. Luke's. There were four ambulances lined up in front of the Trauma Center, and I could hear a soft *whump, whump* from the helicopter located on the roof.

Dr. Augustin parked his Jeep in Hillsborough 20, which, to my amazement, was relatively close to the main Emergency entrance. We hurried across the asphalt and up the sidewalk to a set of automatic doors that slid open as we approached. It was like being on the Starship *Enterprise*. Inside, though, the scene was more like something out of *Earthquake*.

There were over two dozen people scattered around the waiting room, at least six of which appeared to belong to one family. The patient, an adolescent male, was holding his right arm close to his body. The four adults in the party were speaking high-speed Spanish and gesticulating wildly. The boy looked embarrassed.

Babies cried from several locations around the room. A large black woman moaned loudly and dramatically from a prone position on one of the couches, while a black man, presumably the woman's companion, pleaded from across the room for somebody to hurry and help Wilma, who was "dying sure as rain." Wilma looked like she had a ways to go before she passed on.

Two police officers, one on either side of a young white

man, stood in front of the glass cage labeled RECEIVING. The young man had obviously been in a fight. His face looked like raw meat. I wondered which of the cops had been responsible. The man appeared to be considerably under the influence, although at that moment, he didn't look terribly combative.

Suddenly, a little girl vomited, which caused several of the non-patients, including most of the Spanish entourage, to hurry out into the parking lot. This lowered the noise level appreciably. Then the woman at the Receiving desk pointed down the hall, and the cops dragged their prisoner in that direction.

Dr. Augustin lost no time in taking the cops' place at the Receiving window. The woman, an attractive redhead with a well-polished beauty pageant smile, looked up from her computer terminal, no doubt ready to recite her usual "Please sign in and be seated, and someone will be with you shortly" line. One look at Dr. Augustin, however, rendered her speechless.

"We're looking for William O'Shea," Dr. Augustin said over the screaming child to our left. "An ambulance brought him here a short time ago. Carbon monoxide poisoning."

The woman absently fluffed her hair and chewed on her lower lip. "Well," she drawled, "let me see." She punched a few letters into the computer. "Mr. O'Shea was taken upstairs. You'll need to go to Admissions. Second floor." She waved a dainty, red-tipped finger into the air over her head.

"Thanks," said Dr. Augustin, and he hurried toward the automatic doors before Miss Strawberry Festival could respond.

We hiked a quarter of a mile around to the main entrance and followed the green stripe to Admissions. As we passed the Information desk, I smiled at the man sitting in front of the little TV. He was about sixty, with lots of snow-white hair and a nice tan. He did not look up. He was watching a baseball game so intently he wouldn't have noticed if Marilyn Monroe had walked by.

Admissions was a large room, with a waiting area on one side and six individual booths, or stalls, separated by floor-to-ceiling partitions, on the other. Each booth had a computer terminal, a staff person seated at the terminal, a desk and chairs for the patient and one companion. A table at the entrance was manned by yet another volunteer, a woman by the name of Peltz, who evidently took your name and called you when an Admissions booth became available. A sign on the desk said, PLEASE SIGN IN AND HAVE A SEAT.

Dr. Augustin, who periodically loses the ability to read, never even paused. He went around Ms. Peltz's desk and up to a booth that had just been vacated. Ms. Peltz jumped to her feet and raced after him.

"Sir, sir!" she cried. "Please, you must register first. It's a rule. There are other people waiting."

I felt sorry for the woman. Carefully trained to carry out this one simple function, she could not deal with someone as ruthless at disobeying rules as Dr. Augustin.

"It's all right, Dianne," said the young lady in the booth. "I'll handle it."

Dianne glowered at Dr. Augustin, then went back to her post. I acted like I had never seen him before in my life. I sat down in one of the chairs in the waiting area and picked up a copy of *Better Homes and Gardens*. I pretended to read but was trying to hear what was being said in the booth.

Dr. Augustin told the woman he was the man responsible for saving Bill O'Shea's life and wanted to know how he was doing. I couldn't see his face but knew from the young woman's expression that he had his eyes cranked all the way up. Needless to say, she was ever so impressed by Dr. Augustin's selfless act of heroism. After punching a few keys on her terminal, she quickly gave him Bill's room number, as well as a promise to call the head nurse on duty there to say Dr. Augustin would be stopping by. Dr. Augustin thanked her. Apparently he smiled, too, because she blushed and fluttered her eyelashes and looked woozy.

I put my magazine back on the end table and got up.

"Let's go," he said over his shoulder, as he breezed past me.

He grinned at Dianne. Dianne, on the other hand, frowned at him. Obviously, she was one of those rare women immune to Dr. Augustin's charm.

I caught up with him at the elevator. "You should be ashamed of yourself," I admonished.

"*Moi?*" he asked innocently.

The elevator doors opened, and we got in. Dr. Augustin pushed the button for the fifth floor

"Bill is in A507," he said. "This wing, fortunately. I guess he's out of the woods, because they haven't put him in Intensive Care."

"That's a relief," I said. "Means we won't have to sneak around pretending to be volunteers."

"I was just about to ask if you had your badge in your purse. You, at least, look the part in that uniform. Bloodstains and all."

I glanced down and was horrified to see a large red blotch on my otherwise clean uniform top. "You could have said something back at the clinic," I growled.

"The condition of your uniform was hardly a top priority at that time, if you'll recall."

The elevator stopped at 5, and we got out. Visiting hours were obviously over. With the exception of two nurses and a doctor, the hallway was empty. We followed the room numbers backwards, down the left corridor. Room 507 was next to the Patient Lounge. I caught a glimpse of juice and soda machines and a small refrigerator, which reminded me I hadn't eaten supper yet. The ways things are going, I thought, breakfast will be my next meal.

We'd obviously avoided the nurses station. I don't know why I expected Dr. Augustin to check in with them, anyway.

Bill O'Shea was alone in a dusk-filled semiprivate room. He was hooked up to an oxygen port on the wall behind him and an IV that hung above his head. Electrodes were just visible beneath the sheet that covered him almost to his chin.

"Bill?" Dr. Augustin said quietly. He put a hand on Bill's shoulder.

Bill opened his eyes. It took several seconds for recognition to alter his dazed expression. "Lou?" he managed. His voice was weak. "They said you found me. Thanks." He coughed lightly. "I owe you my life."

"Think nothing of it," said Dr. Augustin. "Can't have one of the city's most determined watchdogs checking out prematurely."

Bill smiled, albeit faintly. His face was suffused with red, as if he had gotten too close to a camp fire.

"What happened?" asked Dr. Augustin. "Sarah Milton—her place is across the street from Arnie's—called me around eight and said someone was inside Arnie's house. Was that you?"

Bill nodded. "Ralph asked me to find some insurance papers for him. The hospital is giving him a hard time about his tab. Anyway, I think I was coming out the back door . . . yes, I had locked the door and was halfway across the porch when someone nailed me from behind. Slugged me." He brought his right hand up and touched the back of his head. He winced.

"I don't suppose you got a look at the guy?" asked Dr. Augustin.

Bill shook his head, then squeezed his eyes closed. When he opened them, he looked like he was about to throw up. Dr. Augustin grabbed a stainless steel pan that was on Bill's end table. But Bill took a deep breath and relaxed.

"I haven't a clue about who would want to kill me or why. The bar is mortgaged to the hilt. Everyone knows that. About the only thing I own outright is my car. And my relatives are welcome to that." He stared at the dark TV screen on the far wall. "I had the papers Ralph wanted in a manila envelope. The police said it wasn't on the porch or in my car."

"Samantha and I will go back and look around."

"Thanks, Lou."

Dr. Augustin looked around the room, spied a chair, and dragged it over. He sat down. I searched for a second chair and, not finding one, hopped up on the empty bed.

"Maybe you know something that could incriminate the guy who tried to bump you off," said Dr. Augustin. "Something about Arnie's death."

Bill had been looking at Dr. Augustin. His eyes suddenly darted to the door, then to me. He turned his head slightly and stared at the wall.

"I don't know what you mean," he said.

Dr. Augustin leaned back in the chair and laced his fingers over his abdomen. "I think you do, Bill. I think you're scared something will happen to Ralph if you talk to the cops."

Bill didn't move. He continued to stare at the wall. I noticed he was breathing more rapidly, though, and I silently willed Dr. Augustin to cease and desist, before Bill lapsed into unconsciousness.

Dr. Augustin leaned forward and put his hand on Bill's arm. "Relax, Bill. I'm not here to cause you or Ralph trouble. I just want to find out who killed Arnie. He was *my* friend, too. Not a close friend, mind you, but a friend just the same."

Bill was silent for several seconds, as if trying to decide whether or not he could trust us. Then he drew in a deep breath and looked at Dr. Augustin.

"Arnie and I worked as printers in D.C. For the government. Nothing elaborate, just plans and budgets. Covers for some of the millions of documents that come out of Congress." He smiled. "We did do one of those fancy invitations to dinner at the White House." The smile faded.

"About five months ago, Arnie was approached by Howard Nichols, that guy from St. Luke's the cops found murdered. He wanted Arnie to help him make counterfeit money. Not a lot, he said, but enough so he could spend what few years he had left in high style. He was dying of emphysema, apparently."

Bill paused and drew in another deep breath. I knew he was still oxygen-starved, and all the effort he was expending by talking certainly wasn't doing him any good. Dr. Augustin could be very single-minded and insensitive at times. It made me angry.

"Maybe Bill can tell us about this tomorrow, when he's feeling better," I said, without looking at Dr. Augustin.

Bill shook his head. "I'm all right. Besides, I've wanted to tell somebody what I know ever since Arnie . . . died. I've just been too scared. Not for me, but for Ralph." He smiled at me. "Thanks anyway." He looked back at Dr. Augustin and continued.

"I figure someone at the bar must have told Nichols about Arnie's printing background and about his son's financial predicament. Ralph's medical bills would make even an honest guy like Arnie think twice about a plan to manufacture counterfeit currency. But Arnie would have no part of it. He lied and told Nichols his eyesight wasn't good anymore. That he wouldn't be able to do a credible job. Thanks but no thanks."

Bill coughed. "Of course, Nichols dropped a few hints that Ralph would never live long enough to get a new liver if Arnie went to the police with what he knew. Arnie made me swear I'd never say anything to anyone." He closed his eyes, then opened them. "It's pretty obvious Nichols found someone else to help him, isn't it?"

"Why do you suppose Nichols didn't ask you? He must have known that you worked with Arnie back in Washington."

"I can't answer that. And don't think I haven't tried."

"Well," said Dr. Augustin, "whoever Nichols got to do his counterfeiting must have decided to get rid of anyone who could point the finger at him, including Nichols. He must have felt you knew more than you profess to know."

Dr. Augustin rubbed the back of his neck. It had been a long day for everyone.

"Can you think of anyone at the bar who might have told Nichols about you and Arnie being printers?" he asked Bill.

Bill shrugged. "Lots of people knew. It could have been anyone."

Yeah, I thought. It didn't have to be Mick.

Just then, the door swung open. A short, balding man in his late fifties, wearing an exquisitely tailored chocolate-brown silk suit, a lemon shirt, and a chocolate and gold paisley tie, burst in. He had a file with him, and he did not look like he was in a particularly affable mood. He saw Dr. Augustin and me and stopped. I expected him to bellow at us and scream for security. But a smile as big as any politician's suddenly consumed his face, and he stuck out his hand, like Dr. Augustin was the Godfather or something.

"Lou!" he said. "Great to see you. *Muchas gracias* for saving Bill's life."

Dr. Augustin got up. "It's been a while, hasn't it, Norman?"

I hopped off the bed and positioned my purse over the bloodstain on my uniform. Dr. Augustin glanced my way.

"Samantha, I'd like you to meet Rosco's owner, Dr. Norman Friedman."

Dr. Friedman surveyed me like he might a cut of meat. I tried not to cringe.

"How do you do?" I said. I did not offer my hand, afraid if he touched me, I might be unable to disguise my feelings. It was clear Dr. Augustin wanted to keep him as a client, for whatever reason.

"Just fine, Samantha," he said. There was no respect in the way he said my name. Evidently, my position in life did not deserve any.

Dr. Friedman turned his attention to Bill. "How do you feel?" he asked, no real concern in his voice.

"I've felt better, that's for sure," Bill answered. "Can you do anything for this headache?"

Dr. Friedman flipped open Bill's chart and wrote in it with his Mont Blanc pen. "I'll have the nurse give you something, as soon as I finish here."

Dr. Augustin looked at me and nodded toward the door. "We'll check in tomorrow, Bill," he said, touching Bill's shoulder. "You take care, you hear? And don't worry about a thing." He shook hands with Dr. Friedman. "Don't be such a stranger, Norman."

"If I could squeeze a few extra hours out of each day, it would help," said Dr. Friedman. "Things have been a little stressful lately." He frowned, then turned his attention to Bill's chart.

We had obviously been dismissed. I smiled at Bill and followed Dr. Augustin out into the hall.

"So that's the great Norman Friedman," I said, as we waited for the elevator. "He sure knows how to dress. That suit looked like an Armani. I'll bet it cost him over a thousand dollars. The tie was another hundred or two."

Dr. Augustin grinned. "Your claws are showing, Samantha."

"I can't help it," I said. "I hate men like Dr. Friedman. They think of their patients in terms of country club memberships and fancy clothes. Believe me, I know." I punched the down button several times, even though I could hear the elevator approaching. "Bill shouldn't have had to ask for something to stop the headache."

Dr. Augustin didn't say anything. We got on the elevator and rode it down to the second floor in silence.

The lobby was quiet, the gift shop and florist closed. A few people sat on the pastel sofas and love seats reading or staring out into space. I could only imagine why they were still there. Visiting hours were over, but they wanted to be close to a loved one, wanted to be available in a hurry should the need arise. I had never lost anyone I cared about, except my grandfather. He had died suddenly and unexpectedly in his sleep. That was how I wanted to go. The thought of my mother sitting all alone in the waiting room of some large, impersonal hospital, while I lay upstairs dying, depressed me.

Dr. Augustin and I walked back around the building. As we started out across the driveway that ran beneath the Emergency Entrance portico, I heard the automatic doors whoosh open. I turned in time to see a woman in white dash out, nearly bumping into me.

I didn't recognize her at first, but she was so close I could see the name printed on her ID badge. "Ramona James." I stopped and watched her as she hurried down the sidewalk. Then I drew in a quick sharp breath. Her hair was pulled back into a ponytail and secured with a wide white ribbon that seemed to phosphoresce in the light of the mercury vapor lamps. The ponytail was why I hadn't recognized her right away as Ralph's nurse. Her figure, particularly from the back, was unmistakable, however.

"That's Ramona James," I said to Dr. Augustin. "Ralph's day nurse."

Dr. Augustin stopped and looked at the disappearing figure.

"I'm almost positive she was in the Paper Moon a week ago last Saturday," I continued. "Having words with Mick Peters." I stopped suddenly, realizing that Mick's association with the James woman was one more piece of evidence to support Dr. Augustin's theory.

"Oh, really?" said Dr. Augustin. He continued to stand there and stare, long after Ramona James had rounded the corner.

CHAPTER 25

•

Wednesday, July 22

On the way back to Arnie's house Tuesday night, Dr. Augustin stopped at McDonald's and bought us each a Quarter Pounder with cheese. It was almost eleven, and the kids in the kitchen had dumped the grease and turned off the grill. From the condition of the bun and the temperature of the meat, I figured our sandwiches had been sitting under the heat lamps for a couple of hours. I ate mine anyway, because I was starving. Every bite made me think of Luther and Martha.

We didn't find Bill's manila envelope. Either he was so confused, he forgot what he did with it, or the guy who mugged him had it, although I couldn't imagine what value a bunch of insurance papers could possibly have. Unless it wasn't insurance forms Bill had gone there to get.

"So who attacked Bill?" I asked, as Dr. Augustin stopped in front of my apartment building. "Mick Peters is in jail." There was a slight smugness in my voice I hadn't intended. Or had I?

"Mick obviously has another partner," he replied. "I never said he was acting alone when he killed Arnie and Howard Nichols. Maybe this unknown partner is the person who framed Mick for Tyndall's murder. Maybe they had a falling-out."

I was too tired to argue with him, so I picked up my purse and got out of the car.

"See you Thursday," he said and drove off.

I can hardly wait, I thought.

• • •

I finally made it to bed Tuesday just after midnight. I was exhausted and decided not to set my alarm. The cats could get me up. However, at 7:30 A.M., before Priss and Tina got the chance, the phone woke me.

"Hello?" I mumbled into the receiver.

"Samantha, it's Michael. I didn't wake you, did I? I figured you'd be leaving for work about now."

"This is Wednesday," I said. "We're closed on Wednesdays." I heard him click his tongue against the roof of his mouth.

"I forgot, Samantha, I'm sorry."

"That's okay," I lied. "My alarm was about to go off, anyway."

Miss Priss and Tina suddenly jumped up onto the foot of the bed and began staring at me. I could feel their telekinetic powers moving me toward the kitchen.

"I have some information about Dr. Augustin's three murder victims that may or may not be significant," Michael said. "I was going to stop by the hospital on my way to the office." He paused. "I wonder if I might drop in on you for a short while this morning."

The apartment needed cleaning. I glanced over at my end table. It wouldn't have surprised me to see the words "Wash me" scrawled in the dust.

"Give me twenty minutes to get showered and dressed," I said reluctantly.

"Will do. And a pot of coffee would be nice."

"Sure," I said. "I can do that."

I took a shower and dried my hair in record time. Then I wasted ten minutes trying to decide what to wear. I finally put on a pair of baggy shorts and a light blue oversized T-shirt. Nothing could be as bad as my uniform, and that's what Michael usually saw me in.

At 8:10 the doorbell rang. When I opened the door, I found Michael dressed in a suit and tie and holding a large white bakery box. I let him in. A faint odor of butter and cinnamon floated along behind him.

"I hope the coffee's hot," he said. "I've brought our breakfast."

We went into the kitchen. I took out plates and coffee mugs. While Michael arranged enough bear claws and blueberry Danish for four on the plates, I poured our coffee.

"Do you know, Michael," I said, grinning, "that except for your little visits to the clinic, every time we get together we eat?"

I was practically drooling, as we carried our coffee and the plates into my living room. Miss Priss, yawning widely, materialized from wherever cats disappear to during the day.

"I invited you to go sailing with me to St. Thomas," he said quietly. "That's something new."

Suddenly, angrily, I realized I had blundered into the matter of Michael wanting a cat for company. I attempted a laugh. "Didn't you tell me you ate lobster nearly every day you were there?" I picked up a bear claw and added hastily, "So, what have you found out about the murder victims?"

Michael sipped his coffee and looked at me. His blue eyes, normally like a calm tropical sea, were overcast, unsettled. He blinked and put down his mug. When he looked back at me, he was all business.

"According to the coroner, the three men were all murdered by different means. And death was the only thing they had in common. Two smoked, one—Arnold Silor—did not."

"Great!" I said. "So where do we go from here?"

"The two who smoked shared the same doctor, which I think is interesting."

"Who?" I asked.

"Norman Friedman."

I thought about this, then frowned. "He's a noted internist. Lots of people, especially those over forty, go to internists. It's a coincidence, that's all."

Michael finished his coffee. I noticed he hadn't touched any of the goodies on his plate. I, on the other hand, had devoured a bear claw and was working on a piece of Danish.

"You're probably right. However, there are sixty-six internists in Brightwater Beach and adjacent communities," said Michael. "A large number of whom are board-certified. And

Dr. Friedman, although certainly among the most successful as far as income goes, is not the most highly decorated, as it were."

"Where did you find all of this out?"

"It's a matter of public record, Samantha."

I put my plate, one last piece of Danish untouched, on the coffee table. My mother, who never quoted the line, "There are children starving in Africa," when I was growing up, firmly believes it is unseemly for a woman to clean her plate.

"Maybe his office was the most convenient for the two men," I said.

Michael shook his head. "I checked. Friedman's office was convenient for Luther Tyndall, but not Howard Nichols. And another thing. Nichols and Tyndall weren't the first patients of Norman Friedman to die under suspicious circumstances."

"What do you mean?"

"Over the last several months, there have been eight deaths in and around Brightwater Beach that the police cannot, with complete certainty, attribute to natural causes. They aren't calling them homicides, either."

I stared at him.

"Six of those went to Dr. Friedman for one reason or another," he said.

Suddenly, I remembered Bill O'Shea. "Last night, someone tried to kill a friend of Arnold Silor," I said. "His name is O'Shea, and he owns a bar on the beach called the Paper Moon. He's Ralph Silor's godfather." I swatted Miss Priss on the rump, as she began to ease a paw toward my plate from beneath the coffee table. "Dr. Augustin and I went to see him at the hospital right after it happened. Guess who his doctor is?"

Michael smiled. "Norman Friedman."

"Right. And something else we learned. Arnie and Bill O'Shea were government printers before they retired to Florida. Howard Nichols found this out and wanted Arnie to help him print counterfeit currency. Arnie told Nichols his eyesight wasn't good enough. Then Nichols threatened to have Ralph killed right there in the hospital if Arnie went to the police with what he knew." I paused. "Of course, now Howard Nichols is dead."

"Let me see if I can find out anything else about Dr. Friedman," said Michael. He looked at his watch and got up. "I'm late. I'll call you."

He started for the door, then turned around. I was still sitting on the sofa. I looked up at him and smiled, but only briefly. His face had that sad, wistful expression it got now and then, an expression I always attributed to some fleeting memory of his dead wife. The longing always made me want to get away from him.

"You must know how I feel about you, Samantha," he said.

I waited, unwilling either to hurt or encourage him by answering. But it obviously wasn't a question.

"What I need to know is how you feel," he said. "About me. About us."

He came over to the sofa and sat down beside me. I couldn't have felt more trapped had he been Arnie's killer. I stood up.

"How about another cup of coffee? I think there's some left."

"Samantha!" he snapped. "Sit down!"

I sat. "Of course I care about you, Michael," I whined. "It's just . . ." I stared dumbly at the piece of Danish on my plate.

"I know about your ex-fiancé, David Ketchum," he said gently. "How he failed to show up on your wedding day."

I silently vowed to kill Cynthia the first chance I got. "Cynthia had no right to tell you that," I said through clenched teeth.

"Cynthia only wants what is best for you." He put his hand over mine. "If it's any consolation, David Ketchum was a fool."

I looked at him, and he smiled. He was the kindest, gentlest man I had ever met. The last thing I wanted to do was hurt him. It would be easy, I thought, to pretend David was the reason I didn't want to make a commitment just yet. String Michael along with some plea for more time. Time to heal. Time to trust again. Except that the real reason I didn't want to make any promises to Michael still eluded me.

"I need more time, Michael," I said, feeling guilty. I eased my hand out from under his. "Please don't be angry."

"How could I be angry, Samantha? I . . ." He touched my cheek, then stood up. "We'll take it one day at a time. How's that?"

"That sounds like a plan," I said.

I walked him to the door and put my arms around his neck. "Thank you, Michael," I whispered. "For being so patient." I felt like a heel.

Michael reached up and brought my arms down, then took my face in his hands. His kiss was filled with such passion, I was startled by it. I stared at him, suddenly intrigued.

He let go of my face, turned, and opened the door. "I'll call you tonight or tomorrow," he said quickly, over his shoulder. "As soon as I do a little more research on Dr. Friedman." He wouldn't look at me. He went out onto the landing and pulled the door closed.

CHAPTER 26

•

Thursday, July 23

Tracey was late. My evil twin sister took great pleasure in this. I knew better, though, having been tardy myself on numerous occasions.

At 8:25 she came running down the hall, face flushed, tiny beads of perspiration adhering to her forehead and nose like glitter.

"I overslept," she said in a breathy voice before disappearing into the bathroom. She came into the lab a couple of minutes later looking better, although she was still perspiring. "I'm sorry, Sam," she said. "I forgot to set my alarm. Thursday used to be my day off, and somehow I got confused."

I wondered how she could get confused after having Wednesday off, but, before I could inquire, Dr. Augustin called me into the surgery. He was early for a change. That was fortunate, since we had an emergency c-section to do, followed by a full surgical schedule.

"I already did the workup on the c-section," I told Tracey, as I was leaving. "Dr. Augustin will need both of us to help with the puppies, so try to get the blood work on at least one of those spays done pronto."

She nodded, smiling sheepishly, and took a syringe out of the drawer. I hurried down the hall.

The dachshund had four puppies in her. The first, a large male, had become trapped in the birth canal and was dead. The remaining three were nice and healthy. Tracey and I cleaned them off and rubbed them briskly, until they were squeaking like rubber chew toys and breathing on their own. Then I put them in the surplus pediatric incubator Dr. Augustin had gotten from St. Luke's, and Tracey went back to her lab duties.

"Two reds and a black and tan," I said, as I watched them wiggle fitfully in an effort to locate their mom, who was still on the table. "All females. Mrs. Garrison should be happy."

"Undoubtedly. It means more money. Anyway, enough to pay me."

I knew he was grinning under his mask.

"She can still have more puppies, can't she?" I asked, pointing to the dachshund.

"Unfortunately." He finished closing the incision and stripped off his gloves. He slid the mask down off of his face. "She's getting a little old for this kind of thing. Remind me to suggest spaying her to Mrs. Garrison."

"I will," I said.

I unhooked the dog from the anesthesia machine and disconnected her IV line, then slipped a rubber cap over the catheter in her foreleg. "Michael came by my apartment yesterday," I said. "He found out that Howard Nichols and Luther Tyndall were both patients of Norman Friedman. And"—I paused dramatically—"there have been six other patients of his who have died recently under 'suspicious circumstances,' as Michael put it. Surely all of them weren't involved in Mick Peters's counterfeiting scam. The fact that they were Norman Friedman's patients is purely coincidental, right?" I hesitated. "You don't think Dr. Friedman is somehow involved in their deaths, do you?"

Dr. Augustin carried the dog to a recovery cage. Then he took off his gown and threw it on the table. His pale yellow cotton shirt was damp with sweat.

"I've known Norman Friedman for several years. I even went to him, myself, when I needed a physical. He's a greedy SOB, but he isn't a bad person. Not really." He went over to the sink. "No, I don't think he had a hand in the deaths. What on earth would he have to gain by knocking off his own meal tickets, anyway?" He paused. "And you didn't mention Arnie, so I assume he wasn't one of Friedman's patients." He pumped the soap dispenser a couple of times and began lathering up his hands. "But I would like to know more about that nurse. Ramona James. And just exactly what her relationship with Mick Peters is."

His back was to me, so he couldn't see the expression on my face. Too bad. I knew what was coming—a trip to St. Luke's and still another day sneaking about like some sleazy PI.

But, instead of telling me to spend the afternoon disguised as a physical therapy student, he reminded me that this was commission meeting night.

"I want to leave by six," he said, drying his hands. "That sewage treatment plant is on the agenda again, and I don't want to be late."

I thanked the Almighty and took a spay pack out of the cabinet.

Our first appointment of the morning was Ms. Leitel. Her two Himalayans were in to have their sutures removed. Dr. Augustin and I were still in surgery, so I asked Tracey to handle it.

"I'm really busy, Samantha," she said into the intercom speaker. "How much longer are you going to be? Maybe she can wait for a few minutes. Until you're finished."

I looked over at Dr. Augustin. He was frowning. I took a deep breath.

"I'm afraid you'll have to take care of Ms. Leitel, Tracey," I said calmly. "Whatever else you're doing can wait." How fortuitous, I thought, that Dr. Augustin can hear this conversation.

Tracey groaned. "Oh, all right," she snapped. The intercom clicked off.

I took a few seconds out from gloating over Tracey's performance to wonder what had gotten into her. It had never occurred to me that she might lack experience dealing with clients. Sure, Dr. Farmington used Tracey in the lab, not in the rooms, but suture removal was so easy, a first-year technology student could do it. For that matter, Ms. Leitel probably could have done it herself, if she'd had someone to hold her cats.

Dr. Augustin continued to work. He didn't say anything, so

I didn't either. But I was pretty sure he was as perplexed as I was.

At eleven, Vivian Porter stopped by. I saw her come through the door, just as I was about to escort our next client into a room. I took a quick detour into the lab. After a minute or so, Cynthia called my name and, when I failed to respond, came looking for me.

"Samantha," she said sternly, her eyebrows drawn together forming a little V over her nose. "Didn't you hear me calling you? Vivian Porter has decided to give that stray a home." She lowered her voice. "She says she'll be bankrupt if it continues to stay here."

I finished straightening the already straight row of bottles on the pharmacy shelf and turned around.

"She is going to ask me if I've spoken to Irma Shoaf in Physical Therapy," I said. "I don't have a good excuse this time, so I would appreciate it if you would kindly tell her I am in a coma or lost in the Everglades. Something to get her off my back. Tell her I got leprosy from an armadillo and have been banished to a sanitarium somewhere. Anything."

Cynthia grinned wickedly. "What'll you give me?"

Before I could think of some snappy comeback, Dr. Augustin appeared in the doorway to his office. "Samantha, could I see you in here for a minute?"

Cynthia whirled around and headed for the reception room. I trudged past Dr. Augustin and sat down on the daybed.

He closed the door. "This is a golden opportunity for you to question Vivian about Ramona James without anyone overhearing you," he said. "I'll tell her we need to take a radiograph of that leg before letting the cat go home. That you'll bring him to her house tonight after work."

"She's going to ask me why I haven't been to the hospital to start my volunteer work," I said. "I haven't even talked to the woman in Physical Therapy who is in charge of the schedule."

"So?"

"I don't want to lie to Vivian. And you know she's going to be curious."

"So, don't lie." He looked at his watch. "Tracey can fill in for you over lunch. You can go to St. Luke's, check in with whoever you're supposed to check in with, and be back here by two." He had it all planned out.

I shook my head. "I can't. I'm supposed to get my hair cut at noon."

"Your hair looks fine, Samantha. Besides, this can't wait. Have Cynthia reschedule your appointment for tomorrow." He opened the door to the reception room and went out, smiling.

"Vivian," I heard him say, "what a pleasant surprise."

I looked around for someone to punch, but Frank was back in the kennel.

Both exam rooms were full and three additional clients were waiting, apparently none too patiently. Cynthia was a nervous wreck. A Newfoundland, a rottweiler, and a hyperactive Welsh corgi, all males, were threatening to turn the reception area into a boxing arena. Frank had already made two trips up front with the mop. Earlier, he had told me he wanted to leave by 4:30 to check out the new sound system at the Chilly Bin. Now it was almost four, with no end in sight, and he was getting cranky. To top it all off, Tracey hadn't said three words to anyone all day. Strangely, though, Dr. Augustin seemed to be taking it all in stride, which, to me, was most unsettling.

I was about to open the door to Room 1 when the phone rang. I picked up the hall extension to save Cynthia the trouble. She couldn't have heard the caller, anyway.

"Sam, this is Mick Peters," the voice said. "I was wondering if I could come get Jonesy this afternoon."

I thought for a minute. "Aren't you in jail, Mick?" Then I added hastily, "I mean, we read about Luther Tyndall in the paper. Of course, Dr. Augustin and I think you're innocent." I didn't elaborate. Innocent of the Tyndall murder, maybe. But what about Arnie and Howard Nichols?

"Thanks, Sam. You must believe me. I did not kill Luther Tyndall." He sounded even worse than he had Monday morning. "So, can I come get Jonesy? My lawyer got me out on bail Tuesday evening. I had to sign over my business to cover the bond."

"Why don't you leave Jonesy here awhile longer?" I said.

"He isn't any trouble, and you probably have enough to worry about already."

Mick forced a laugh. "You don't know the half of it, Samantha." Then he sighed audibly. "Okay," he said. "But give him a hug for me. Tell him I haven't forgotten about him. Will you do that?"

"Of course, Mick."

"Thanks. I'll check in later this week." He hung up.

I put the receiver back in its cradle and started, once again, to open the door to Room 1. Then I stopped. Tuesday. Mick said he was out of jail Tuesday. The day Bill O'Shea was attacked over at Arnie's. I shook my head, sadly. I hated to admit it, but Mick's innocence was becoming more and more difficult to defend.

Tracey's mood improved as the day wore on. At six, she and I were in the reception room, waiting for Cynthia to finish adding up the deposit. Dr. Augustin had already left for City Hall.

"Are you doing anything tomorrow, after work?" Tracey asked me.

I put the June issue of *Cat Fancy* back on the magazine rack. Vivian's stray peered out at me from the carrier next to my leg. He looked like he was ready to chomp on a few fingers, if someone would be so kind as to stick them through the little holes for him.

"Why?" I asked.

"Frank's band is playing at the Chilly Bin," she said. "I told him I'd stop by. I thought you might like to come along. We could have a couple of beers and stay for a set."

Cynthia looked up from her computer screen.

"I can't," I said. "I've got plans." I studied the linoleum.

"If it's a date, bring him along. It'll be fun."

Losing one's hearing to a bunch of overgrown teenagers who treat electric guitars like extensions of their penises is anything but fun, I thought. "He's not into rock music," I said.

Tracy laughed. "It's Michael Halsey, isn't it?"

"What if it is?" I snapped.

"Hey, I didn't mean anything." She got up, slung her purse

over her shoulder, and headed for the door. "I guess I'll see you tomorrow, then," she said, without looking at me. She turned the dead bolt and let herself out.

I watched her get into her car, a white Nissan 300ZX. "Where do you think she got the money for that little number?" I asked Cynthia.

"I wouldn't know." She licked the night envelope and sealed it. Then she turned off the computer. "You should give the poor girl a chance, Samantha. She's really very nice."

I continued to stare through the window.

"By the way," Cynthia said suddenly. "Did you know that Ms. Leitel is Tracey's mother?"

I looked at her and felt my eyes bug out.

"I overheard the two of them talking in Room One. They didn't seem to be on the best of terms, but Tracey did call her 'Mom' once or twice. I'm certain of that."

CHAPTER 27

•

Vivian told Dr. Augustin she planned to be home around six and would be expecting me. Unfortunately, she didn't mention anything about Dresden. Like where *he* would be and whether or not he would have eaten his dinner by then.

I hadn't talked to Irma Shoaf, although I did go to the hospital at one. Irma was having her nails done. Lucky her. I spoke with a man who said he was Irma's boss, but he didn't know where Irma kept the schedule sheet and wasn't familiar with the procedure for signing up new recruits. He took my name and number. He referred to himself as *Dr.* Smith, which explained a lot.

I parked my car in the alley behind Vivian's house and, cat carrier in hand, walked up to the gate. I stared at the gold and red sign. If Vivian was home, Dresden was probably in the house with her. I could risk it and let myself in, or I could stand there in the alley and scream Vivian's name. Neither option was very appealing. A cowbell hung on the gate would be nice, I thought.

While I was trying to decide what to do, the door to the kitchen opened, and Dresden came flying out, ears flapping, tongue lolling, his stub of a tail whipping to and fro like a high-speed metronome. He came to a screeching halt at the gate and smiled up at me, panting.

"Come on in, Miss Holt," said Vivian from across the yard. "Dresden, sit!"

The dog took a couple of steps in reverse and sat down. His peculiar, almost reptilian eyes watched me intently.

I opened the gate and passed through, closing it behind me. Dresden continued to sit, but when the occupant of the carrier started to rumble, the dog's entire body suddenly snapped to attention, and he stared through the door of the carrier with the single-mindedness of a pointer. He was drooling, but I didn't know if that was the result of his romp across the lawn or the prospect of dinner.

I moved quickly up the walkway to the house.

"Welcome, Miss Holt," said Vivian. "Please, come in." She was wearing a grey skirt and a pale pink polyester blouse. She had on an apron that said, "Don't hassle the cook," beneath a cartoon drawing of a man in a chef's cap holding up a butcher knife.

I stepped inside. Vivian released her dog from the "sit" command, then followed me into the kitchen and closed the door. Dresden remained outside.

I had expected Vivian's kitchen to be in keeping with the exterior of the house—vintage 1930, full of nostalgia and checkered oilcloth. Where mothers and grandmothers (or cooks who looked like Mrs. Butterworth) made cakes from scratch with real butter and eggs, oblivious to the fat, cholesterol, and calories they contained, and dishes were washed by hand.

Instead, I saw modern appliances, including a large-capacity dishwasher and a built-in microwave oven, and countertops covered with gleaming white ceramic tile. Numerous cabinets encircling the room were of varnished natural pine. An island in the center of the kitchen featured two electrical outlets and an inlaid ceramic cutting board. Pots and pans hung from *s* hooks on a black wrought-iron rectangle suspended over the island.

The floor was alternating squares of black and white tile. There was an enormous dog dish, licked clean, and a pan of water large enough to double as an infant bathtub on the floor at one end of the island. There was, however, no evidence that a kitten had ever been in Vivian's kitchen.

I put the cat carrier on the island. "This is beautiful," I said. "My mother would be envious."

Vivian opened one of the cabinets. "I enjoy cooking," she said, patting her hip, "and I'm afraid it shows." She began taking out coffee cups, saucers, and dessert plates. She arranged the dishes on a large black tray. "I hope you drink coffee, Miss Holt," she said, her back to me.

"Oh, yes, I love coffee. And, please, call me Samantha."

Vivian took a brown sack out of the freezer half of an enormous side-by-side, opened it, and poured coffee beans into a small grinder. She placed the lid on the grinder and pushed down. The resulting noise caused the cat to jump. His carrier wobbled and moved backwards a few inches.

The aroma of rich coffee and hazelnuts was powerful. I watched Vivian spoon grounds into the basket of a twelve-cup coffeemaker.

"How do you think Dresden is going to handle having a cat in the house?" I asked. "I assume he hasn't been around one before."

Vivian filled the coffeemaker with water and switched it on. She turned around. "I'll have to keep them separated, I suppose. At least until Harvey's leg is healed and he can defend himself."

"Harvey?"

Vivian smiled impishly. It made her cheeks puff out. They looked like plump muscadine grapes.

"That's what I've decided to call him," she said. "I don't know what brought that name to mind, but I like it."

I looked at her and thought, Harvey was an invisible rabbit that Jimmy Stewart liked to talk to.

Vivian pointed at the carrier. "Shouldn't we let him out?"

"I guess so," I said. "Where do you plan to keep him? We should let him out there, so he can learn where his litter pan and food dishes are."

Vivian went around the refrigerator and opened a door. "In here," she said. "It's the utility room, but there's plenty of space." She turned on a light.

I picked up the carrier. Harvey started to rumble again. I looked through the metal bars. He was scrunched as far back in the carrier as possible. All I could see was a lot of black and white hair and two very large eyes, mostly pupil. Then he opened his mouth and hissed at me.

I followed Vivian into the utility room and put the carrier down on the floor. In addition to a washer and dryer, the room contained a sewing table and chair, two sets of built-in storage shelves painted white and filled to capacity, a swing down ironing board, and several clothes boxes like the one Vivian had used to transport the cat to the clinic.

On the floor next to the sewing table was a new litter pan filled with clean litter, a red food dish containing dry cat food, and a water bowl. Beside the dryer, a red and yellow beach towel had been folded into a nice bed. All the comforts of home, I thought with some amusement. Because, despite her earlier refusal to adopt the cat, Vivian had obviously spent some time planning for the new arrival.

"I have an old radio here," Vivian said, pointing to one of the shelves, "that I can turn on so he has some company."

I leaned over and opened the door to the carrier. Harvey hissed again but did not budge.

"Let's leave him alone," I said. "He'll come out when things calm down."

We went back into the kitchen.

"Why don't you go into the living room, Samantha," said Vivian, indicating a door to our left. "And I'll bring along the coffee, as soon as it's done. Shouldn't be long now." She opened the refrigerator. "Do you take cream and sugar?"

"Black is fine, thanks." I hesitated, then pushed open the door.

If Vivian's kitchen had caught me by surprise, the rest of her house, at least the part I could see, was more what I'd expected. I went into the dining room. It was an estate auctioneer's dream come true. A massive trestle table and eight chairs with dark blue brocade seat cushions made the room look small, although it probably would have occupied half the downstairs in the average suburban house.

Pale green wallpaper with vertical rows of tiny blue forget-me-nots covered the bottom half of each wall, while the top portion was solid green. A wooden chair rail stained and varnished to match the table and chairs separated the two halves. An elegant chandelier hung over the table, its tiny glass teardrops moving only slightly in the otherwise imperceptible breeze created by the air-conditioning system.

A green and blue Oriental rug covered most of the polished hardwood floor. The rug looked old and expensive. It was worn in a uniform pattern around the table, where I imagined elegantly attired ladies and gentlemen, their feet touching the rug beneath their chairs, had raised wineglasses in countless toasts to the host and hostess. And then I wondered about the host. Because, of course, there must have been one. But I just couldn't imagine Vivian married. Perhaps it was her father's house, I thought, or an uncle's.

I looked in the glass-fronted china cabinet. There were at least two different china patterns represented on the lower shelves, enough for a small army of diners. One pattern was basically white, with a one-inch band of blue, green, and gold scrollwork. Very English. The other was black, with gold and red feathers. Very Oriental.

The top shelf contained porcelain and glass knickknacks, undoubtedly souvenirs from someone's travels or useless but expensive wedding gifts. I spied a badly tarnished candlesnuffer in the shape of a tri-cornered hat. People still send gifts like that, I thought. The richer the family, the more useless the gifts, it seemed. I had gotten a sterling silver clothes brush with David's initials engraved on it. It was one of the few gifts I enjoyed sending back.

I continued on into the living room. Despite the air-conditioning, I detected a faint musty odor, the odor of disuse, mingled with lemon Pledge. It was fairly obvious that Vivian hadn't entertained in that room for some time. Even so, every surface, from the butler's table that served as a coffee table in front of the sofa, to the various occasional tables to the mantel above the fireplace, was dust-free. Someone evidently kept up the place.

I stared at two china figurines, one on either side of the ornate gilt-framed mirror over the mantel. There was a hand-painted inscription, done in gold calligraphy, beneath each figurine. The inscriptions were worn. I could just make out

"Wednesday's Child" beneath the girl on the left. I tried to remember. "Wednesday's child is full of woe." Wasn't that it? According to my mother, I had been born on a Wednesday. That thought, together with the loneliness of the room, brought Michael to mind. When are you going to tell him the truth? I asked myself. And just what is the truth? What, exactly, are you looking for, anyway?

"Harvey is investigating his cat food," said Vivian. She came across the room and put the black tray on the butler's table. A plate containing four little tarts, each filled with a pale yellow custard and topped with a slice of kiwi fruit, sat next to the coffee cups and dessert plates. "Let me get the coffeepot," she added.

When she came back, she proceeded to pour us each a cup of coffee.

"These are Key lime tarts," she said. "I have a tree in my yard. The soil isn't exactly right, but it still produces for me." She picked up one of the tarts with a cake server and slipped it onto a plate. She handed it and a fork to me.

"You made these?" I asked. I hadn't meant it to sound so incredulous.

Vivian smiled demurely and nodded.

"The crust is so perfect," I said. "However did you get them fluted? Mine would be chipped and crumbled."

"I won't say they all turned out. There were a few casualties. They make nice topping for ice cream."

I could hear Dr. Augustin telling me to dispense with the small talk and get to the point. But I wasn't interested in Ramona James. I wanted to know about Vivian Porter. I wanted to know about the candlesnuffer and Wednesday's Child.

I tasted the custard. It was tart, yet sweet and as smooth as satin. I took a sip of coffee.

"I tried to reach Irma Shoaf today," I said reluctantly, "about getting on her schedule. She wasn't in. Her boss, a Dr. Smith, took my name and number."

Vivian eyed me over her coffee cup. "I am just a little concerned about you, Miss Holt—Samantha," she said. "A volunteer has to be reliable. If you say you're going to be there on a certain day, you must show up. I mean no offense by this, but you seem less than enthusiastic about volunteering at St. Luke's. It's almost as if you have some reason other than community service for wanting to be there."

It is difficult to act nonchalant while choking on tart crumbs. I grabbed one of the little napkins Vivian had placed next to the coffeepot and covered my mouth. After several heartfelt coughs, the kind that bring tears to your eyes, I was finally able to speak.

"The truth is," I said, my voice cracking, "I don't really have the time to volunteer. But Dr. Augustin is determined that his staff become involved in some local cause or community service project." I smiled at her. After all, it wasn't actually a lie, was it? I simply hadn't specified the type of project Dr. Augustin meant for us to become involved with.

Vivian seemed unconvinced. "Not to appear in any way disrespectful," she said, "but if Dr. Augustin wishes his employees to get involved in community matters, then he should set an example by volunteering some of his own time."

Amen to that, I thought. Then I remembered the commission meeting. "Oh, Dr. Augustin does his share, trust me. Right now, he's at the Brightwater Beach City Commission meeting arguing for a new sewage treatment plant. At least that's what I think the issue is. Other than that, he has very little spare time. He certainly couldn't be counted on to stick to a schedule, what with emergencies, house calls, and everything." To myself, I added solving murders, chasing bad guys, risking life and limb. And not always his, either.

Vivian refilled our coffee cups. "Do have a second tart," she said, picking up the cake server.

I shook my head. "They are delicious but, no, thank you. I really need to watch my weight." Then I cleared my throat. "By the way, a friend of mine is in the sixth floor intensive care unit. I was wondering if you could check in on him from time to time. I assume you get to the B wing in your travels around the hospital."

"Yes, indeed," she said. "But I usually don't see the patients. Except to deliver flowers and mail. I'm sure he is in good hands, though."

"I'm sure he is, too. His nurse, Ramona James, seems quite

competent." I waited, the caffeine not doing my already agitated nervous system any good.

Vivian stared across the room for a moment, her face blank. Then she smiled and nodded. "Oh yes, Ramona," she said. "A lovely girl."

"You know her then?"

"Not well, but she and I have talked. About our pets, mostly. Ramona is the one who convinced me to adopt Harvey. I tried to get her to take him, but she said she couldn't, because she had recently acquired a kitten." Vivian shook her head, sadly. "Poor little thing has some sort of birth defect."

That time, it was the coffee I nearly aspirated.

CHAPTER 28

•

We rounded the corner just as the light changed. Grateful for the excuse, I stopped and panted loudly. The stitch in my side that had begun two minutes out was still with me. I tried to ignore Jeffrey. He was next to me, running in place and, as usual, hardly breathing.

The light changed, and we took off again. We were half a mile from our apartment building. I wasn't sure I could make it. I had agreed to run five miles, instead of my usual three, and every breath was agony because of the cramp in my side. To make matters worse, Jeffrey was humiliating me by running up and down every side street we passed, just to show me how slow I was. I knew he didn't mean to hurt my feelings, but the performance was demoralizing, just the same.

Finally, like an oasis in the desert, our building appeared, and I picked up speed.

"Smell the barn, do you?" Jeffrey joked.

The fact that he could talk so easily after five grueling miles (well, they were grueling to me) only added insult to injury. I dropped back to a walk when I reached our parking lot.

"I should know better than to listen to you," I managed between gasps. "'There's a cool breeze tonight, Samantha,'" I mocked. "'I promise to go slow, Samantha.'"

I straightened up. My cramp was better. "It is definitely *not* cool tonight, Jeffrey, and we covered five miles in very nearly what it normally takes me to do three." I bent over and used the bottom half of my T-shirt to wipe my face.

"Sorry," Jeffrey said. He started up the stairs. "I'll get us some water. You finish cooling down." He pranced up to his apartment. He was barely damp.

I walked out to the canal behind our building. In the growing darkness, I could just make out one of the many stray cats in the neighborhood carefully picking its way along the old oyster shells piled up next to the seawall. It was hunting rats, an ancient and honorable profession. I wished it well.

I sat down on the seawall and stared at the black water. A light breeze, smelling faintly of seaweed and rotten eggs, made the sweat on my face prickle. Palm fronds rustled softly above me. A gull, cruising in the light of the causeway, laughed suddenly. It was an eerie, ominous sound.

After returning from Vivian's house, I had phoned Dr. Augustin. I was eager to tell him about Ramona James. Unfortunately, I got his machine, then remembered he was at the commission meeting and probably wouldn't be home until late. I decided not to leave a message. I wanted to see his face when I told him I was pretty sure I had found Pearl's missing kitten. The question now, of course, was how Ramona had gotten the kitten and what, if any, role she had played in the murders of Arnold Silor and Howard Nichols and the attempted murder of Bill O'Shea.

"Samantha?" It was Jeffrey. He spotted me and came across the lawn with a large glass of water and a beer. He handed the glass to me and sat down on the seawall. "I figured you wouldn't want a beer," he said, "but if you do, just say the word, and I'll go get you one." He burped.

I took a long drink of water. "This is fine, thanks." I put the glass down next to me. "Jeffrey, you spend a fair amount of time at the Paper Moon. Do you know anything about a woman by the name of Ramona James?" When he didn't answer, I added, "Attractive brunette. Wears her hair in a ponytail. She's a nurse at St. Luke's."

Jeffrey shook his head. "Can't help you. Is this another one of Dr. Augustin's 'cases' you're working on?"

"Of course," I said, laughing.

Jeffrey burped again. "When you mentioned the Moon, I thought you were going to ask me about that cute bartender.

Toby Reynolds. All I can tell you about him is he's straight, unfortunately. But then, you already know that, don't you?"

"What do you mean by that crack?"

"Hey, lighten up, Samantha. I only mean that since you went out with him, you must know what his preferences are."

"How do you know I went out with him?" I asked. Was the whole town keeping tabs on my love life?

"Jeez Louise. Don't get so hostile. I was off Friday and decided to put in a few miles. You guys passed me over by Durante's Gym."

I put my hand on his arm. "I'm sorry, Jeffrey," I said gently. "I didn't mean to yell at you. It's just that Dr. Augustin has been bugging me the last few months about who I date. It's getting on my nerves."

"Give the guy credit, Sam," Jeffrey said. "Maybe he's trying to keep you from getting hurt again."

"Yeah, right."

Jeffrey smashed his beer can and folded it in half. Then he got up. "I'm going for another beer. Are you sure you don't want one?"

I handed him my empty glass. "Thanks anyway, but I'm beat. I think I'll take a shower and hit the sack." I struggled to my feet. "And the next time you suggest I run five miles with you, it had better be in January!"

The phone rang. I reached behind the shower curtain and turned off the water. Then I ran into the bedroom.

"Hello," I said, hopeful it was Dr. Augustin.

"Samantha? It's Mike. I'm not disturbing you, am I? I asked around about Dr. Friedman and thought you'd want to know what I found out."

"I certainly do, and no, you aren't disturbing me."

I could hear him breathing on the other end of the line. It was like he was right there beside me. I looked down. I was standing next to my bed, stark naked. Suddenly embarrassed, I pulled an edge of my bedspread up in an effort to cover myself. Then I felt foolish.

"Dr. Friedman has been married five times," Michael was saying. "His first wife died. His second wife left him after they lost their son, Mark, to cystic fibrosis. Apparently, a controversial transplant procedure could have saved the boy's life, but Friedman wouldn't allow it."

"What?" I asked, surprised that a father wouldn't agree to almost anything to save his child's life.

"It required a portion of one of each parent's lungs. Evidently, Dr. Friedman was afraid Mrs. Friedman might not survive it, because she suffered from asthma and wasn't a terribly strong person as a result.

"Anyway, Mrs. Friedman blamed her husband for the boy's death and divorced him soon thereafter. Dr. Friedman hasn't been the same, according to several of the people I talked to. Although he has been married since then—three times, as a matter of fact—he's never gotten over Sondra."

"Sondra?" I asked, sitting down on the bed.

"She goes by her maiden name now. Leitel. Sondra Leitel. I found out Dr. Friedman has been openly courting Ms. Leitel, even though he is currently married to Anna Rhodes Friedman. From what I hear, Dr. Friedman and wife number five aren't getting along."

"I wouldn't imagine so," I said, "under those circumstances." Sondra Leitel, Tracey's mother. Now isn't that interesting? I mused.

Michael paused, then cleared his throat. "Samantha . . . about yesterday morning . . ."

I waited, thankful I couldn't see his face, thankful he wasn't there to put his warm hand on mine or touch my face.

"I apologize if I made you uncomfortable. I let my feelings get the better of me."

Good for you, I wanted to say. "You have nothing to apologize for, Michael," I said instead.

"I can't promise it won't happen again. But I'll do my best to be a gentleman."

"You are always a perfect gentleman, Michael," I said softly.

CHAPTER 29

•

Friday, July 24

Tracey was already in the lab when I got to the clinic at 7:45. Since she still didn't have a key, I figured Frank had let her in.

"Morning," I said, as casually as I could. I put my lunch in the refrigerator.

She did not turn around. "Good morning," she responded, her words sharp like icicles.

"I'm sorry I snapped at you yesterday. I guess I'm a little overly sensitive about my relationship with Michael Halsey."

Tracey shrugged. She still had her back to me. "I wasn't trying to be nosy," she said.

"I know you weren't," I replied. She didn't look anything like Ms. Leitel. I wondered where Mr. Nevins was. "Listen, is that offer of a beer tonight still good?"

At that, she turned around and smiled. "Sure. Is seven-thirty okay?"

The Brightwater Beach City Commission voted unanimously to begin plans to upgrade the oldest of the city's three sewage treatment plants. The mayor had summed up the argument by saying that the city could not risk paying fines on an old, outdated plant. It was either upgrade it or put a moratorium on new development. According to the *Times*, the word *moratorium* caused representatives of the local Chamber of Commerce to suggest the mayor wash her mouth out with soap. Or words to that effect.

Cynthia folded up the City and State section of the paper and stuffed it in the lab's trash can. She poured herself a cup of coffee. "Dr. Augustin should be pleased," she said. "That sewage treatment plant is all he's been interested in lately."

Not entirely, I thought. "Of course, now Tracey will have to wait another two weeks to see the *real* Dr. Augustin," I said.

Tracey looked up from her microscope. "*Real* Dr. Augustin?"

Cynthia frowned at me. "Don't pay any attention to her, Tracey. Samantha is just trying to be funny. Dr. Augustin gets a little worked up about local politics occasionally, but he's all bark and no bite."

Right, I thought. Try telling that to Tracey's predecessor. For that matter, tell it to *my* predecessor.

Edna Carlyle brought Rosco in at 8:15. I was in the supply closet behind Cynthia's desk when I heard Edna cry out.

"Lordy mercy!" she exclaimed.

Then I heard a lot of squealing and laughing. I stuck my head around the corner to see what mischief Rosco had gotten into and was surprised to find Edna and Tracey hugging and crying like classmates at their twenty-fifth reunion.

"Child, let me look at you," Edna said, holding Tracey at arm's length. "Why, you're nothing but skin and bones. What you need is a good home-cooked meal."

Tracey shook her head. "All those calories and fat grams. Besides, I'm a vegetarian now."

"What?" Edna asked.

"Vegetarian. I don't eat animal products. Well . . . just eggs and cheese."

Tracey seemed quite embarrassed by this flagrant violation of vegan ethics. But it was lost on Edna, who shook her head in disbelief.

"You'll waste away," she said. Then she grinned. "You have a boyfriend yet? I remember that cute blond boy with the earring you used to date. Drove Dr. F. crazy with all that long hair."

Tracey glanced over at Cynthia. Then she smiled at me, as

if to say, Okay, so I know how it feels. "Let's not talk about him, Edna," she said.

I heard a noise in the parking lot and turned my head. "It's Serafina," I said. "Our spay/declaw." I looked at the wall clock. "Dr. Augustin should be here shortly."

Tracey and Edna hugged each other one last time. Then Tracey promised to stop by the Friedman mansion for a visit.

"Your momma came to the house last week," Edna said, as Tracey was leading Rosco across the room.

Tracey stopped and turned around. "You're kidding, right?"

Edna laughed. "Now, would I kid about a thing like that?" She paused. "Anna was out of town."

At that moment, Serafina's owner pushed open the door and walked in, her kitten under her left arm. Rosco was busy snuffling the hallway door frame and did not appear to notice. Serafina, however, took one look at Rosco and proceeded to haul herself up onto her owner's shoulder, where she puffed out like a cobra and hissed venomously. Rosco, now curious, abandoned the door frame and turned his attention to the new arrival. Then he surprised everyone by lunging at the cat.

"Rosco!" shouted Edna. "You stop that."

The dog looked up at Edna and promptly sat down, his enormous front feet slewed out in typical basset hound fashion. His sad eyes moved from Edna to the kitten and back to Edna again. Tracey leaned over and grabbed Rosco's collar. She dragged him across the room and into the hallway.

"Talk to you later, Edna," she said, still leaning over. Then she let go of Rosco's collar and began pulling the unwilling animal down the hall by his leash.

At nine, Dr. Augustin came through the front door carrying a Krispy Kreme box. Pearl had been sitting like a sphinx in the front left corner of the reception room, watching lizards chase each other across the parking lot. At the sight of Dr. Augustin, she spun around and disappeared down the hall.

Dr. Augustin frowned, then continued on into the lab. He put the donut box on the counter next to Edna Carlyle's Tupperware container.

"I told the girl to give me a couple of apple fritters." He smiled. "Just for you, Samantha."

"Gee, thanks," I said.

With some difficulty, I ignored the goodies, told Tracey to put Pearl back in her cage, and joined Dr. Augustin in the surgery.

"I went to see Vivian last night," I said, after Serafina was asleep on the table, and her belly had been clipped and scrubbed. "She doesn't have Pearl's kitten."

"Of course she doesn't," said Dr. Augustin. He pumped a ribbon of antiseptic soap into the palm of his left hand. "Why would she?"

"I don't know. She works at the hospital. She has access to Ralph and had access to Howard Nichols. Originally, I thought maybe she was somehow involved in all of this."

"Vivian? That's ridiculous. Vivian Porter has more morals, and more money for that matter, than she knows what to do with. Her husband was an Episcopal minister, and her father was an ambassador to Japan or Australia. Somewhere over there." He waved a foamy hand over his shoulder.

I opened a gown pack for him. "Why didn't you tell me about Vivian?"

"You didn't ask." He picked up a sterile towel and dried his hands. He tossed the towel on the counter and picked up the gown. "Is that all you found out? That Vivian doesn't have that kitten?"

I tied the gown closed in back and opened his glove pack. He pulled on each glove, snapping the latex cuff smartly over his gown sleeves.

"No, that's not all I found out," I said, just as smartly. "I think Ramona James has it. The kitten, I mean. Vivian said Ramona mentioned she had acquired a kitten with some kind of birth defect."

Dr. Augustin stopped and looked over his mask at me. "Oh, really?"

"Yes, really."

He took a drape out of the spay pack and positioned it over the cat's abdomen. "Now we're getting somewhere," he said.

I knew he was smiling under his mask. His eyes glowed like polished onyx spheres.

"I have plans tonight," he said, "but I think you and I need to pay Ms. James a little visit tomorrow after work."

At first, I didn't say anything. In truth, I was less concerned about his plans for Saturday evening than I was about his plans for *that* evening. Then I remembered what Michael had told me.

"Tracey is Dr. Friedman's stepdaughter," I said. "Her mother is that Leitel woman with the Himalayans. Leitel is her maiden name."

Dr. Augustin was reaching for the scalpel. His hand stopped in midair. "Who told you that? Tracey?" He picked up the scalpel.

"No, Michael did. He called last night. He's been checking up on Dr. Friedman. I know you don't think Norman Friedman has anything to do with the murders, but Michael volunteered to check on him, anyway."

Dr. Augustin chuckled. "Good old Michael Halsey," he said.

I was probably being a trifle paranoic, but I thought he put emphasis on the word *old*.

I quickly changed the subject. "So, is our visit to Ramona James's house intended as a social call or another late night B&E?"

Dr. Augustin looked up at me. "What do you think?" he asked. Then he winked.

CHAPTER 30

•

I got to the Chilly Bin about 7:15. The parking lot was full. After circling the block twice, I decided to leave my car in front of a nearby Winn-Dixie. It seemed like a safe place, despite the bearded man standing at the curb. His faded Tampa Bay Buccaneers T-shirt, not the Bible he clutched in his right hand, made me suspicious. He smiled at me. He was missing most of his front teeth. He was, nevertheless, able to "praise the Lord" several times when a woman exiting the grocery store tossed a dollar bill at him.

I hurried across the street. In the background, I could hear the man begin to quote a verse from the book of Revelation, his voice deep and filled with emotion.

"'And the sea gave up the dead which were in it; and death and hell delivered up the dead which were in them: and they were judged every man according to their works.'"

Tracey met me at the entrance to the Chilly Bin. She was wearing bright red bib overalls, a red and white striped shirt, and white tennis shoes with red laces. The overalls hid her stick-thin figure. Farmer's best never looked so good.

"Where did you have to park?" she asked me.

"In front of the Winn-Dixie," I said, pointing down the street.

"Me, too." She laughed. "Did you get a load of that preacher man?"

While we waited in line to get in, we chatted, mostly about harmless, inconsequential things. Like, how can anyone possibly eat a hamburger knowing it was once a big, dumb, warm, furry, brown-eyed cow? And how to make soy burgers taste just like hamburgers. What wasn't mentioned was why a vegetarian would want to do that in the first place.

Then Tracey noticed my earrings. "These are nice," she said, fingering the left one.

"Thanks," I said. "A friend brought them back from St. Thomas." Why did I find it so difficult to admit my relationship with Michael to her? Perhaps because he was old enough to be her father. But the way she smiled told me she knew who I was talking about.

We had our IDs checked at the door. The guy who looked at mine grinned as he handed it back to me. I started to ask him for a cane but thought better of it.

Once inside, it took a few seconds for our eyes to adjust. The walls were painted dark blue, with big green swirls overlaid with an intricate, recurring black and white design. It was an interesting color scheme and probably would have been attractive in the daylight, but the dark paint only accentuated the cavelike atmosphere of the windowless establishment.

Tracey spied a table in the corner and took off. I followed her, nearly colliding with a girl in purple bicycle shorts and a yellow and purple spandex midriff top. She looked like an x-rated Easter egg. She frowned at me. Her eye makeup reminded me of a raccoon.

It was obvious after a minute or so spent surveying the room that I was one of the few over-thirty people there. In fact, the average age of the patrons in the Chilly Bin fell somewhat short of legal. At the door, a man with an indelible glow-in-the-dark marking pen had been painting *x*'s on the hands of those under twenty-one. Evidently, it allowed the cocktail waitresses to keep track of who was drinking age and who wasn't. The luminous green tattoos bounced up and down from all corners of the room like a swarm of fireflies. To make matters worse, every male I passed took one look at me and straightened up as though his mother had just entered the room. If Michael Halsey had come along, I thought, they'd call him "Gramps" or "Pops" and offer to get him a glass of prune juice.

Tracey went to the bar to get us a beer, since our waitress was still several tables away. I was happy she volunteered. I certainly didn't want to venture out into kiddyland, but we only had twenty minutes of relative quiet, until Frank's band started playing. I wanted to question Tracey while I could still hear her answers. What most interested me was Tracey's relationship with her stepfather. Had Dr. Friedman given her the car? Or did Tracey hate him enough to . . . ? To what?

I saw Frank emerge from a side door. He waved at Tracey, then went over to the stage, where he began to fiddle with an enormous amplifier. I suddenly wished I had brought along some earplugs.

Tracey put two Steinlagers and a couple of paper coasters on the table. "Isn't Frank wonderful?" she asked, wiping off the mouth of her bottle. Her expression—the rolling eyes and flushed cheeks—reminded me of the look Cynthia gets whenever Michael comes to the clinic.

"We *are* talking about Frank Jennings, aren't we?" I asked in genuine amazement. Had I missed something?

Tracey gave me a sideways glance. "He works hard all day so he can pursue his art," she said. "I think that's, well, pretty noble, don't you?"

Noble wasn't one of the adjectives I routinely used to describe Frank, but I wasn't going to argue with her.

I watched as a second male with shoulder-length hair and a grinning demon on his T-shirt joined Frank. "So why did you leave Dr. Farmington?" I asked Tracey.

She shrugged. "I needed a change." She took a drink from her beer bottle.

I was pretty sure there was more to it than that. I prayed she hadn't left a perfectly good job in the hopes of finding a boyfriend someplace else. Had I been that irresponsible and immature at twenty-one?

Suddenly Tracey looked up. "Have you ever been harassed? I mean, sexually?"

I stared at her. "Dr. Farmington?" I asked. Surely not. The guy had four kids and coached Little League.

"Not Dr. Farmington," Tracey said. "Dr. Shaw."

I thought back and remembered the way he had looked at

me. "God, Tracey, what did he do? Better yet, what did *you* do?"

"At first, I tried to ignore him. You know, I'd be working in the lab, standing by the sink or the blood machine, and he'd go for something in a bottom cabinet and brush against me as he stood up. Stuff like that. And he'd make little suggestive remarks or tell dirty jokes where only I could hear him." She cringed. "His eyes, the way he looked at me . . . Then, late one afternoon when he and I were alone, he asked me out. I said I couldn't, and he dropped it. Boy, did I feel relieved. But then he tried again a couple of days later. I said no, again, and that time he hinted that he was responsible for my evaluation, which was due the following month." She stopped and stared at a couple making out two tables over.

"So what did you do?"

She looked down at her hands. "I went out with him."

I didn't say anything. The implication was there, plain as day.

She shivered. "But I didn't go to bed with him, if that's what you're thinking."

I had been, of course, and I was relieved. I wasn't crazy about Tracey, but I despised men like Dr. Shaw.

"After the restaurant," she continued, "I asked him to take me home. I'd spent the entire meal listening to his raunchy jokes and trying to keep his hands off my legs, and I was exhausted." She took another drink of beer.

"When we got to my apartment, he insisted on walking me upstairs. I knew he'd try to get in, so I pretended I'd lost my key. It meant we had to go to the manager's office. I guess Dr. Shaw realized he wouldn't be able to force his way into my apartment with Jim there."

"Did you say something to Dr. Farmington?" I asked.

She gnawed on a fingernail, then held her left hand out and studied the remaining nails.

"Well, did you?"

She picked up her beer, then put it down again. She shook her head.

"Why not? Don't tell me you were afraid of Dr. Farmington. You don't seem like the type."

Tracey lifted her shoulders and let them drop. She reminded me of a little kid just then. I expected her to say, "I dunno."

"Dr. Farmington had spent eight months trying to find an internist for the practice," she said instead. "His requirements were really tough. Dr. Shaw met every one. How could I complain about him?"

"That's very 'noble,' Tracey, to use your word. But what about the next technician Dr. Shaw harasses?"

She didn't say anything.

"So that's when you decided you needed a change?"

She nodded. "I knew Norman Friedman took Rosco to Dr. Augustin and had since the dog was a puppy. Norman says Dr. Augustin is a better doctor than a lot of Norman's MD friends, which is pretty impressive, when you think about it. Anyway, I couldn't believe my luck when you mentioned there was a job opening at your clinic. Naturally, I jumped at the chance." She paused. "Dr. Farmington let me go without the usual two weeks' notice. I think he knew there was a problem between me and Dr. Shaw."

I looked at my watch. I was running out of time.

"I didn't know you were Norman Friedman's stepdaughter," I said, rather abruptly. There wasn't any point in beating around the bush.

Tracey downed several ounces of her beer. She wiped her mouth on her hand. "I try not to dwell on the past," she said.

"I know about Mark and the surgery that could have saved him."

Tracey looked at me, her expression less than friendly. "You're wrong," she said. "You don't know anything about it." She drank some more and stared across the room, her back very straight.

"What I mean is, I know that when Mark died, your family suffered terribly for a lot of reasons."

Tracey lowered her eyes and pretended to read the label on her beer bottle. Her whole body seemed to collapse inwardly, like a cake suddenly falling.

"Norman loved—loves—my mother more than anything in the world," she said, her voice breaking slightly. "He was so convinced she would die if he agreed to the transplant that he was willing to let Mark die to save her." She looked at me. "Norman is Jewish, and Mark was his only son. Do you know what that means?"

I thought she might cry then, but she straightened up and looked me square in the face.

"My mother ditched Norman. I'll never forgive her for that." She looked at her empty beer bottle, then searched for a waitress.

An ear-shattering screech suddenly emanated from one of the amplifiers. That was followed by a loud tapping sound. I looked up. The band had assembled, and Frank was pecking at the lead singer's microphone with his right index finger. Apparently satisfied that it was working, he walked over to his drums and sat down.

"She tried to turn me against Norman," Tracey continued. "And for a while, it worked. I moved out of the house. Refused to go back, even to visit poor Edna. But then I got to thinking. If Mom *had* agreed to the surgery and Mark had died anyway, would things be any different? She and Norman weren't getting along. Mark's death was an excuse to leave. I realize that now. I sometimes wonder if my dad left us, or if we left my dad. I don't think my mother is into long-term relationships. She's had three chances, and she's blown every one of them." She smiled wryly. "Of course, I have to admit, Norman isn't the world's greatest husband, either. But he was a good father, despite what other people may say."

Our waitress arrived just as the band started up. Tracey screamed her order to the woman, but finally had to hold up her bottle and two fingers. The waitress, evidently used to sign language, nodded and left.

I watched Frank pound on his drums. I hated to admit it, but he was a pretty fair drummer. What really amazed me, though, was the fact that he could clean and bathe dogs all day long after mimicking a whirling dervish for half the night. Endurance, rather than nobility, was what came to mind when I thought of Frank Jennings.

Our waitress came by with our beers. I tried to pay for them, but Tracey wouldn't let me. She handed the woman a twenty. I wanted to intercept it and look for the polyester ribbon, but I just watched, while the waitress made change. Tracey gave her a two-dollar tip.

The first song ended, and the crowd cheered and whistled their appreciation, either for the music or for the sudden cessation of noise. Then, before our ears stopped ringing, the lead guitar cranked up again. It was obviously a dance number, because a herd of patrons immediately started a stampede to the parquet floor in front of the band. The Easter egg was among them. Her companion was a boy around seventeen. He had more hair hanging in his face than he had on the back of his head, and his baggy trousers were so low on his hips, his boxer shorts were showing. They had red hearts on them.

Two dozen variously shaped bodies wearing a variety of strange and unusual outfits writhed and bounced and sweated, elbow to elbow, never actually moving, at least not laterally. It hadn't been so long ago that I couldn't remember the thrill of being packed like sardines on a dance floor, trying not to get stepped on while gazing into the eyes of your partner. It helped if you were a little inebriated.

When the music ended, the dancers scurried back to their drinks and their verbal flirting. Many of them, I felt certain, would continue the exercise in a more private setting. What was the going slogan on billboards these days? "Get high, get stupid, get AIDS."

But when you are young, nothing can hurt you.

"I didn't mean to bore you with my private life, Sam," said Tracey, as if the musical interlude had never occurred. "Let's talk about something else. Like what made you move to Florida. I would have thought New York or Boston would be more exciting. You know, not as many old people." She smiled and sipped her beer.

I wasn't interested in discussing my private life, either. Fortunately, the band was taking a break. I saw Frank grab a Coke from the bartender. As he drank it, he let his eyes move over the room. When he spotted Tracey and me, he headed in our direction.

"Hey, you made it, Samantha," he said happily. He looked like he always did—T-shirt drenched, hair plastered to his face and neck. The odor of flea shampoo had been replaced by a less pleasant aroma. "So, what's your opinion?"

"Not bad," I said. "Not bad at all. I mean it."

Tracey gazed up at Frank adoringly. I needed to leave before I started laughing.

"I have to go," I said, getting up.

Frank instantly commandeered my chair and took Tracey's hand.

"I'll see you in the morning," I said, apparently to deaf ears. Then I grinned. "Don't forget, Frank, tomorrow is bath day."

"Sure, Sam, bath day." He never took his eyes off of Tracey.

I threaded my way through the crowd and stepped outside into the heat and humidity. The line at the door was all the way around the building. It was composed mostly of teens, but a surprising number of the Generation X crowd had joined the pack.

I hoped Frank was getting a percentage of the take. Maybe I've underestimated him, I said to myself. Maybe Tracey is a better judge of character than I am. After all, I didn't like Tracey in the beginning, either. But as I got in my car and headed for home, I couldn't shake the feeling that she was hiding something from me. Something important.

CHAPTER 31

•

Saturday, July 25

That suspicious feeling stayed with me. I was having trouble concentrating on the business at hand.

"Why is there a litter pan in that Yorkie's cage?" asked Dr. Augustin. He stood, hands on hips, in the doorway between the surgery and Isolation.

I refused to look directly at him. "I meant to put it in Randy's cage," I said. "Something must have distracted me." I finished loading the autoclave and switched it on.

"Yes, well, let's get it together, shall we? It's bad enough Frank decides to sleep in on a Saturday without you nodding off." He barreled past me and went across the hall to the kennel.

I heard him snap at Tracey. Then, to my amusement, Tracey responded in kind.

"I am working as fast as I can, *Dr. Augustin*," she yelled over the noise of the dryer. "You could help by combing out that Persian." It was obvious that Dr. Augustin didn't frighten Tracey one bit.

Dr. Augustin muttered something unintelligible. I was grinning broadly, when he suddenly reappeared in the doorway.

"Wipe that smirk off your face, Samantha," he snapped, "and get in there and help her!" He looked at his watch. "Our first client is due in fifteen minutes, and both of you had better be ready." He gave me a departing scowl, then huffed off down the hall like a snotty kid.

"Typical male," Tracey said angrily, after I had joined her in the kennel.

She was bathing a black Labrador. It was hard to tell which of them was the more lathered up.

"He gets this way sometimes," I said. "He'll forget all about it, though, trust me. In an hour, he won't even remember he was back here." Who did I think I was kidding?

I took the Persian out of the dryer cage and began brushing his tangled orange coat. The cat was used to it. He growled softly, just to let me know he wasn't a pushover, but didn't try to bite me or escape.

"I guess Frank isn't coming in," I said. "Thanks for picking up the slack."

"No problem."

I wondered when she had left the Chilly Bin. If she had waited until the place closed and the band packed up their gear, she certainly didn't show it.

Tracey lifted the Lab out of the tub. His legs flailed, and she staggered a bit, but she was managing, so I continued to comb out the Persian.

"I wanted to thank you, Sam," she said, after transferring the dryer to the dog's cage and setting the timer.

"For what?"

The Labrador squinted, as the stream of warm air hit his face. He turned around and let the dryer blow on his tail.

"For being nice. For going to the Chilly Bin with me last night." She paused. "I . . . we kind of got off to a bad start, didn't we?"

I worked a mat out of the Persian's belly.

"I was just so happy to get away from Dr. Shaw," she said. "I guess I *was* a little cocky that first couple of days, wasn't I?"

I ran a slicker over the cat and put him back in his cage. He looked beautiful. "Think nothing of it," I said. But I kept my eyes on the cat.

Tracey turned off the light to quiet the dogs, and we headed for the lab.

Before we got there, however, Cynthia's voice crackled out of the intercom speaker. "Samantha," she said. "Mr. Clark is here with Mad Max. Max will be boarding until Monday." She sounded extremely amused.

I groaned and started down the hall. "You'd better hope Frank gets here soon," I told Tracey over my shoulder. "This dog weighs twice what you weigh and has a neck like a cast-iron pipe." I could already feel my shoulder separating.

Tracey laughed nervously. "I don't guess we get hazardous duty pay, do we?"

We were busy with clients all morning and, at lunch, Tracey and I had to finish bathing and dipping, while Dr. Augustin enjoyed an Italian meatball sub from Mario's. My earlier feeling of uncertainty was replaced by an almost overwhelming desire to turn the largest, wettest dog I could find loose in Dr. Augustin's office.

At three, we had a cancellation. Dr. Augustin went into his office carrying a stack of files that Cynthia said were seriously in arrears and needed his attention. She told him she had done everything she could to get the money out of the clients, and now it was his turn.

Such a large number of overdue accounts did nothing to improve Dr. Augustin's mood. He rattled papers and punched the keys on his adding machine with such a vengeance, I avoided him like the plague.

At four, our last client left, and Tracey went back to the kennel to turn the dogs out and feed everybody. I had just started treatments when Dr. Augustin called my name. I closed the door to Benji's cage and went into his office.

"I think we should wait until dark to pay Ms. James a visit, don't you?" he asked. He was smiling, his black mood clearly buoyed by the prospect of our impending felony.

For the second time that day, I came close to handing him my resignation. I was tired of being taken for granted.

"Well?" he asked. He was staring at me.

"Sure," I said, kicking myself mentally. "Should I wear black for the occasion?"

CHAPTER 32

•

I went home to feed my cats, change clothes, and eat dinner. Over a bowl of canned vegetable soup and a BLT, minus the *B*, I watched the news and thought about the prospect of jail time. Life was so much simpler, I told myself, when a bad day meant Dr. Augustin had caught someone undercharging a client for flea shampoo.

At 8:30, I got into Dr. Augustin's Jeep. I noticed he had changed his T-shirt. The current one suited the occasion—all black except for a tiny white line drawing of a scuba diver and a much larger drawing of a great white shark, jaws open wide. A small balloon emanating from the diver's mouth had the words, "Oh shit!" printed in it.

"If she isn't home, we'll find a way inside and look for the kitten," he said matter-of-factly, like he was giving me instructions for setting my VCR.

"What if she's there?"

He was quiet for a minute. "I'll think of something," he said finally.

I just bet you will, I thought.

There was no Ramona James in the phone book, but an R. James lived twelve blocks from the hospital on Riviera Drive. Dr. Augustin drove by the house, a typical Florida retirement home—concrete block rectangle, identical to its neighbors except for the color of the shutters. Where pigmy date palms and bird of paradise swim in a sea of gravel, and pink plastic flamingos constitute the area's only wildlife.

We left the Jeep around the corner and walked back to the James residence. No one appeared to be home. The house was dark, the carport empty. It was almost nine o'clock. A small but feisty dog barked wildly from somewhere close, but nothing came of it. I was starting to sweat and not entirely from the heat. Dr. Augustin was apparently feeling it, too, because when we reached the carport, he stopped and dug a gumball out of his pocket. He offered it to me, and when I declined, he popped it in his mouth and started to chew. Sometimes I wonder why he doesn't suffer from some type of jaw disorder. Something that would necessitate wiring his mouth closed to repair would be nice.

I followed him around to the back of the house, noticing that R. James had real grass and several large rosebushes. A bird feeder hung from the carport roof. I had to dodge it as we walked between the James house and its neighbor to the left.

Dr. Augustin switched on his flashlight and aimed it through a window. Then he switched it off. He handed me a pair of surgical gloves, put on a pair of his own, and went to work on the back door lock. I noticed he had graduated to the big time, with the acquisition of a set of lock picks. He'd obviously been practicing, too, because we were inside in under a minute.

He closed the door and switched his flashlight back on, then played the beam slowly around the room. We were in the dining area. The kitchen was to our left, the living room straight ahead. Dr. Augustin studied the items on the small dinette table. He picked up a pale green, legal-sized envelope, a power bill, by the look of it.

"This is the place," he said softly, reading the name on the envelope.

I turned my head away from him, toward the kitchen. "Listen," I said quickly. "Over there."

Dr. Augustin pointed the flashlight into the tiny kitchen. Stainless steel and chipped avocado enamel reflected the light back at us, and shadows from various small appliances moved across the countertop like ghosts. I half-expected to see a rottweiler or Vivian Porter's Doberman crouched in the corner, ready to tear our throats out. But the source of the noise wasn't a dog. Shoved up against the wall next to the refrigerator was a large animal crate. I went over to it and knelt down. Dr. Augustin handed me the flashlight, and I pointed the beam inside.

A roly-poly black and white kitten, slightly larger than Randy, sat atop a small stuffed bear and cried its heart out at me. Then the kitten tumbled off the bear and made its way across the crate to the door. It poked a tiny paw through the chicken wire.

I handed the flashlight back to Dr. Augustin and opened the crate. The kitten fell out in its haste to reach me, then began to climb up my leg.

"Let's have a look, shall we?" said Dr. Augustin, plucking the kitten off of my shorts.

I took the flashlight and directed the beam into the cat's mouth, which Dr. Augustin had pried open. The cleft was obvious but, like Randy's, not severe.

"Similar to the cleft on the kitten back at the clinic," said Dr. Augustin. He was still refusing to call the cat Randy.

"So what do we do now?" I asked, hopeful he would say we could leave. Take the kitten and retreat to the safety of the Jeep.

The little dog with the big mouth started to bark again. The sound unnerved me but apparently had no effect on Dr. Augustin. He put the kitten back in its crate and closed the door.

"Check around for anything that might tie Ramona to the counterfeiting. See if you can find a sample of her handwriting. One we can compare to the note in the basket." He took something out of his pocket, then handed me the flashlight. "I'll use this," he said. He was holding a small penlight. He turned it on.

"We know there's at least a fourth party involved," he said. "With Howard Nichols dead and Mick in jail and Ramona James at the hospital, someone else obviously tried to kill Bill O'Shea."

"Mick wasn't in jail," I said quietly.

Dr. Augustin aimed his penlight at me, and I squinted. "What?" he barked. He didn't sound the least bit pleased.

"He called Thursday," I said, "to see if he could come get

Jonesy. He told me his lawyer got him out on bail Tuesday afternoon."

Dr. Augustin lowered the penlight. "You should have told me that, Samantha. It changes things just a tad, doesn't it?"

"I forgot," I lied. "Besides, you still need proof that Ramona James is involved, don't you? And proof that Mick killed Arnie and Howard Nichols? Maybe a fourth party really does exist, and that person killed all those people. Maybe Mick isn't guilty of anything, and we should be helping him, not trying to put him away."

I heard a noise and pointed my flashlight into the crate. The kitten was perched on the bear again.

"Maybe," said Dr. Augustin. "To tell you the truth, I'm not sure of anything anymore."

"That's too bad," said a familiar voice directly behind me.

Suddenly the kitchen was filled with a brilliant, painful white light. I squinted and turned around. Toby Reynolds stood in the hall doorway. He had a gun pointed at me. I stared at him.

"You can put down that flashlight, Samantha," Toby said, his voice almost pleasant. "You, too, Dr. Augustin." He pointed toward the dinette table. "And then we can wait for Ramona to get home." He nodded his head toward the living room. "Samantha, you first."

I put the flashlight on the table and walked slowly across to the living room. I sat down on the sofa. The inner supports creaked and groaned, and the brown tweed cushions, nearly threadbare in places, gave off a faint odor of sweat. Dr. Augustin followed me and started to sit down on one of the two recliners in the room, but Toby clucked his tongue and shook his head.

"Next to Samantha, please." He switched on a light.

Dr. Augustin shrugged and took the opposite end of the sofa. He looked at me briefly. His eyes were very black.

Toby sat down in one of the recliners. It appeared to be new, upholstered in a deep wine-colored fabric, and was the kind that swiveled. He put his right hand on the chair arm, gun barrel pointed at my throat.

"I like you, Samantha," he said, smiling. "But you should

stay out of the private detective business. It isn't healthy." He laughed suddenly, then stopped, just as suddenly, and frowned. "And you, *Doctor* Augustin, are responsible for putting Samantha's life in danger. Don't you feel ashamed of yourself?" His emphasis on Dr. Augustin's title was exaggerated and sarcastic.

He was still gorgeous, still had his wreath of golden curls and beautiful bronze biceps. But his eyes were cold, his mouth a thin, hard line.

"So where is this going?" asked Dr. Augustin.

Toby looked back at me and, for a very brief moment, I saw indecision cloud his features. "Nowhere, somewhere," he said. Then he smiled again.

I heard a car approach. It slowed, then turned into the driveway. It came to a stop in the carport. Pretty soon, Ramona James opened the kitchen door. She stepped inside.

"Toby?" she called.

She was dressed in her uniform. Her hair was down, and a little nursing cap sat atop her head like a white dove, wings outstretched. When she saw the gun, and Dr. Augustin and me sitting on the sofa, she stopped. Her eyes grew very wide, and her face lost some of its color.

"Toby? What's going on here? Where did you get that gun? And what are they doing here?" Very slowly, she walked over to the dinette table and put her purse down. She never took her eyes off the gun.

"I found these two sneaking around in your kitchen," said Toby.

"Maybe you should call the police," Dr. Augustin offered. He was clenching and unclenching his left fist, like he frequently does when he is tense.

They both ignored him.

"I asked you where you got that gun," said Ramona. She started around the table, then stopped.

"From Bill O'Shea," said Toby. "I figured he owed it to me." He pressed his left index finger into his temple and winced. "The bastard fired me. Said he didn't like my attitude."

I could feel myself start to tremble. I looked over at Dr. Augustin. He was watching Toby intently. It was difficult to tell, because of the beard, but he seemed pretty calm then. And both hands were motionless, one on the sofa arm, the other by his side. He probably has a plan, I told myself, and tried to relax.

A siren sounded several blocks away. It grew louder, and I prayed the neighbor with the dog had seen our flashlight and called the police. But the wailing passed us by, and then it was gone.

Toby waved the gun back and forth. "So, Ramona, darling, what should we do about the good doctor and his lovely assistant?"

"Let them go, Toby," she said. "Please let them go."

Toby clucked his tongue. "Tsk, tsk, Ramona, dear. You're not thinking. If we let them go, they'll run straight to the cops. And the doc, here, knows too much already, don't you, *Doctor* Augustin?"

"How many people have you killed to date, Toby?" asked Dr. Augustin, his voice low, his eyes drifting over to Ramona. "Eight? Nine? Let's see, there was Arnie Silor and then Howard Nichols, followed by that Tyndall character. Who else have you done in?"

Ramona ventured a few steps in Toby's direction. "What is he talking about, Toby?" she demanded. "You said Mick killed Arnie and Howard, because he didn't trust them to keep quiet. That Mick was losing it. I thought that's why you needed to know where Mick's parents lived. You said it was our insurance policy in case he took off with the money."

"Okay, so I lied," Toby said, looking over at Ramona. He chuckled. It was a mirthless cackling sound. "That nerd Mick Peters hasn't got the balls to get himself out of hock, let alone kill anyone."

I watched Ramona's expression evolve from one of confusion to one of terror. "Oh my God," she said. She backed up and placed her hand over her mouth.

"The rest of them were dead, anyway," Toby said, looking back at Dr. Augustin. "Or close to it. I just hurried up the process." He laughed. "Hey, you guys should thank me, actually, for getting rid of a bunch of drunks and smokers. Besides, Norman Asshole Friedman was just keeping them alive so he could continue sucking money out of their insurance companies. I'll bet he's having a hard time explaining why his patients are dropping like flies. Maybe the bastard will lose his license. Wouldn't that be lucky for us? Hell, I did a lot of people a favor."

The kitten started to cry, and Ramona looked over at it. "What's the matter, Katie, honey?" she crooned. "Are you hungry?"

She smiled. It was an odd expression—vacant and mindless—and I realized the woman was probably in shock. She went into the kitchen. I heard her open the refrigerator. Then the microwave started to hum. She must be getting ready to feed the kitten, I thought. And I wanted to help her. More than anything, I wanted to hold that little fur ball under my chin and let its purring calm me.

I was beginning to feel dizzy, and my hands and feet were numb. Without realizing it, I had been hyperventilating. Not overtly panting, but hyperventilating just the same. Which suddenly gave me an idea. If Dr. Augustin had a plan, and I sincerely hoped he did, he would need a diversion. So I continued to breathe in and out as rapidly as I could, careful not to attract Toby's attention.

In high school, Lisa Jaffe could pass out at will. It was a neat trick and useful, too. She could postpone exams, avoid PE and biology lab whenever the need arose. Fainting was also useful when you wanted to attract the attention of big strong basketball players who otherwise might not give you the time of day. What red-blooded American teenage male can pass up an opportunity to help a lady in distress?

There were tiny white spots exploding across my field of vision.

"I don't feel well," I said.

To help things along, I abruptly stood up. The tiny white spots coalesced and then turned to black. My legs buckled, and I was floating somewhere very warm, and then a sharp pain across my forehead and a loud crack intruded into the darkness. I had bounced off the coffee table on my way to the floor.

Since, at that point, I was fully conscious, the impulse to open my eyes, groan in agony, and check my head for signs of damage was pretty great. I resisted, however, and feigned unconsciousness. The pain in my head pulsed with each surge of blood.

"Oh great!" I heard Toby exclaim.

Then I heard someone walk across the rug. A blunt object—a foot—shoved me onto my back.

"Get away from her," Dr Augustin hissed.

"Toby, for God's sake," Ramona pleaded from the dining area, her voice very shrill. She apparently was holding the kitten, because its mewing was loud and insistent.

"Okay, okay," Toby said impatiently. "But shut up that damned cat, before I do." He paused. "Put her on the couch."

I felt Dr. Augustin's arms slide beneath my shoulders and knees. I knew it was him, because I could smell his bubble gum. That damned gum, sickly sweet artificial flavor and all, never smelled so good. It was grape. And suddenly, inexplicably, an image of the Fruit-of-the-Loom guys popped into my head. I almost smiled.

"Hurry it up," snapped Toby.

Dr. Augustin's muscles flexed, and he lifted me off the floor without too much effort, then eased me onto the sofa.

"She's bleeding," he said. His hand, ice-cold—the only indication I'd had so far that he was the least bit afraid—smoothed the hair back off my forehead.

I opened one eye briefly. Dr. Augustin smiled through his beard.

"It's nothing. A scratch," Toby said. "Now sit down. Over there."

The recliner by the front window creaked. "At least let me put a cold compress on her head," Dr. Augustin said. "If you're going to kill us, don't you think it would be more sporting for Samantha to be awake when you do it? I don't think even you could shoot an unconscious person." He paused. "I've got a better idea. You could give us a running start. That would be really sporting, now wouldn't it?"

"Shut up!" Toby hissed.

"Just trying to help," said Dr. Augustin.

"I'm warning you, *shut up!*"

Dr. Augustin had started that little dialogue for a reason. He was not one to babble, and when he was mad, he tended to be rather closemouthed. Either he wanted Toby to do something stupid, like shoot us both and be done with it, or he was trying to send me a message. Now what had he said? Something about a running start.

I heard Toby's recliner creak. "Okay, Doc, you can get some ice for the little lady. But keep in mind, I won't think twice about plugging you. Or her."

"Sure," said Dr. Augustin.

Someone walked past me to the dining area. I risked cracking an eyelid. Dr. Augustin evidently had gone into the kitchen, because I couldn't see him. Toby was standing by the dinette table, his back to me. I opened both eyes and looked at the front door. It had a dead bolt. If Toby had come in that way, and I was pretty sure he must have, then maybe it wasn't locked. If it was, I still might be able to turn the dead bolt and open the door before he heard me. I didn't think Toby would really shoot me. I wasn't sure why, but I didn't. I couldn't say the same about Dr. Augustin's fate, however.

Suddenly, a loud crash, followed by the sound of ice cubes dancing across the kitchen floor, caused Toby to step just out of sight.

I got up, winced as my head started to throb, ran lightly to the door, and turned the knob. I pushed the door open. Behind me, Toby cried out.

"Hey!"

I stepped out onto the front porch while Toby yelled at Ramona to shoot Dr. Augustin if he so much as twitched. Then I took off across the lawn.

CHAPTER 33

•

Like a terrified cat or dog, I ran down the street with no idea where I was headed. I could hear Toby a short distance behind me. He was wearing loafers, and his soles smacked the pavement with a frighteningly quick tempo.

I guessed he had given the gun to Ramona, so she could guard Dr. Augustin. Toby won't need a gun, though, I reminded myself, if he manages to catch me. And then I thought of Arnie and Howard Nichols and Bill O'Shea and my throat began to constrict from the fear. I was beginning to rasp and wheeze. Stop it! I told myself. Stop it!

I was nearing the intersection of Riviera and Gulf Drive. I knew the Brightwater Beach Police Station was on Gulf Drive, a couple of miles or so from the hospital. What I couldn't remember was which way—north or south of the hospital. I took a chance and turned north, toward St. Luke's.

Traffic was heavy, mostly teenagers cruising the beach on a Saturday night or tourists looking for someplace to eat. I considered stopping one of them. I could claim I was being chased by a rapist. But given the general fear tourists in Florida have of strangers, I figured no one would dare roll their window down to speak to me, much less let me into their car.

The neon signs up and down the beach, advertising everything from fast food and two-dollar T-shirts to time-shares, make streetlights unnecessary. The effect is garish and haphazard. Hotels and motels, lounges and overpriced eateries are jammed so tightly together, only the required public access corridors every few blocks allow passing motorists a brief glimpse of west Florida's famous shimmering white sandy beach and bathwater-warm Gulf of Mexico.

The odor of fried fish, hamburgers, and suntan lotion, mingled with exhaust fumes, was making me nauseous. And I was getting tired of dodging people, most of whom were too self-absorbed to give way when I approached. So I moved off the sidewalk onto the roadway. I was running with the traffic, which is never a good idea, but I didn't want to slow down or, worse, have to stop altogether until the light changed.

Toby was gaining on me. I could see him over my left shoulder without turning my head more than a few degrees. I should have had an advantage. I was wearing running shoes, and by his own admission, he was not built like a runner. I thought about Jeffrey. He would tell me to reach out, lengthen my stride, relax my shoulders and arms. Take nice even breaths.

I picked it up, surprised my head wasn't throbbing and I hadn't developed a cramp somewhere. I passed the hospital. I knew I could use one of the pay phones in the emergency room to call the cops. I didn't even need a quarter. But that would take too long. And how could I be sure they would actually respond? Toby certainly would head back to Ramona's. And then what? "Plug" Dr. Augustin?

I glanced over my shoulder again and was relieved to see that Toby had fallen behind almost a full block. And he was running awkwardly, his arms high and tight, his feet barely leaving the pavement.

I smiled and ran on ahead. It would take him a while to reach Ramona's. He would have to walk, and that would give the cops time to rescue Dr. Augustin. Assuming the police station was up ahead somewhere.

I ignored a red light and crossed Ibis Avenue, dodging traffic as I went. Several cars honked. One joker suggested I do an unnatural act on myself, but I was too focused to suggest he do likewise. However, from the great cloud of white smoke the guy's car emitted as he whipped past me, and the temporary tag taped to his rear window, it seemed some crafty used car salesman had already worked him over but good.

The police station appeared suddenly like a beacon in the night. I ran up the sidewalk and through the front door.

"Please help me," I gasped. I bent over and tried to breathe. "A man back there is chasing me. He's already killed three people and now I think he's going to kill my boss if someone doesn't stop him." I straightened up.

A woman behind the half-wall/counter got up from her desk and slowly approached me. "Do you know the man?" she asked.

Another woman came over and stood beside her. They both eyed me suspiciously, like I had just escaped from the state mental hospital. I saw the second woman press what I gathered was a silent alarm located under the lip of the counter. I couldn't hear anything, but a moment later, a man in a patrolman's uniform came through a side door. He joined the two women.

"What seems to be the problem here?" he asked, his expression very stern.

I took a deep breath. Sweat trickled down my face and neck. I could only imagine how I looked. Then I realized I didn't have any identification on me.

"My name is Samantha Holt," I said quickly. "I work for Dr. Louis Augustin over at Paradise Cay Animal Hospital. It's a very long story, but the man who killed Arnold Silor and that purchasing director from St. Luke's—Howard Nichols—and another man whose name I can't remember just now was holding Dr. Augustin and me at gunpoint at his girlfriend's house. We figured out he did it, and now he is threatening to kill us. I got away and ran here, but Dr. Augustin is still at the girlfriend's house, and he is probably on his way back there right now to kill Dr. Augustin." I stopped abruptly and wiped the sweat out of my eyes with the sleeve of my T-shirt.

"Who is 'he'?" the cop asked.

"He?" I thought. "Oh, sorry. His name is Toby Reynolds."

"What is the girlfriend's name and address?"

I told him, then watched as he punched three numbers on

the telephone at a nearby desk. He spoke briefly into the receiver. Then he hung up and turned back to me.

"We'll send a patrol car by the James house, Miss Holt. Please have a seat until we can sort this thing out." He indicated a row of chairs along the wall.

I got the distinct impression that he meant to hold me there whether I liked it or not and, quite honestly, I didn't blame him. So I walked over to one of the chairs.

"I could use a glass of water," I told one of the women as I sat down.

She nodded. "I'll get one for you." Then she disappeared through the same door the patrolman had used.

Pretty soon she was back carrying a paper cup filled with cold water. She came through a swinging door and handed it to me. I thanked her, and she went back behind the half-wall and sat down. But I noticed she periodically stood up and glanced in my direction.

Several patrolmen and plainclothes officers came and went while I sipped my water. They paid no attention to me whatever. Most of them paused briefly to tell one of the women something or to drop off a sheet of paper or a file or to sign something. Then they continued on through the main door to the left of the entrance.

Two of the uniformed officers had a young man in tow. He wasn't cuffed but looked extremely embarrassed. The taller of the two officers filled out a form, while the woman I had originally spoken to went into a room labeled "ID and Fingerprinting." The officers escorted the young man into the room, presumably to fingerprint him. It was a procedure I was familiar with, having undergone it myself as a result of Dr. Augustin's last murder investigation, the one in February involving his ex-wife.

I shuddered. What will happen to me this time? I wonder. A night in the pokey, perhaps? And I began to conjure up images of prostitutes and drug pushers and drunks. Everyone was staring at me and laughing.

I was brought out of my reverie by a voice I recognized from that same fateful February.

"Miss Holt?"

I looked up. Detective Sergeant Peter Robinson smiled down at me.

"What on earth are you doing here?" he asked.

"If you have a few minutes, I'd love to tell you all about it," I said.

So he sat down beside me. Then, like a beer suddenly sprinkled with salt, I let go and told him everything I knew, including the part about the counterfeit twenties and the Secret Service and Toby Reynolds. The detective made me stop several times and back up and start again, but somehow I got it all out.

He didn't say anything immediately. He stared at the ceiling and let my words float around in his head, presumably comparing what I had told him with what he already knew about the murders, to see if my version made any sense. Evidently it did, because he got up and spoke to someone on the telephone, then came back over to me.

"They've got Ms. James," he said. "Dr. Augustin is fine. What say we take a ride down there?"

I glanced over at the two women behind the half-wall. "Don't they want me to give a statement or something?" I asked.

"We'll worry about that later," he said, holding the door open for me.

Three patrol cars, their lights flashing, and two unmarked cars were parked in Ramona's driveway and at the curb in front of her house.

Detective Sergeant Robinson pulled up behind one of the unmarked cars, and he and I got out. As we walked toward the house, I noticed Ramona James sitting in the backseat of one of the patrol cars. She was staring straight ahead and didn't see me or, if she had, she didn't let on.

Dr. Augustin was standing by the front porch. He had the kitten in his arms. It was investigating his beard with its paw. I wished I had a camera.

Detective Robinson left me and walked through the carport to the backyard. I went over to Dr. Augustin.

"Toby is still out there," I said quietly.

Dr. Augustin was silent. He stroked the kitten. I could hear it purring. We watched the cops milling about Ramona's house, trampling her rosebushes.

"Ramona honestly believed Mick Peters killed Arnie, Howard Nichols, and Luther Tyndall," said Dr. Augustin. "Apparently she didn't know about the others. And Reynolds had her convinced that Mick was the mastermind behind the counterfeiting scheme. The computer whiz kid who finally found a gold mine in all that high-tech stuff he peddles. Ramona stayed pretty much out of the whole affair, except when Reynolds needed her for something, although she admitted she was looking forward to the money. I gathered her relationship with Reynolds was a means to an end. She didn't love him."

He paused, then looked down at me. "Ramona told me she called Reynolds," he said, "right after she caught you in Ralph Silor's room. That he asked you out to see what you and I knew."

He had a right to be angry. I hadn't been entirely honest with him. But I felt the need to defend myself, anyway. "He didn't ask me anything relevant. In fact, we didn't really talk at all. He never even made a pass at me. It was the strangest date I have ever been on."

"The fact that it was so strange should have told you something," he countered.

I chewed on my lip. He was right. Toby hadn't been the least bit interested in me. In fact, he'd seemed more interested in Dr. Augustin.

Detective Robinson came out of the house and stood on the front porch. "I suggest you two watch yourselves until we catch this guy," he said. "Stay with friends. Keep a lot of people around you. I don't think he'll try anything in a crowd."

He pointed at the car Ramona was in. "The James woman has agreed to cooperate, so I expect we'll find Mr. Reynolds presently. In any case, I'll let you know the minute we have him." He glanced at his watch. "I need to get back. Let's postpone the statements until tomorrow." He looked at me, then at Dr. Augustin. "Do you folks have a way home?"

Dr. Augustin nodded. "My car is around the corner," he said. "Thanks for getting here so quickly. I wasn't worried about Ramona, but I can't say the same about Toby Reynolds."

The sergeant shook Dr. Augustin's hand, patted the kitten on the head, and started toward the car. Suddenly, he turned around and smiled. "And try to stay out of trouble," he said. "Control the urge to break into anyone else's house." He winked at me and continued across the lawn.

Dr. Augustin and I walked around the corner to his Jeep.

"I don't think you should stay at your place tonight, Samantha," Dr. Augustin said, as he unlocked the passenger side door. "I'll drop you off at Tracey's apartment. I'm sure she won't mind, and I doubt Toby will think to look there."

I got in, and he handed me the kitten. The idea of spending the night with Tracey Nevins did not thrill me in the least.

"I don't have a toothbrush or a change of clothes," I said. "And I need to feed my cats."

He slid behind the wheel and shut the door. "Call Jeffrey and have him feed your cats. He's got a key, hasn't he?" He looked at me. "I mean it. This guy is nuts. And he has nothing to lose by getting rid of us." He started the engine.

"So where are you going to stay?" I asked.

"Don't worry about me," he said. "I'll be fine. Besides, it's tough to nail a moving target."

I had no idea what he meant, but at that point I was too tired to care. I tucked the kitten up under my chin and closed my eyes.

On the way to Tracey's, Dr. Augustin stopped at a convenience store so I could buy a toothbrush and he could telephone Tracey to warn her. I had hoped she wouldn't be home, since it was Saturday night. I figured she would be at the Chilly Bin. But no such luck. She told Dr. Augustin she would be happy to have me over.

Dr. Augustin let me out in front of Tracey's apartment building and waited until she opened the door to drive off. He had taken the kitten from me and, after seeing the look on my face, assured me nothing would happen to it. He even suggested Randy might like to have a sister to play with. The fact that he had referred to Randy by name was encouraging.

As I watched him turn the corner, I realized, too late, that he was headed for the clinic, alone and unarmed and, most probably, straight into Toby's sights.

CHAPTER 34

•

I called the sergeant as soon as I was safely inside Tracey's apartment. I told him I thought Toby might head for the clinic and that Dr. Augustin would probably be there. Robinson said he would send a patrol car by and not to worry.

When I hung up the phone, Tracey was standing in the bedroom doorway, a puzzled look on her face.

"What's going on?" she asked. "Dr. Augustin said you couldn't stay at your apartment tonight. He didn't say why. What is this about Toby?"

"You know Toby Reynolds?"

She came into the room and sat down on the bed. I continued to stand.

"He's in trouble, isn't he?" she asked. She pulled her legs up onto the bed and wrapped her arms around them. She looked cold, but the temperature in the room was somewhere in the upper seventies.

I sat down on the bed next to her. "I'm afraid he is," I said. "Remember that man I told you about? The one the cops found in the canal? Arnie Silor? His cat Pearl is staying at the clinic, along with her kitten, Randy."

She nodded, then began to rock back and forth.

"It's beginning to look like Toby murdered him. And that guy from the hospital. Howard Nichols. I don't know if you read about that in the paper. And five or six other people." I paused. "Toby was making counterfeit money. That's why we think he killed Arnie and Howard Nichols. The rest of the victims were patients of your stepfather. Why he killed them is still a mystery."

Tracey stopped rocking. She got off the bed and walked into the kitchen. I followed her and sat down on one of two bar stools.

Tracey opened the refrigerator and took out a half-full bottle of wine. "Want some?" she asked.

"Sure," I said. I wanted her to tell me about how she knew Toby, but I wanted it to be on her terms. If they'd been lovers, the shock of finding out she'd slept with a murderer had to be traumatic. I, for one, found it a lot easier to think I'd eaten spinach lasagna with a thief than with a serial killer.

Tracey poured wine into two plastic cups and handed me one. Then she sat down on the second stool.

"Toby Reynolds is my brother," she said calmly. "Half brother, actually."

I stared at her in disbelief.

"Same mother, different fathers." She took a drink of wine. Her hands were shaking. "Mom was very young when she got pregnant the first time. And the guy took off when he found out. So Mom named the baby after some great uncle of hers. Tobias Lancaster Reynolds."

I realized I was holding my breath and exhaled sharply. I picked up my glass and took a long, slow drink while trying to compose myself.

"Toby is extremely smart," Tracey continued. "He could have been a successful surgeon. But after Mark died, he sort of went off the deep end. He dropped out of med school. He went to work as a med tech at St. Luke's, then as a sales rep for a surgical supply company. That didn't last. Then he got it in his head to open a health club."

"Are you and Toby close?"

"We talk occasionally, but we're hardly close." Suddenly she started to cry. "Oh, Toby," she said, sniffing. She got up and tore a paper towel off the roll on the counter next to the refrigerator.

"Toby is the stubbornest person I know," she said, shaking her head. Her eyes shone. "Norman offered to help finance that stupid club, but Toby refused to even talk to him. He said he didn't need Norman's help. Ever." She looked over at me. "But why would Toby kill people? Innocent people?"

"I don't know, Tracey," I said. "Since Toby's father abandoned him before he was born, maybe he felt Dr. Friedman was abandoning Mark by not agreeing to the surgery. Maybe Toby is punishing your stepfather for what his real father did to him."

She refilled our cups, and we went into her living room. I felt sorry for Tracey. Life hadn't been particularly easy for her, I realized. Of course, my life wasn't a bowl of cherries either. It became apparent that, despite the difference in our ages and our divergent tastes in music and clothes, Tracey Nevins and I had a lot of things in common.

Around 4:30 we finally decided we were tired enough to turn in. My head was starting to throb, and aspirin wasn't having any effect. Tracey let me use her bed. She assured me that, at five foot three, she could afford to sleep on the sofa. At five foot ten, I couldn't and didn't argue with her.

CHAPTER 35

•

Sunday, July 26

The phone rang at noon, rescuing me from a totally nonsensical, yet strangely disturbing dream. Two headless marble statues, both males, both nude, somehow had come to life and were wrestling in a shallow pool of oil. At least, I thought it was oil. It was dark and gooey. In my dream, the statues moved jerkily, like Claymation figures or characters in an old, poorly done science fiction movie.

Without thinking, I reached across the end table and picked up the receiver. "Hello?" I mumbled. I could hear someone breathing. It lasted for about ten seconds, then the line went dead.

Instantly, I was awake, the remnants of my dream swept away by a sudden feeling of apprehension. As I replaced the receiver, Tracey appeared in the doorway to her bedroom. Her hair stuck up on top like porcupine quills.

"Who was that?" she asked, rubbing her eyes.

"I don't know. They hung up."

She stared at me. "You don't suppose . . . ?"

The telephone rang again. That time, Tracey answered it.

"Yes?" she said cautiously. Then her eyes met mine, and she mouthed the word "Toby." "She spent the night here," she said into the phone. "Because the police told her you might try something, and she shouldn't go back to her place, that's why." She had suddenly become agitated. "Yes, well you sure have a strange way of showing it." She chewed on a finger. "So where are you? Oh."

She sat down on the bed. "I'll see what I can do, Toby. But it wouldn't surprise me if he refuses. And I can't say I'd blame him." She ran her hand over her hair, trying to flatten the sleep-induced Mohawk. "Sure." She stood up. "I said I'll try. That's all I can promise. Yeah, you, too." She hung up.

I let her stare at the phone for a few seconds. Then I cleared my throat.

She turned around. "He's in jail. They caught him this morning. He didn't say where. Now he wants me to ask Norman for help. Can you imagine? After all he's put Norman through, Toby wants Norman to send over his best lawyer. If it was me, I'd let him rot."

"You don't mean that, Tracey," I said. "He's your brother. And he's sick. You said so, yourself."

She sat down on the bed next to me. "You're right. Of course, you're right."

"Listen," I said. "You go ahead and take a shower and get dressed. Then, if you don't mind, you can drop me off at my apartment. I'll get cleaned up there. The thought of putting sweaty clothes back on after I've had a shower is too much, and I doubt anything you have would fit me."

"Okay," she said. "Give me fifteen minutes."

It was hard to tell if Jeffrey had come over the night before to feed my cats. Tina and Priss weren't saying. They met me at the door acting like Sudanese waifs at a relief station. If it is possible for cats to purposefully lay a guilt trip on their owners, mine should get some kind of prize.

It was almost three when I finally reached Dr. Augustin. He was at the clinic and answered the phone one ring before Cynthia's recording cut in.

"The police found Toby at Jewel Graphics," he said. "He and the owner, Chris Fleig, were busy stuffing counterfeit twenties and fifties into a shipping crate addressed to someplace in Mexico."

I heard the sound of a cage door closing. He was obviously in the kennel.

"How's your head?" he asked.

"Okay, I guess. A little black-and-blue, but my bangs hide it pretty well. I still have a headache, though."

I told him about Tracey being Toby's half sister. And about his hatred for Norman Friedman. "I feel so sorry for Tracey," I said. "Now she'll have to live with the fact that her brother is crazy as a loon and a murderer to boot."

"Everyone has a skeleton or two in their closets, Samantha," Dr. Augustin said.

"I guess."

"Why don't you meet me at the Moon in an hour," he said, "and I'll buy you a hamburger and a beer. You'll feel better."

"Make it a grouper sandwich," I said. "I'm not into warm, brown-eyed, furry things just now."

"What are you talking about?"

"Never mind," I said. "I'll see you at four."

When I arrived at the Moon, most of the patrons had evidently gone outside to watch a volleyball game. I could hear telltale clapping and cheering coming from the beach, and the waitress with shocking pink claws, the one Dr. Augustin had ogled, was just disappearing out the back door carrying two pitchers of beer. Inside, a flock of giggling, glistening, bikini-clad nymphs was comparing notes in the hallway while waiting for their turn in the ladies' room.

There were only four people at the bar, all of them ancient and wizened. Every cocktail lounge and pub in the country has them—retirees who live nearby and have nothing better to do with their days than drink beer and watch ESPN in the air-conditioned bars.

A tall, skinny guy, who was mostly legs and obviously a runner, was operating the beer pulls. He had medium-length brown hair and reminded me of Jeffrey. He looked up, caught me staring at him, and smiled. I smiled back, then turned away, relieved I hadn't felt anything. I was beginning to wonder if Dr. Augustin had been right about me, after all.

Bill O'Shea and Dr. Augustin were at Bill's table in the corner, where they were busy polishing off a couple of beers. From their relaxed postures, I gathered it wasn't the first for either of them.

"Pull up a chair, Samantha," Bill said.

I dragged one over from a nearby vacant table and settled myself. Bill signaled the bartender for another round.

"I'm glad you're feeling better," I said. "I guess Dr. Augustin told you about Toby Reynolds."

Bill nodded. "When I fired him, he looked at me like he could have throttled me on the spot. To tell you the truth, I never really trusted Toby, but he was a good bartender, and the women really liked him."

Dr. Augustin eyed me, and I could feel my face redden.

"Fortunately, there was quite a crowd here yesterday when I let him go," Bill continued. "But I lost no time in checking the .38 I keep in the office to make sure it was loaded. Except it was gone. Toby had it."

The bartender came over with a pitcher and an extra glass. He poured beer for each of us, then tossed a wad of napkins on the table.

"Can I get you folks anything else?" he asked.

Bill looked at Dr. Augustin, then at me, then said, "How about three grouper sandwiches? Extra tartar sauce."

"Make mine a hamburger, all the way," said Dr. Augustin.

"You got it," the young man said. He glanced at me, then left for the kitchen.

"That's Jason Cox," Bill said. "He may not be as appealing to the women as Toby was, but I trust him a whole lot more."

Except for his lunch order, Dr. Augustin hadn't said a word since I arrived, and it was beginning to bother me. I knew he was angry, or at least disappointed in me for not telling him about my date with Toby, but I couldn't tell how angry, since his beard covered up the more expressive parts of his face. All except the eyes, and I was avoiding them.

My mind began to play tricks on me. I could see Dr. Augustin lying on the surgical prep table. He was unconscious, and I was standing over him, holding up the clinic's heavy-duty electric clippers. The clippers were buzzing loudly, and I was laughing.

I rubbed my fingers over the cool, wet surface of my beer glass, then touched them to my lips. I had tossed and turned all night because of the bump on my head and the wine.

"What was Toby doing at that graphics place?" I asked. "I

thought they were using computer equipment at the hospital. You told me it was probably some computer setup Howard Nichols bought from Mick."

"Either Mick couldn't or wouldn't provide them with what they wanted," said Dr. Augustin. "Anyway, Ramona said when the computer equipment at the hospital didn't work out, Reynolds and company—remember, she thought Mick was in on the thing from the start—went looking for another printer. Arnie was dead and, for some reason, Bill, here, wasn't an option. Then Reynolds discovered that Chris Fleig had filed for bankruptcy. Apparently, Fleig was one step away from losing everything he owned as a result of some bad investments, and that made him susceptible to the counterfeiting scheme. Which, as we now know, was originally Reynolds's idea, not Howard Nichols's. He's the one who contacted Nichols. I guess Nichols figured he had nothing to lose, so why not make a little extra money so he could enjoy his final days. Except Reynolds had Nichols do all his dirty work to avoid having anyone at the bar suspect him."

Dr. Augustin drained his glass, then lifted the pitcher and refilled it. "Anyway, Fleig used photo offset to print the money."

"Color copiers and laser printers do a good job of reproducing a color image," said Bill, "but photo offset is far superior. Gives much better definition. That's probably why Nichols approached Arnie."

"Ramona volunteered all this information while she had you at gunpoint?" I asked sarcastically, wishing *I* had him at gunpoint.

"Ramona James wasn't about to kill me," said Dr. Augustin. "But after realizing that Reynolds was a murderer several times over, she was terrified of what he might do to her if she let me go. Apparently he used her to get the victims' names and addresses from Friedman's files. She worked for Friedman before taking the job at the hospital. She didn't say how Reynolds managed to get the information without arousing her curiosity, but apparently he did."

He leaned back in his chair and balanced his beer glass on his stomach. The glass never even wobbled. "I think she knew, deep down, that Toby Reynolds was unbalanced, but the promise of all that money was worth the risk, I guess."

The girl with the claws came out of the kitchen and over to

our table, a large tray on her left shoulder. After she had placed three red plastic baskets on the table, each stuffed with a sandwich, fries, and the most enormous dill pickle slice I had ever seen, she started to go.

"Don't forget the extra tartar sauce, Patty," Bill said patiently.

Patty drew in a little breath and placed her right hand on her chest, just over the word "Moon" on her crop top. "I don't know where my brain is today, Mr. O'Shea. I'll be right back." She turned and hurried off toward the kitchen, her behind swaying provocatively.

I admired the way she avoided the hands that tried to intercept her as she passed by the bar. No matter what Bill is paying you, I thought, it isn't enough. Then I noticed Dr. Augustin lift up the top of his hamburger bun, together with the lettuce leaf, onion ring, and slice of tomato, and begin pouring ketchup liberally over the meat patty.

"So Toby killed Luther Tyndall," I said. Suddenly I wasn't very hungry.

Dr. Augustin took a bite of pickle. "Ramona said Reynolds went over to Mick's periodically. 'Planning sessions' he called them. My guess is he went there to scare Mick into keeping quiet. I'm sure he ran into Tyndall once or twice. He noticed Tyndall's bronchitis, found out the guy was one of Norman's patients, and killed two birds with one stone, so to speak. Got rid of Tyndall and pinned it on Mick." He picked up his hamburger. Ketchup and meat juices dripped back into the little basket.

I swallowed. "Why didn't he just kill Mick? I mean, that would have shut him up. Permanently."

Dr. Augustin shrugged. "He's crazy, Samantha. Who knows why he did what he did? Presumably he wanted to get back at Norman, and killing Mick wouldn't accomplish that."

"Then why did he kill Arnie?" I asked. "Arnie wasn't one of Friedman's patients. And why did he cut off Arnie's hands?"

Bill suddenly pushed back his chair and got up. "I wonder what happened to Patty?" he said. "I'll go check on her." He headed for the kitchen.

Dr. Augustin frowned at me. "You could have phrased that a little better, Samantha."

I didn't say anything.

Then he smiled. "You're not eating."

"I'm waiting for the tartar sauce," I said. "So, why did he do it?"

"Kill Arnie and cut off his hands? Probably because Reynolds thought Arnie had somehow managed to steal some of the counterfeit money. Ramona admitted she took the kittens from Arnie's place. And she swiped the three hundred bucks you found in the basket with them. Took it from Toby's apartment one morning. She wrote the note, of course. She said she couldn't just leave the kittens without leaving us something to pay for their care."

He shook his head. "Reynolds was smart enough to know he couldn't pass the money locally. That it needed to leave the country. But Ramona didn't know that. She blames herself for Arnie's death. And her guilt was made all the worse because of what his death did to Ralph."

I picked up a french fry and took a bite. "What do you think will happen to Mick?"

Dr. Augustin reached for his glass. He was looking at something over my shoulder. "I don't know. Why don't you ask him yourself?"

I turned around. Mick Peters was standing by the front door with Cindy. I waved, and they came over to our table. The dark circles under Mick's eyes were even darker, and he had lost weight. Cindy looked her usual happy self, though. She was dressed in pink OshKosh overalls and a matching T-shirt.

"I want to thank you, Dr. Augustin," Mick said. "You, too, Samantha. For leading the cops to Toby Reynolds. Sergeant Robinson said they'll probably drop the charges against me tomorrow or the next day." He sat down in Bill's chair and lifted Cindy into his lap. "My mom and dad drove up this morning with Cindy. I couldn't stand to be away from her another minute." Then he frowned. "I know I should have gone to the cops as soon as I figured out what Nichols wanted from me."

Cindy was eyeing my grouper sandwich.

"Why don't you and Cindy share this?" I said, pushing the basket toward Mick. "I ate before I came."

Mick didn't argue with me. He cut the sandwich into quarters and gave one to Cindy. She bit into it hungrily. Then Mick looked over at Dr. Augustin.

"A couple of weeks after I'd made delivery to St. Luke's and helped Nichols get set up, he called me," he said. "He told me he was having problems and could I stop by the hospital. I did, and after beating around the bush, Nichols finally blurted out what he wanted to do—make counterfeit money."

He put a fry in his mouth and chewed. "I told him I couldn't help him. I said what he needed was a really good color copier. That a laser printer wouldn't do any better of a job. I thought he would leave me alone after that." He looked around the table. "Is there any tartar sauce?"

"Bill went for it," I said.

"But of course at that point I was a risk," Mick continued. "Then Toby paid me a little visit. More than once. I swore I wouldn't tell anyone, but the way he looked at Cindy scared me to death. I finally sent her to Ft. Myers to stay with her grandparents." He kissed the top of his daughter's head.

"You know, there's something really evil about that guy. Shortly after he started working at the Moon, regulars, at least the ones who smoked or drank too much, began to die. It seemed like we were drinking more and more toasts to the dearly departed. Then I noticed a pattern. Toby would say something about a customer's cough or ask how much they weighed and if they'd seen a doctor. You know, act real concerned. Then the guy would turn up dead.

"I decided it had to be Toby, that in addition to everything else, he had something against people who weren't health freaks like him. That's when I quit smoking. I figured, even if I kept quiet about the money, he was going to get me if I didn't watch out. I started jogging, gave up coffee."

"Did you know Ramona James was involved with Reynolds?" asked Dr. Augustin.

The tartar sauce was slow in making an appearance, so Mick took a bite of one of the sandwich quarters. He chewed rapidly and swallowed.

"Not at first," he said. "You see, I met Ramona at the hospital while Janine was . . . sick. Ramona was very kind and caring. And I needed a friend, anyway. Then last month I finally asked her out." He laughed. "Let's face it, I'm no Don Juan. So I didn't expect her to say yes. But she did. We went to a movie. The whole evening she acted sort of weird. She asked a lot of questions. Like where I was born, were my parents still alive. Where did they live. I got a little suspicious when she asked me who Cindy's baby-sitter was."

Jason Cox came over to our table with two glasses of water. "Need anything?" he asked.

"A glass of milk, if it isn't too much trouble," said Mick.

"You bet," said Jason, and he left for the kitchen.

"Anyway, a couple of weeks ago," Mick continued, "my mother called to say she'd gotten a strange phone call from a guy who claimed he was my partner. He was calling to see how Cindy was. Mom knows I don't have a partner. She wanted to warn me. That's when I realized Ramona had to be working with Toby Reynolds. A few days later, I saw her here at the Moon and told her if anything happened to Cindy she'd be sorry. She said she didn't know what I was talking about."

Mick shivered. "You just can't imagine what my life has been like these last few months. I kept praying Toby would make a mistake, and the cops would arrest him." Suddenly he brightened. "And then you guys came along."

"Jonesy will be mighty glad to see you," I said.

"Jonesy!" exclaimed Cindy.

Mick grinned. "How's he doing, anyway? I sure do miss that mutt."

"He's fine, Mick," said Dr. Augustin. He looked at his watch. "Samantha has to go back to the clinic to medicate a boarder and feed everyone. Why don't you go along with her and get Jonesy? There's no need for him to stay at the clinic another night."

I stared across the table at Dr. Augustin. He was finishing his hamburger, looking positively innocent.

"Me?" I said. "This is my day off. It's *your* weekend to do treatments." The thought of having to wrestle with Mad Max after less then a full eight hours of sleep filled me with dread.

Dr. Augustin popped the last of the dill pickle in his mouth and chewed slowly. Then he aimed his optical ray guns at me and smiled. "Call it penance," he said.

EPILOGUE

•

Life at the clinic had returned pretty much to normal by Labor Day. Dr. Augustin shaved off his beard. He said the heat was getting to him. I think he was referring to his staff's sarcasm, rather than the temperature outside.

After the cops arrested Toby Reynolds, Dr. Augustin acted pretty cocky for a couple of weeks, as if he single-handedly had exposed a big-time counterfeiting ring, as well as solved at least nine murders. The fact that he withheld information from the police and the Secret Service must have slipped his mind. Fortunately, the fact that I almost got him killed by withholding information from him had also slipped his mind. Or maybe he was saving it for a rainy day. That would be more like him. At least he had taken care of Irma Shoaf. He told her (and Vivian Porter) he needed me to be on call Wednesdays, in case there was an emergency, so I wouldn't be able to do any volunteer work in the immediate future. I was so grateful, I almost forgave him for getting me mixed up with St. Luke's Volunteer Services in the first place. Almost.

It was Saturday. We'd been extremely busy since ten, with two emergencies and a full schedule. At four, Cynthia reminded me that she wanted to leave promptly at five. She'd been driving me home and picking me up since Thursday, because my car was at Phil's Body Shop having the front bumper replaced. A little old man had run into me in the grocery store parking lot. Phil assured me he could do it in a day. So much for dependability.

I was about to tell Cynthia I didn't see a problem, since we only had two appointments left, when a taxi pulled up in front of the clinic. Even before the driver could get out to open her door, Sarah Milton emerged. She stood, none too patiently I presumed from her posture, and waited while the young man lifted the cat carrier out of the vehicle.

"You may have to leave without me," I told Cynthia.

Sarah trudged up to the front door and pulled it open. The taxi driver was right behind her, but wasn't quick enough to catch the door before it shut in his face. I walked across the room, opened the door, and the guy handed me the carrier. I smiled at him.

"I'm here to see Dr. Augustin," Sarah announced, oblivious to the look the driver gave her as he left. She'd apparently already paid him, but I felt certain she hadn't given him a tip.

"Sarah," I said, putting the carrier on the floor next to her, "you're just the person I wanted to talk to."

She peered at me suspiciously.

"We've got a couple of adorable kittens here who are looking for homes. Would you be interested?"

Sarah put her hands on her hips and leaned forward. "Are you *crazy*?" She pushed the carrier toward me with her foot. "I need another kitten like a hole in the head."

Cynthia grinned. I frowned at her, then bent down and looked in the carrier. A scrawny black cat, not much over six months of age lay on her side. Three tiny kittens, one black and two grey, were nursing. I put them at two days old, max.

"Found 'em in a cardboard box outside my back door," said Sarah. "Some horse's ass left them there this morning." She opened her purse and pulled out a brown paper sack. "One died already." She handed the parcel to me. "Mother's too young to have kittens."

I picked up the carrier and started toward the hallway. "Let's put you and your little friends in an exam room, Sarah. Dr. Augustin will be along shortly."

She didn't budge. "He'd better not charge me for that dead

one," she said. "And I ought to get some kind of discount. For being a good Samaritan."

I tried not to laugh, although Cynthia was making it difficult. "I think we can work something out, Sarah," I said.

With that, she hiked up her clam diggers and followed me into Room 2.

Sarah left with her new foster children at 4:30. The same taxi driver who'd brought her arrived to take her home. He didn't look pleased. After she was gone and our last appointment of the day was in a room with Dr. Augustin, I went up to the front to relieve Cynthia.

"Isn't it wonderful that Dr. Farmington is going to do the surgery on those kittens free of charge?" she asked me, as she gathered up her purse and the newspaper.

"Not entirely free of charge," I said. "Dr. Augustin is going to assist him."

"Still, I think it's nice."

The phone rang. Cynthia looked at the clock, hesitated while it rang a couple more times, then shrugged and picked up the receiver.

"Yes, Samantha is right here," she said, in her little girl voice. She grinned and handed me the receiver. "It's Mike."

I took it. "Hi, Michael," I said.

"Greetings," he said.

I frowned at Cynthia and pointed at the clock. She looked hurt, but took the hint and headed for the door.

"I was wondering if you'd like to go to the ballet tomorrow afternoon. It's something different. We don't even have to eat dinner if you don't want to."

"Sure," I said. "I think that would be very nice." I covered the mouthpiece. "He's asked me to the ballet tomorrow," I said to Cynthia. "Are you happy now?"

She blushed and hurried out the door. I had made her day, I was certain of it.

"Actually, I'm glad you called. You remember you said you wanted a cat?" I didn't let him respond, since I knew the cat thing was only an excuse. "Well, I have two adorable kittens, brother and sister, that Dr. Augustin will neuter for free. And we'll make sure they have all their shots, so you won't have to pay for a thing. How about it? They're absolutely precious. I just know you'll love them right off. And take it from me, two cats are a lot more fun than one. They can play together and entertain each other while you're at work." I drew in a deep breath.

He didn't say anything.

"Michael?"

He laughed. "You're a tough customer, you know that? All right. I'll take them on one condition."

"What's that?" I asked, suddenly wary.

"You promise to come by and visit them at least once a week."

I thought about this. "I'll try, Michael."

"Well, that's a start. Listen, I'll pick you up at three tomorrow, okay?"

"Sounds good," I said. "And we can eat afterwards, if you want."

He laughed. "Bye, Samantha."

I turned the answering machine on, then wandered across the hall to Isolation, where the kittens were wrestling in their cage. Pearl ambled in, jumped up on the counter by the sink, and stared at her children through half-open eyes.

"Hi, Pearl," I said. "What's up?"

Pearl blinked and kneaded the air a couple of times with her right paw. Her purring sounded like the rumble of distant thunder.

Charlie, who undoubtedly had just finished eating Pearl's dinner, having long since finished his own and anyone else's whose cage he could open, came into the room licking his lips. He sat down and began cleaning himself, apparently unaware of the cat directly above him.

Pearl casually switched her gaze to Charlie. The end of her tail, which had been curled around her feet, began to move, slowly, almost imperceptibly at first, then more violently. Her ears began to flatten out, and her pupils opened up. You could almost hear the wheels turning in her head, as she hung low over her prey.

Suddenly, she sprang into the air, landing lightly a few

inches in front of Charlie. Her paw lashed out, and she carved her initials on his nose. Then, before he could react, she dashed almost gleefully down the hall. Charlie yowled and hissed, but it was too late.

"Good for you, Pearl," I yelled after her.

Dr. Augustin came through the treatment room and stood in the doorway. "What's going on in here?" he asked. "Why are those cats still out? Where is Frank?"

"Pearl finally got even with Charlie," I said. "It's about time, don't you think? We women need a little more respect around here." I smiled playfully.

He shook his head in apparent disgust and went into his office. Buoyed by Pearl's sudden aplomb, I followed him.

I sat down on the daybed. "Do you think Ralph is going to get that liver transplant?" I asked. "Bill said he was pretty close to the top of the list."

Dr. Augustin was making notes in a boarder's file. He shrugged. "There are people all over the country waiting for new livers. All we can do is keep our fingers crossed."

The picture of Dr. Augustin and the woman on the rocky ledge caught my eye, and suddenly I couldn't stand it any longer.

"So, who's the woman in the photo?" I asked.

Dr. Augustin turned around in his chair, a quizzical expression on his face. I pointed to the image taped to the wall. He glanced at the picture and smiled.

"Kathy Berrill, an old vet school buddy of mine." He looked back at me. "We were lab partners." He was staring with his black eyes shining, his mouth still curled at the corners.

I should have said something like, "The two of you look as if you were having a pretty terrific time." What I really wanted to say was, "Is she married? Are you dating her?" Instead I mumbled, "Oh."

Dr. Augustin continued to stare at me for a moment. Then he laughed. "Her husband borrowed my camera for that shot," he said finally, as if reading my mind. "Bernie Berrill, DVM. They're quite a pair."

His eyes were like magnets. I couldn't look away, no matter how much I wanted to, and I could feel my face grow hot.

"Oh," I said again, relief all too evident in my voice.

"Who do you think took that picture," he asked me, "some woodlands creature?"

He was fortunate there weren't any sharp objects within my reach.

"By the way, Samantha, did I ever thank you for sending the cavalry to my rescue back in July?"

"No," I said.

"I guess I've sort of been taking you for granted lately, haven't I?"

He paused, but I didn't say anything.

"Well, anyway, thanks." He seemed embarrassed, which did not suit him.

"I was right about Mick Peters, wasn't I?" I asked.

"I had my doubts about his guilt. I told you that." Then he winked. "And *I* was right about Toby Reynolds."

"You said he was a steroid junkie," I countered, "not Dr. Death."

He wasn't going to admit he was wrong. I could see that. His comment about taking me for granted was the best he could do in the apology department.

He got up. "Come on," he said. "I'll help you do treatments, then take you home. Maybe even buy you dinner on the way. Something a step or two up from McDonald's. It's the least I can do."

The least, indeed, I thought, and grinned.